DEBORAH E. HAMMOND

Melissa
I hope you will
enjoy.

Deborah
Hammond

BOOKS BY DEBORAH E. HAMMOND

In The Eye of the Storm
The Big Sky
The English Rose
Until You
To Woo a Wife
The Calling
In Another's Shoes
Someone to Watch Over Me
The Scot's Bride
As Time Goes By
Storm Chaser
Storm Season
Monocacy Crossing
One Shining Knight
A Knight's Errand
All books are available in paperback and kindle versions on Amazon.com.

Copyright

DEDICATION

To the people of Berkeley County, West Virginia; thank you for your wonderful support of my endeavors for over twenty-five years. I share this book with you as the inspiration for many of the beautiful locations referenced in this story and to Bill - With you all things are possible. You are my home.

At the time of this story, Berkeley County was part of Virginia. The story begins, therefore in Berkeley County, Virginia. Berkeley County was part of Virginia until 1863 when the new state of West Virginia was formed and the Eastern Panhandle, where we live; became part of the new state of West Virginia.

To my Scot's ancestors and all Scot's immigrants to this country; thank you for what you brought to the great American experience and to the beautiful tapestry which is our immigrant history. A Scot's Gaelic dictionary is included in the author's notes for those who wish to reference.

Table of Contents

BOOK ONE

BERKELEY COUNTY, VIRGINIA –
OCTOBER 1785

CHAPTER ONE

Morgana Mackenzie sat in her still room with a cup of tea before her. Taking the last swallow, she turned out the leaves to study her own future. She had studied many times for the people of her new community; searching the leaves, examining the hands and looking for signs; confirming the sight that she had inherited from her mother and her mother's mother and on and on before her and back and back again to Scotland, where it had all begun. As she had been taught since childhood; the sight was a skill that only grew with time, age and maturity. Others might fear the gift and the power that came with it, but Morgana and her family knew the strength of the sight, just as the chieftains and lairds of her native Scotland had known. One with the sight was frequently at the right hand side of the laird as he made decisions for the clan. It had been so with her mother, her mother's mother and on and on; but that time was gone now and would never return.

This time the life before her was her own. Her grandparents had come to this new land after the time of troubles in the Highlands of Scotland. In 1745 many of the Highland chieftains had rebelled against the Hanoverian King George II of England. The Highlanders had supported the Catholic Stuart King James and had risen to overthrow the Protestant King George II. The resulting defeat of the Stuart cause had resulted in the destruction of the clan system and the Highlander way of life forever. Nothing left behind to hold them; her grandparents had walked out of the Highlands of Scotland and never looked back. They had come to the American colonies in search of the Highlands of this new land. They were told that mountains such as the Highlands existed in the western part of Virginia. They had sought to travel there, but her grandfather too heartbroken by the war and suffering for all that he had lost in his homeland, had taken ill. Now both her grandparents and her parents were gone and she was alone in this new land; Berkeley County, Virginia, in the new country of America in the year of our Lord, 1785.

Morgana searched the leaves and her palm for the future. For the first time, she saw there a sign. She checked it twice not believing her own eyes. Her own future now lay before her. He was coming; one of her own was coming for her. For the first time, she saw a traveler; one of her own Scot's brethren coming into her life. He was a Highlander, as her mother had known would come for her. She knew the old ways, taught to her by her grandparents and her parents and she knew the power of the sight which had been gifted to her from her mother's line.

Morgana's eyes rose from her cup and her palm. He was on his way; the Highlander was on his way to claim her and the life that they would build together. She would be ready and look carefully for any additional signs. She tidied her cup and returned to making her herbs and tinctures which she sold in this new land to make her way. Her own Highlander was on his way and he would soon arrive and her new life was about to begin.

CHAPTER TWO

The body had been found in the still room of the family house. The hands still contained the marks of death upon them; the marks there for those who knew and could interpret such things. How many would know these signs in this small community and how many would endeavor to assist? Sheriff Lucas Holter believed he had a murder on his hands. He contacted the state authorities and they replied that they would be sending an investigator. The investigator was renowned for his cunning and intelligence. He was a Highlander by birth and by tradition, arrived in this country to practice his trade and his modern ways of detection straight from Edinburgh, Scotland. Until his arrival, Sheriff Holter would place the body in the family ice house. The grieving family spoke of evil visited upon the family and wanted the local priest consulted. The local priest had only recently arrived from Alexandria, Virginia himself and was unknown to the community at large and to the Sheriff.

The Sheriff saw no reason for the priest to be called, unless to provide solace to the remaining family members. The family could be consoled while the matter was sorted. He would consult with Morgana Mackenzie, however. As the local healer, Morgana had considerable knowledge of herbs, tinctures and all manner of healing. As she said many times, she also had knowledge of the evil that could come from the good earth. Just like the Garden of Eden in the bible, the earth could provide both sustenance and death. For those who knew the plants, there was life from the earth and also the ability to bring death. Morgana was also consulted for a variety of other needs as well, some including social and counseling concerns. She was a person who had knowledge unknown to anyone else in the community and closely guarded the secrets that were shared with her. She was therefore essential to any murder investigation and Lucas would call upon her frequently in the days and weeks ahead.

Besides which, she was a bonny lass and to hear her speech, was like a return to his youth and the voices of many who had come to this new land, seeking their own fortune and new life. Upon leaving the grieving family, Sheriff Holter headed out to Bella Vista to consult with Morgana. She would know much and could assist him and the Inspector upon his arrival.

Bella Vista was a beautiful property in the farmland outside of Martinsburg, Virginia. Built of local stone, a small cottage on the property had been provided as a grace and favor gift to Morgana after she saved the owner's life from a serious illness. She had brought to the new land the medicine of the old world, as her mother and grandmother before her had both been healers. Morgana had learned the powers of the tea leaves, the palm, the sight and most importantly, the healing arts at her Mother's knee. Though she tried hard to leave the superstitions of the old land behind her, the people of her new land viewed her with a mixture of awe and fear. She was consulted in secret and her opinions were well received, but she was not openly accepted except by Sheriff Holter himself. He sought to bring reason and logic to his new job as Sheriff of the community only recently formed as a new county in 1772 before the American Revolutionary War. He hoped to leave behind the old superstitions and practices, hence his contact with the state authorities and their best man; another Highlander, Sheriff Holter looked forward to working with him and learning from the man.

Upon arriving at Bella Vista, the Sheriff saw Morgana's dark head bent over her herb garden. Her potions and concoctions were highly prized by those in need, as much as her readings of leaves and palms. The Sheriff had never consulted her for that reason, but only for official matters relating to prisoners who took ill and those with mental issues not brought on by the drink. She smiled at his arrival and welcomed him in for tea.

"Morgana, I believe we have a murder on our hands, lass. I have placed the body of the victim in the family ice house until the arrival of the inspector from Alexandria. He is coming soon and should be here by the end of the week. He is a Highlander, Morgana so he will want to talk to ye if for no other reason than to hear your honeyed speech and the ways of the old country that ye hold dear. Morgana lass; I think the death may be murder, so I will need yer help," Sheriff Holter said earnestly.

"Of course Sheriff; it is October so I think the body will keep. Who is the victim?" she asked.

"Deacon, Morgana; Dirk Deacon; do ye know him?"

"Oh aye Sheriff, I know him and I know his secrets as well," Morgana replied frowning.

"That is what I was counting on, Morgana. All this I will need and the Inspector when he arrives. Was Deacon one who sought your skills then, Morgana?" Sheriff Holter asked warily.

"Aye, Sheriff; he thought himself possessed because he was in love with a woman who was not his wife," Morgana replied softly.

"Do ye know if he acted on his feelings, Morgana?" the Sheriff asked frowning.

"Aye that was the case, Sheriff, but I do not know the identity of the woman. Had she been married also, Sheriff; a husband perhaps or his wife's family could all be possible suspects," Morgana said gravely.

"Aye, the Inspector will have it sorted in due order no doubt," the Sheriff replied. "How do you fare, lass? Do you find it hard staying on here on yer own? Ye know ye can always stay with the wife and me in town," Sheriff Holter offered.

"I know Sheriff and I appreciate it. But here I have my garden and I am close to a wee mountain. The garden is for my work and gives me the herbs for my tinctures; the wee mountain is for my soul, ye ken. Ye know I will help ye

5

anyway I can. How is yer shoulder doing then, Sheriff?" she asked anxiously. "I will give ye some lotion to take with you and Mrs. Holter can use it when the pain comes on. It will help with the soreness, Sheriff. The cold will have brought the stiffness and in a few short weeks, the pain will be with you when the cold comes on hard," Morgana stated smiling.

"Thank you Morgana for your kindness. I should be going. I will have the Inspector visit ye when he arrives. God be with ye Morgana," the Sheriff stated.

"And also with ye, Sheriff," Morgana replied. She watched him as he climbed his horse and headed back into town. So, she thought; the Highlander comes. My signs were correct; the Highlander comes and he comes not only for the murder; but he comes for me, she thought with a shiver. The Highlander comes for me, she thought again.

CHAPTER THREE

Himself arrived on a black prancing stallion at the end of
the week. He went directly to Sheriff Holter's office and the
particulars of the case were laid before him. "I have someone
I would like you to meet with, Inspector. She is a local healer
and very knowledgeable of medicines, herbs and such like. In
addition, many of the local folk seek her out for her
knowledge both of the medical arts and for her special skills.
She has information that she keeps close to herself except
when needed by the law and then she will share it. I believe
you will find she will be useful to you, Inspector. She also
has the sight, Inspector and uses it to assist all who pursue
the truth and to uphold the law," Sheriff Holter stated
proudly.

"Hmph," was the only reply; a reply only known and
understood by a fellow Highlander.

"I will give you instructions on how to find her Inspector.
You may wish to visit tomorrow," Sheriff Holter stated.

"I will begin my work today, Sheriff. Thank ye for the
information. I shall visit yer source directly," Inspector
Macpherson replied. He headed out of the Sheriff's offices,
down King Street and towards North Mountain to interrogate
Morgana Mackenzie.

As the dusk approached on that October night, an autumn
sky lie before him. His prancing stallion picked up the scent
of autumn; the wood fires burning to heat the interiors of the
homes and he felt the crisp, cool day come to a close. Ever
since they had left Alexandria, he had felt the draw of the
mountains. To a Highlander born and bred, the mountains
were like the mother herself. Inspector Macpherson let out
the sigh that he had been holding for the past hour and felt
the draw of the mountains ahead of him. Had he still not been
on duty, he would have let loose his queue and let the breeze
take his hair. "Feel the chill boy; we sleep near the mountains
tonight," James Alexander Macpherson said smiling to his

horse. "We sleep near the mountains tonight, lad," he said again with a sigh.

Nearing the Bella Vista property, Inspector Macpherson spied the stone buildings that he had been briefed to seek out and looked for the tiny cottage identified by Sheriff Holter. The woman would be interrogated for purposes of the file and no more. He saw no use for civilians when professional investigations were underway. Spying the cottage and its two chimneys as described to him by the Sheriff, he pulled his horse into the garden and tied him to the post. The sight indeed, he said shaking his head. We are in the new world now and all the nonsense of the old should be left where it belonged; in the old world, along with the belief in fairies and the healing power of the stones and the springs.

As he came to the door, he smiled at the fact that it was a mere doll house as far as he could see. He would have to bend to get through the door. Since an old crone must live here with her bent back and bent head, she would have no problem in navigating that entrance, he thought smiling. He knocked and a few minutes later a dark head greeted him at the door, her eyes were as bright blue as the sky and as bottomless as a Scots loch, her skin like ivory or marble, and her lips like the red of a flame. Surely not marble, he thought to himself; for that skin would be warm to the touch and not cold like marble. She was wearing a dress of the Mackenzie clan tartan and the blue of the plaid was the same color as her eyes. The dress was finished with a white fichu and she wore a matching white apron. "May I help you, sir?" replied the bonny lass.

"Aye, mistress; may I speak with yer mother then?" the Inspector asked gravely.

"My mother's been dead near two years, sir. Would it be me ye would be wanting?" the bright eyes asked.

"Perhaps so, lass; are you Mistress Mackenzie, then?" the stranger asked frowning.

"Aye, I am Morgana Mackenzie. Can you come in then? You must be *Himself;* the Inspector that was expected. Sheriff Holter told me of yer coming," Morgana said smiling.

Inspector Macpherson bent low to navigate under the door frame and into the front room of the cottage. Built for a doll for sure and she must be the doll that it was built for, he thought wistfully.

Himself, as Morgana now thought of him, consumed her little cottage. He was a good foot taller than she, as she was but five foot three. He had deep red, nearer to reddish brown hair pulled into a queue with a leather tie. His eyes were as blue as hers, his cheekbones high with a full, straight mouth. Though he stood at parade attention, she could see the crinkle of smiles past at his eyes and mouth. For all his stern looks, this was a man capable of laughter, even if he showed no evidence of it at the present time. He wore a great coat and a uniform with dark blue coat and blue colored breeches and boots that would have reached Morgana's thighs. She tried not to notice, but could not help but think he was a fine figure of a man. Her first but not last thought was of *Himself* in the kilt of the Macpherson clan and what a sight that would be to behold.

"Would ye join me for supper then, Inspector? You can question me and have your supper at the same time. If you have ridden straight through, ye must be starved. Its haggis and single malt whiskey I offer you tonight," Morgana said smiling.

One eyebrow raised as *Himself* accepted the kind offer. He took off his great coat and relaxed in one of the offered chairs. "So the Sheriff tells me you are knowledgeable of the healing arts, Mistress," Inspector Macpherson stated.

"Aye Inspector; I learned at my mother's knee and my grandmother's before her and back and back again to the Highlands of Scotland," Morgana replied.

"Do you also have the sight then, Mistress?" Inspector Macpherson asked staring intently at Morgana.

Morgana blushed at the intensity of the look. "Ye know of the sight then, Inspector? Ye understand the way of it; not the forgeries of some, but those truly born with it? I can read the leaves and palms and I have the sight in some matters, but not all," Morgana replied. "The folks here consult me for my healing skills mostly, although I can do readings as well," Morgana said placing the steaming haggis before Inspector Macpherson. He took in the aroma with a deep breath and slowly cut the haggis waiting for the first bite of a delicacy dear to a Scots heart. Morgana saw the look of bliss on his face and filled his glass with the aged single malt. A rare smile creased his lips as he took the first bite.

"Did you learn this at your mother's knee as well, Mistress?" Inspector Macpherson asked smiling.

"I did Inspector. My grandmother brought the recipe with her from the Highlands and it was then brought down to me from my mother. Let me know when you'll need more," Morgana stated smiling. There were no questions through the remainder of the supper. *Himself* would not intrude upon haggis with official business. After his meal was concluded and the dishes taken away, Morgana filled the Inspector's glass once again and they returned to business. He noticed that she drank only tea.

"So, Mistress; you were known to the victim?" Inspector Macpherson asked.

"Aye, Inspector; he sought me out as he feared he was possessed of demons," Morgana replied calmly.

"Stuff and nonsense," he snorted inelegantly; "and why would that be, lass?" Inspector Macpherson asked intently.

"He was a married man, Inspector; with three wee bairns. He told me that he had fallen in love with another woman and could not help himself. He thought himself possessed. I knew he had no such ailment. His problem was of the soul, not the body. I gave him teas to calm his mind, but knew I could not cure his affliction," Morgana explained.

"Do you know the name of the lady in question?" Inspector Macpherson asked.

"I do not know, Inspector; he did not share that detail of information. I did tell the Sheriff that were the lady also married, her husband could mayhap be a possible suspect, as well as the wife and her family. I am sorry that I do not know further on that topic," Morgana replied.

"The Sheriff seems to think that it could be poison, Mistress. Were you to go with us in the morning, could you tell by the signs; if any still remain after several days?" Inspector Macpherson asked earnestly.

"I will be happy to go with ye, Inspector. But I have seen the body when the murder first occurred, so that I could report to ye when ye arrived. It was poison, of this there is no doubt. I will help you and the Sheriff in any way that I can," Morgana replied quietly.

"How have ye come to ken such things, Mistress; if it is not so forward of me to ask?" the Inspector said with a frown.

"Not at all, Inspector; I ken these are strange facts for a person to know. My ma'am had access to books back in the old country. They were in the Latin and she was taught the Latin by the old laird. The books spoke of many poisons and its affects and what to do if encountered. Ye must ken the poison itself before trying to treat the patient. Some poisons will cause more damage when coming up then if remaining in the body. The old ones used charcoal to filter the damage and to try to protect the vital organs in the process. It was all in the books, ye see; the ones that my ma'am learned from when she was but a girl. She taught all to me as I grew and came to have interest in the herbs and healing," Morgana replied smiling.

"Ye have a rare gift, Mistress and a rare talent. I wonder how many here realize just how special your skills. Well, I must be off. Good then; I will come for ye in the morning and we will see what more we can discover," Inspector

Macpherson stated staring again intently at Morgana. "Good night then, Mistress and thank ye for supper. I have not had a better haggis since I left the Highlands and the single malt was pure nectar," he said with a bow. He gifted her then with one of his rare smiles. Putting on his great coat, he bent again to exit the door and once again entered the garden. The full moon shone down upon his prancing stallion. The black horse had picked up the scent of the fireplaces and the autumn chill. "Oh aye, Duncan; she is a bonny lass; a Highlander through and through. A man could get lost in those blue eyes, Duncan and that is no lie. Och, here am I talking to my horse about a lass I have just met. Ye will think me possessed if I keep carrying on so, Duncan." Right, steady on, man; ye have only just met her, he thought grinning. James Macpherson smiled into the darkness at that statement as he swung up into the saddle and he and Duncan headed back for town.

Morgana for her part smiled over her dishes. The haggis had been a success. What better way to a man's heart than through his stomach, as her mother had always said? Was he the Highlander her leaves had foretold? Had he truly come for her? Only time would tell, she thought smiling. Only time would tell, but Morgana knew that she would dream of this man tonight. His shoulders could hardly come through her front door and he had to bend double to come beneath it. He was an impressive man and a Scot; what a combination, she thought with a grin.

*****

The next day Morgana heard a knock at the front door of the cottage. When she went to the door, the cottage entrance was again filled by the broad shoulders and impressive chest of Inspector Macpherson. "Are you ready then, lass?" Inspector Macpherson called out.

"Aye, Inspector; I will just grab my cloak," Morgana replied.

Morgana eyed Duncan suspiciously upon exiting the cottage and warily caught his eye as she entered the garden. The cool of the morning meant that the proud stallion was again frisky and prancing in wait for his master. "Do ye have a horse, lass?" Inspector Macpherson asked.

"Nay Inspector; my family walked out of the Highlands. I have no experience of horses," Morgana said warily watching Duncan.

"Ye dinna walk across the ocean I'll wager," Inspector Macpherson said smiling and watching Morgana intently again. He whispered into Duncan's ear then and quickly gentled the massive horse.

"Aye, ye would be right about that sure enough, Inspector. My family took passage from Inverness and then into Alexandria and on to here," she replied. As she spoke, she calmed as much by their conversation as the horse at his master's whispers.

"Give me yer foot then, lass and we shall ride double," Inspector Macpherson replied.

Still eyeing Duncan warily, Morgana placed her foot into Inspector Macpherson's hand and he easily lifted her onto Duncan's back followed by himself. After mounting, his hands came around her waist and he gave her a brief hug. "Dinna fash, lass; Duncan is a fine mount. He will not know ye are here, as you weigh nay more than a feather." With that they headed down the road to meet the Sheriff and their appointment with a possible murder victim.

Upon their arrival, Sheriff Holter advised that the family would remain inside the house, as the investigation centered on the body presently located in the ice house. Inspector Macpherson helped Morgana down from his horse's back and she followed the Sheriff and the Inspector into the darkness of the ice house interior. The Sheriff carried a torch to light their path.

The body was laid out on a slab typically reserved for meat in the ice house. Morgana gathered her cloak around her against the damp cold of the ice house. She looked down into the face of Dirk Deacon and crossed herself before proceeding to her work. Inspector Macpherson watched her intently. She noted for the Inspector the presence of the light blue mark at the corner of the victim's mouth that she had seen when first she examined the body and the smell of the faint odor of almonds which had clung to the body. She pointed to the hands, where she had seen the same telltale color and smell. She had found it on the right hand. She looked up at the Sheriff and the Inspector who had intently watched her progress. "Ye see the telltale blue marks were on the right hand and at the corner of the mouth here," she pointed. "There was also a faint smell of almond. This was poison, gentlemen in case there was any doubt on yer part before now," Morgana said gravely.

"I can confirm further for ye, given it has been a week since the death. The tongue here has swollen and ye will ken the blackness around the mouth. These are all sure signs of poison, for those who ken what to look for," she said worriedly.

The Sheriff crossed himself and the Inspector stood stonily taking in the information. "I shall want to meet with the wife and family, Sheriff. I want no mention of Mistress Mackenzie's findings outside of this space. Do ye ken?" Inspector Macpherson asked sternly.

The Sheriff and Morgana both said *aye* and the Inspector walked from the ice house. The Sheriff helped Morgana to her feet and led her outside. Once into the light again, Morgana went to an outcropping of stone and flowers and proceeded to scour it for medicinal plants that she might pick for her stash of medicinal herbs. The Inspector proceeded inside to meet with the widow and other family members.

After forty-five minutes or so, the Inspector came out of the house pulling on his gloves. His face wore a scowl and he pulled at his queue as if to release the hair to the soft autumn breeze. Morgana straightened herself then from her collecting at his approach. The sun caught the glint of the reddish brown hair and Morgana thought again that he was a fine figure of a man, as restless now as his mount and as anxious to be gone from this place of death.

"They had no information of value. I do not believe demons at work when poison is so obviously found on the body. Bloody superstitions," Inspector Macpherson stated heatedly. "There is a logical explanation for all of this and I intend to find it," the Inspector continued heatedly.

The Sheriff and Morgana exchanged looks and then quickly looked to the ground. "Morgana, would you like a ride back to the cottage?" Sheriff Holter asked.

"She rides with me, Sheriff," Inspector Macpherson said testily. The Inspector took Morgana's foot in his hand again and lifted her to the horse's back. After settling her on the saddle, he pulled himself up next. The threesome rode back to the cottage in silence.

Upon arriving at Bella Vista, the Inspector handed Morgana down from the mount. Morgana patted the horse's neck as the Sheriff and Inspector talked. The Inspector was obviously angered by the lack of a trail to follow in his first line of inquires. After a few minutes of conversation, he broke off from the Sheriff and came to stand by Morgana, the Sheriff heading on his mount back to town. "So ye two are becoming friends then, are ye?" the Inspector asked. He gifted Morgana with another of his rare smiles which may have also been directed towards his mount, she was not sure.

"We are indeed, Inspector. Most creatures respond to kindness; do ye not think?" she asked shyly.

"Aye Mistress, but there is precious little of it in this world to go around," he said sharply, and then broke the grimace with another rare smile. "Will ye get word to me if ye hear anything about our murder?" Inspector Macpherson asked.

"Aye, Inspector; I was thinking, ye might want to talk to some of the local orchardists. They all use the poison in their growing and about their properties. They use it to keep away the vermin and to kill the insects that would come at the fruit," Morgana stated. "They could advise ye if any had gone missing or if anyone would have come to mayhap buy some for their own use," she added.

"That is a good lead Mistress; ye have been most helpful. How would they come about such a substance in the growing?" he asked.

"It is possible to make, if ye ken how; from apple pips, cherry pits or peach pits and such which they have in abundance. It is used primarily to keep away the rats that would do damage to the harvest and the warehousing and for other pests while the apples are growing," Morgana replied.

"Just so, thank ye for that information. Thank ye also for dinner last night. I have not had haggis better since I left the Highlands," Inspector Macpherson stated smiling again.

"Aye Inspector; it is rare to find in this new land," Morgana stated smiling shyly again.

"Mistress, keep me informed of any new information that ye may discover," Inspector Macpherson said before mounting. He stopped suddenly before mounting his horse. "Is that . . . heather that I see in yer garden?" he asked suddenly.

"Oh aye, my mam brought a shoot of it when my da and she left Scotland. He laughed at her saying it would never last during the voyage and never grow once she arrived; but she kept a bit of it for each place that they lived," Morgana replied smiling.

"Oh aye, we have had it at each of our houses also," he replied smiling.

"Yer wife saw to it, then?" Morgana asked casually.

"Nay, mistress; my mam saw to the picking and the planting; I am not married," he replied softly.

"Oh, I dinna ken," she replied blushing. She watched as he reached out and brushed his fingers gently against the heather. It was an action that she had watched her parents do many times, as if by touching the heather transplant, they again touched the heather of home and the blessed ground in which the plant had originally grew. She reached down then and broke off a small piece of it and fitted it into the Inspector's buttonhole. "It will give ye a bit of home while ye dwell among us," she replied as she stepped back and admired her handiwork.

"Moran taing, mistress; until next we meet; God be with ye, lass," the Inspector said as he mounted his horse.

"And also with ye, Inspector," she replied.

Morgana stood watching the Inspector leave. She watched until he was out of sight and then picking a piece of heather for herself, went inside to put on the kettle. She hoped the flowers she had picked at the crime scene would help further with the investigation. The leaves when steeped brought her another piece of the puzzle; the letter *E* was plainly before her, but no other clue presented itself at this time. She had no idea the significance of the letter or if it even pertained to the investigation before them. The letter *E*; I must make a note of it and keep it with me until the reason becomes known to me or to the Inspector, she thought. Somehow this is valuable to the inquiry, but how, she speculated. She thought again about the taciturn Inspector. He had told her that he was not married. That was useful information for sure. She had hopes that he would be the Highlander that her mother had spoken of so often. Perhaps, she thought fleetingly, this is he.

CHAPTER FOUR

In response to Morgana's suggestion, the Inspector had the Sheriff take him to the home of one after another of the local orchardists and farmers. They all were questioned about the use of the poison in their growing efforts and whether or not any of the poison would have gone missing or been sought out by one who was not a farmer recently. Most stated that they kept the poison to kill rats and keep them away from the harvest. Some used it in diluted portions to keep the pests from the crop during the growing season. All were convinced that it was such a common household item in the area that it would not be of specific interest to have it possessed by a family. At each homestead, the making of it was a family recipe and each told him of their own private formula. At each household, the Inspector asked also about Mistress Mackenzie and whether or not her skills had been sought out by the family in the past, either for health related concerns or her other more specialized talents.

Each of the families interviewed spoke glowingly of Morgana's skills, even if they did not admit publicly to visiting her themselves. The Inspector received the very real sense that Morgana was a hidden treasure in the community; sought out by all in their time of trouble, but acknowledged by none. He thought it odd that people of this new world would not understand the importance of a healer and in her case; a healer with the sight as well. Perhaps, he thought, this was yet another thing that only a Highlander would understand. At his own family home in Scotland, a healer was present at all times and one with the sight was the most highly prized as a confidante and advisor to the laird. Here it seemed that Morgana was required to keep her highly prized skills hidden, if only to keep from arousing suspicion on the part of her neighbors. Not for the first time Inspector Macpherson felt like an outsider in his new land. It was but one thing that Morgana and he shared; the knowledge of the old world and a feeling of being an outsider in the new.

*****

Two days later a knock came to Morgana's cottage door. When she opened the door, she saw the door frame again filled by the large figure of Inspector Macpherson. "Has there been news, Inspector?" Morgana asked.

"Aye, there has been another development, Mistress. We have a second body and are in need of yer assistance if ye will be so kind," Inspector Macpherson requested frowning.

Morgana gathered her cloak, shut the door and joined the Inspector in the garden. "Ye are old friends now, Mistress, I am thinking," he said smiling at his mount.

"Aye Inspector; he is not so verra tall and imposing; just tall," Morgana said with mischief in her eyes. Macpherson caught the mischief and smiled briefly into her laughing eyes.

"And all creatures respond to kindness, Mistress; do they not?" he replied with one eyebrow raised. Macpherson caught Morgana by the foot again and legged her onto his mount. He patted her foot briefly then before pulling himself into the saddle behind her. His hand came briefly to her waist again, patted her waist and steered Duncan to the location of the latest victim's home.

Sheriff Holter met them at the designated location. Inspector Macpherson lowered himself from his mount and helped Morgana carefully down from his horse as well. He offered his arm this time and they came abreast of the Sheriff. "What do we have here, Sheriff?" Macpherson asked earnestly.

"It looks very much the same as the prior murder, Inspector. I would ask for Morgana's assistance again to verify and confirm that the means of the death are the same," Sheriff Holter stated gravely.

"If ye will be so kind to keep the family at bay, we will ask Mistress Mackenzie to render her opinion," Macpherson stated looking down at Morgana.

Morgana went into the house and pulled her cloak tightly about her. She heard the sound of a woman weeping in the adjacent room. The room in which the body was found was cold and damp, which would help preserve the body, as the ice house had done previously. Morgana knelt next to the victim. Her dark head was so close as if she would take measure of the death and how it had occurred by her sheer proximity. She crossed herself quickly and then proceeded with her examination.

After a few moments, Morgana raised her head to the Inspector and Sheriff. "The death is the same; the telltale blue mark at the corner of the mouth here," she pointed "and again on the right hand here. I found these tiny threads in the hand of the victim as well. They are black threads, Inspector and are perhaps from a cloak, I am not sure. The telltale smell is present as well. There is information also that ye may wish to know about the victim when we can again speak privately." Morgana gently returned the covering blanket over the face of the victim and rose to her feet. She again pulled her cloak tightly about her and asked if she could speak to *Himself* privately in the vestibule of the house.

"Inspector, I would ask if the bins or trash heaps could be inspected for any remaining food stuffs. We did not have that assessment with the first victim, as too much time had passed between the death and our arrival. There has to be a means by which the poison is being ingested. If we can find that, perhaps we will know if there are common food items between the two deaths," Morgana said intently.

"I shall ask the Sheriff to do so. Thank ye Mistress for yer insight," Macpherson said pressing her hand.

"I will wait outside, Inspector; should ye need me further," Morgana stated.

Morgana went outside and breathed a deep sigh of relief. She was relieved to be out of the house and out of the sound of the keening of the widow of the victim. She went directly to the Inspector's horse. They had become friends since the first murder site. She had no treats for him on this day, but he happily accepted her stroking embraces. In that manner of large beasts and small creatures, the two stood like two opposing views of nature. Morgana held to the neck of the Inspector's proud mount and he in turn offered comfort to the tiny healer who had become a central part of this ongoing murder investigation. Morgana who had learned her arts as a healer, found it hard to accept that she had been thrust into the identification of the now two deaths presented to them and that both victims were beyond her healing care.

Inspector Macpherson found them there together as he exited the house; his proud prancing mount and the tiny healer gaining strength from each other. The autumn breeze had picked up and Morgana's curls had come loose from her sheltering cloak. The winds gathered them and they danced along with the circling leaves picked up on the autumn breeze. "Mistress Mackenzie," Inspector Macpherson stated watching the healer and his mount, "do ye have any private information about our victim that ye would care to share with me at this time?" he asked watching her intently.

"I do, Inspector but it may be well that such information be shared with ye in private again, if that is agreeable. The information I have is not fitting for the ears of the family, if ye ken my meaning" Morgana stated quietly.

"Verra well; I shall check on the progress by the Sheriff and rejoin you shortly, Mistress," Macpherson stated.

Morgana continued to stroke and nuzzle the Inspector's horse Duncan. Duncan for his part behaved as if he was her protector in lieu of the Inspector and the Sheriff both occupied by the crime scene. Perhaps the mount of such a respected man of the law understood the need for comfort by those who have viewed grievous bodily harm and require solace thereafter. Regardless, Morgana and Duncan forged a bond that day which lasted them well beyond this place of death and yet another scene of crime.

The Inspector came upon them again in the same posture. He was amazed at the usually aloof Duncan and the tiny healer who stood nuzzling him. He had seen that sign before. She was seeking comfort in another living creature and the warmth and solace of the same in the face of one more death. Inspector Macpherson had seen it many times before and shared it as well. Duncan was an unlikely comforter, but on this day, this healer had reached out to him and he had filled that need.

Inspector Macpherson cleared his throat and Morgana's head came up, not sharply but attentively. She held onto Duncan's head until the Inspector came abreast of them.

"Let me help ye, Mistress." He took her foot again in his hand and helped her into the saddle. Duncan whinnied quietly as if to say all is well. Inspector Macpherson pulled himself into the saddle behind her; gathered the reins in one hand and placed his free hand around Morgana's waist. The great coat he pulled around her shoulders against the lifting breeze.

When they returned to her cottage, Macpherson pulled himself from the saddle and handed Morgana down. She went into the cottage followed closely by the stooped figure of the Inspector. "May I take yer coat, Inspector?" Morgana asked. "Will ye have some tea then?" Morgana offered.

"Nay tea, Mistress but a dram of single malt, if it is at hand," Macpherson replied with a smile.

"Aye, Inspector; just the thing," Morgana replied.

Morgana poured out a dram of whiskey for the Inspector and made a cup of tea for herself. She sat at the still room table and prepared to relay her story to the Inspector. "The victim's name is Donald Carmack. He came to me as a patient, but there was no illness, Inspector. He planned on a connection with a certain lady of questionable virtue that practices her trade in town. His concern was that this lady not become with child as a result of their dalliance and that his wife not be exposed to disease because of his straying ways, beyond the bounds of marriage. It was a request I could not comply with Inspector for several reasons," Morgana stated quietly.

The Inspector was thoughtful for a moment then raised his eyes to Morgana. "He does not sound like a man of honor, Mistress. Ye were correct to deny his request. In any light, your skills would have been used to enable adultery and perhaps worse. Mistress, may I ask ye, do ye have protection here at yer cottage? Ye have patients who are without honor and secrets that make ye verra vulnerable in the hearing. Ye now are assisting both the Sheriff and me in our inquiries. I believe this assistance could make ye even more vulnerable here on yer own as we now investigate two murders which may or may not be related," Macpherson stated earnestly.

Morgana went to her cabinet then and pulled from it a dirk and a sgian dubh which had belonged to her Father and her grandfather before him. "My Father carried these from the Highlands, Inspector; after the time of the troubles. They belonged to his family," Morgana stated with proud, shining eyes.

"Do ye ken how to use them then, Mistress?" Macpherson asked earnestly.

"Oh aye; my Father taught me how, Inspector. I have never had to use them to protect myself, but I know how should the need arise," she replied fiercely.

"Aye, Mistress; that is well. I see the sgian dubh as your best choice because of your size, mind; but the dirk would do well should ye be set upon when outside with more room to maneuver," Inspector Macpherson replied earnestly. A strange look passed over his features and he blinked suddenly and multiple times as if in pain. It was a quick thing and soon over. Only someone with Morgana's skills at diagnosis would have noted it and suspected its cause. She replaced the dirk and sgian dubh in their hiding places in the cabinet and turning thought to assist the Inspector.

"Is the headache upon ye, Inspector?" Morgana asked.

"Aye Mistress; above the eyes as always," Inspector Macpherson said quietly. "It is a small thing and naught for ye to worry about," he continued.

"Is it the queue then, Inspector?" Morgana continued quietly.

"The queue, Mistress; what makes ye say the queue is the cause?" Macpherson asked.

"No Highlander would be comfortable in a queue, Inspector or if so, not for long," Morgana replied smiling. "Will ye have some willow bark tea to relieve the pain?" Morgana asked.

"Nay, Mistress; it will pass. They always do," Macpherson replied quietly.

"May I help?" Morgana asked shyly. She came behind Inspector Macpherson then and unlaced the queue. She then began to massage his temples beginning at the hair line and continuing behind the ears, down the neck and to the base of his skull. He spoke not a word as she quietly went about the work of eliminating his pain. She was a healer again after leaving behind her the second scene of death. Her hands travelled from his neck across the broad shoulders. She knew from experience that headaches frequently resulted from tension in the shoulders and back. She dared not fully extend her touch to his back as a whole without his consent, but thought her ministrations safe if limited to the shoulders. Her hands small but strong, kneaded the flesh then worked their way back up to the starting point at the temples. Once she had concluded her work, she stood for a moment waiting to see if her ministrations had been successful. The answering reply was satisfying.

AN EVIL MOON

"You have healing hands, Mistress; a gentle touch. My headache is gone, Mistress and I thank ye for it," Macpherson stated smiling one of his rare smiles.

"I needed to heal again, Inspector you see; after being with one more beyond my help. I hope ye do not mind, but I wanted to make sure ye were not pained further," Morgana stated quietly. "I have been with those near death many times, but not with those past my helping. These two victims all have one thing in common, Inspector. They are pillars of the community as far as the larger world knows, but they have secrets known only to a few," Morgana continued warily. "Those secrets are not known to many and were they to be released, the victims would have been shamed, Inspector and perhaps would have been forced to leave the community," Morgana replied.

"Aye, Mistress; I ken what you say and I thank ye again for the healing," Macpherson stated tenderly. "There is much information to ponder and much to follow-up on from this day's work," he replied solemnly.

*****

In follow-up to the Donald Carmack murder inquiry, the Inspector made a point of interviewing the lady of questionable virtue with whom Carmack had been well acquainted. The Sheriff had directed him to the tavern and to the second story access of the business run by Carmack's associate. The Sheriff had not taken actions to close the business, as many of the community made it a regular stop in their evening revels, as it lie above a favorite tavern.

The Inspector was no prude and a man who had served in battle and on the side of the law since he was eighteen years old. He knew from experience that fresh faced lads came to such places to become men and men fresh from battle

25

likewise to forget the sounds, smells, and horrors of war in the arms of a tarnished dove, like the women that he would find beyond this painted door.

James Macpherson was a man of the world and a Scotsman in the bargain; practical and no nonsense. He had seen his share of such businesses, but found that they held no attraction for him. The rough, corseted and rouged women within the door that he entered brought to him more feelings of shame and pity for the women concerned and for those who felt themselves compelled to avail themselves of their services. With each new woman who approached him and solicited his interest, the image of a fresh faced, blue eyed lass came to his mind. There was an attraction for him in Berkeley County for certain; but she resided in a stone cottage far from this door and far from the women who resided within.

As he entered an inner door within the establishment, he asked to speak to the proprietor. He was taken to a woman of five and thirty years of age who looked much older than her actual years. Given her profession, this fact did not surprise him. "I have come, madam to make inquiries into the recent death of Donald Carmack. Would ye be the person who would have knowledge of Donald Carmack, then?" Inspector Macpherson asked.

"Aye; you are the Scots Inspector that I have heard tell of. Will ye not take some refreshment and entertainment before your interrogation, Inspector?" the madam stated flirtatiously.

"Nay, madam; I am pressed for time and come only in answer to my inquiries. Would ye have knowledge of Donald Carmack, madam that may prove helpful to my investigation?" Inspector Macpherson continued.

"Aye, Inspector; one could say intimate knowledge," she continued smiling. "I was not with him at the time of his death, as I understand that he died at home. My business interests keep me close to this location at night and I sleep during the day, Inspector. There are those who can account for my whereabouts on the day that he died if that was a question that you wished to ask. Is that a sufficient alibi for you for the death in question?" she asked.

"I am sure, madam. Are there others who could have reason to end the life of Master Carmack and if so, can you share any possible reasons that they may have had to do so?" Inspector Macpherson asked.

"Not that I can think of, Inspector. He was generally liked, although I am sure that some would take issue with his choice of entertainments, if you catch my meaning," she continued flirtatiously. "He was also a man who took what he wanted in business. There are those who would call him sharp in business and sharp in tongue when the time called for it," she continued. "There are some that he has crossed who might wish to see him out of their way, permanently. He was not one who was content with the word no for any reason," she said fiercely.

"Would there be those who you could name who would wish him gone, madam?" Macpherson asked.

"That would be a question for the widow, I do believe Inspector. She also kept the books for his business and might have more to share regarding his known enemies. He did not speak of his business concerns to me generally, Inspector. We had other things to speak of most times," she replied flirtatiously.

"I see, madam and I thank ye for yer time. I would ask if there is any additional information that ye may recall, to get word to me through the Sheriff. Thank ye again, madam for the information," Inspector Macpherson stated as he inclined his head.

"Not at all, Inspector; I hope that we may see you again very soon, in a social setting if not officially," she continued smiling. "Please avail yourself of the hospitality of my establishment, without charge, of course. Call it a professional courtesy, from one professional to another," she said with a coquettish smile.

The proprietress bowed her head and returned to an inner chamber. The Inspector retreated from the space, the image of a blue eyed lass before him on his retreat. On returning to his rented rooms that night, the Inspector took off his great coat, neck cloth and shirt and bathed. There were times such as this that the sordid nature of his work cut him to the bone. Bright, shining blue eyes sustained him on this night, as they had since they first met. He remembered well the feel of her healing hands on his head and shoulders. Not since he had left the Highlands had he felt the same healing touch taking away his pain and the headaches that plagued him since childhood. Morgana, he thought; so far removed from this work, the death and of all the ugliness that I have seen since leaving the Highlands. He sighed again and made his notes from the day's inquiries. Another lead followed and another dead end reached, he thought despondently.

*****

The next day James Macpherson informed the Sheriff of his ongoing work regarding the Donald Carmack murder. The interview with Carmack's lady of easy virtue had not provided any useful information. His principal concern now two murders in, was the effect the ongoing work was having on Morgana.

"Sheriff, do you ken the danger that Mistress Mackenzie is in on a daily basis and worse still, during the night? She lives alone in her cottage, though I ken the master lives nearby. She helps us daily on two murder cases now. Should the wrong person see her give that assistance, there is no telling the impact. We deal with a mad man in this matter;

make no mistake and the wee mistress is alone in a cottage each night," Inspector Macpherson stated heatedly.

"Aye, Inspector, I have asked her repeatedly to come back to town and stay with the missus and myself. She refuses, Inspector as she says she must have a garden for her potions and lotions and such. Folks go to her to cure their ills, Inspector but the trust is not there because of the sight and her other knowledge, I believe. They hold her at arm's length, unless they need her of course. Then she must come to heal their ills right enough," the Sheriff responded heatedly.

"A garden you say, Sheriff; is that all that she requires?" the Inspector asked taking stock of the conversation.

"Aye, she tells me she needs her wee mountain, but I think that is more the Highlander in her, you ken?" the Sheriff said smiling. "Her garden provides the herbs and such that she needs to make her lotions, potions and tinctures. She is a marvel at it for sure," he continued.

"Aye; she needs the mountains as do we all; but not to do her healing, but for her soul. The mountain being close enough can work the same, I reckon," the Inspector stated frowning. He hoped that was the case at any rate, as Alexandria had no mountains. He knew since entering her cottage that he needed to convince her to return with him when this whole sordid affair was at an end. He made no comment regarding his personal feelings to the Sheriff, but made a mental note of what she would need in the future. That was valuable information indeed and he would hold it to his heart until the time was right and his work here was done.

*****

From that day forward, the Inspector made a point of stopping daily to check on Morgana and to apprise her of his round of inquires and what he had gleaned thus far. She was worried about his inquires as it relayed to the lady of questionable virtue and informed him of the same. He smiled with the one cocked eyebrow and informed her that his inquiries had been limited to the murder victim and that verra little progress was made of it and certainly no enjoyment. He was able to verify that the lady had been an associate of the victim, but her alibi had covered the day and time of the death.

"Were any food stuffs able to be uncovered at the scene of the second murder, Inspector?" Morgana asked gravely.

"Nay lass; that is the mystery of it all. The food scraps were checked, bins and trash heaps and no foodstuffs that smelled of the almond that you spoke of finding; nothing that was not also eaten by the family as a whole and no one else taken ill from any meal. Have ye had any images of the sight, mistress that might be of assistance?"

"There is one letter that comes to me. The letter *E* comes to me in the leaves, Inspector; that only so far," Morgana replied quietly.

"Aye, Mistress; the letter *E*, you say. Well, all that ye have said has been born out in truth. What signs ye see I take as fact; that ye can be sure. I understand the Sheriff's reliance on ye, and I thank ye for yer assistance as well. We will keep this information tucked away and ponder on it when the time is right," Macpherson said tenderly.

"Ye are welcome, Inspector. Will ye have a wee dram before ye go?" Morgana asked shyly.

"Aye Mistress; that will not come amiss," Macpherson replied smiling. A wee dram with the tiny healer had become the best part of his day and he looked forward to it as his business concluded for the day and no answers yet provided to the mysterious deaths and who had profited from them.

CHAPTER FIVE

By the third week of his arrival, a third body had been discovered. The body count was growing and the Inspector was in no mood for further delay of the investigation and the discovery of the culprit. The Inspector came to claim Morgana again for her assistance to the Sheriff and himself in this cruel business that had become a serial murder investigation. Her eyes were wide as saucers at the thought of yet another scene of death. She took but a moment to cut an apple for Duncan and wrapped it in her hankie. If the two comrades would spend time together today, she would have a treat for him this time. Inspector Macpherson, who missed nothing, saw her hankie in her hand as he legged her up on the horse's back. "Ye are ill then, Mistress?" he asked anxiously.

"Nay, Inspector; it is a treat for Duncan . . . for after," she replied quietly.

"Aye, Mistress; he is a good mount and a good friend. He gives as much comfort as he accepts, I reckon. He will be happy of the treat," Macpherson said tenderly.

They made their way to the assigned location. The Sheriff was there already and was keeping the family at bay. The victim was laid out again in the stillroom with nothing but a blanket covering him. The Sheriff knowing the routine that had gone before, was collecting trash bins and food heaps to see if any telltale signs of the poison remained. Morgana inspected the body and confirmed the same poison; the distinctive blue color was evident at the corner of the mouth and this time on the left hand of the victim; left handed versus the right handed of the previous victims. Morgana found something more on this victim; a small crumb still remaining in the hand which she looked at closely and felt might resemble a portion of a biscuit or piece of bread with the same telltale smell of almond upon it.

"What do ye make of this, Inspector? The poison is definitely upon it," Morgana stated.

"It is a crumb of some sort, Mistress?" Macpherson stated as he inspected it closely.

"I think perhaps a portion of a biscuit or other piece of bread, Inspector," Morgana stated.

"Bread you say; the texture reminds me more of a communal wafer. Do ye ken anything of the local priest?" Macpherson asked.

"Nay; he is new to these parts, Inspector. Since I moved to the cottage, I have not been able to go to mass. Maybe the Sheriff can cast some light. But why would you ask?" she asked warily.

"Oh . . . just a hunch at this stage; nothing more, Mistress. Just a thought at this point, but I must gather more information before I proceed. I shall go interview the family again if ye wish to wait in the garden," Macpherson stated.

"Aye, Inspector; I shall do so," Morgana replied.

Morgana went to the garden again to wait. She pulled out her hankie and the cut apple slices for Duncan. She smiled when she drew near to him and taking his neck in her hands, began to feed the mount the cut apple slices. He lipped her small hand and the apple contained on the flat surface of her palm. She smiled at the velvety touch of his lips as he enjoyed the treat. He whinnied and bobbed his head with each piece as if in thanks for the snack. Forty-five minutes later, the Inspector came from the house and found Morgana feeding the remaining apple slices to Duncan. He smiled again at the unexpected companionship between the two; the one so large and majestic and the other so tiny. "Do they have anything useful to share, Inspector?" Morgana asked as he approached.

"Nay, no useful information; the victim was alone when he was taken. The family returned to find him dead, just as in the other cases," Macpherson stated sighing.

"It is just a thought, Inspector; but do we ken perhaps if each of the victims were alone when they died?" Morgana asked.

"They were, lass; what are ye thinking?" Macpherson asked frowning.

"Could we speak privately again, Inspector?" Morgana asked.

"Aye, lass; I do not think there is much more to gain here," Macpherson stated.

The Inspector legged Morgana up and picked up her hankie dropped from the ground. He placed it carefully in the pocket of his great coat and then pulled himself into the saddle behind Morgana.

When they arrived back at the cottage, the Inspector followed Morgana into the stillroom where he took off his great coat and she put out two glasses; one which she filled with a dram of whiskey and the other with tea for herself.

"So what do ye ken of this newest victim, Mistress Morgana?" Macpherson asked. Her head came up quickly as it was the first time that he had called her by her Christian name.

"Edward Murphy was his name, Inspector and he was a convicted felon; not in this country mind, but in the old country. He carried the mark from his punishment. I saw it when giving treatment. I never made a comment, Inspector but he found the need to tell the story," Morgana stated quietly.

"I ken ye are a verra good listener, Mistress. People tell ye their deepest thoughts because ye hold confidences as ye hold their limbs for treatment," Macpherson stated quietly.

"Aye, Inspector; I reckon that is the case. It is true that sometimes folk need to talk as much as they need treatment. They need to unburden themselves as they would to a priest," Morgana stated. She frowned then at the thought of her own words; as they would to a priest, she thought again.

"Aye; yers is a very special gift, Mistress Morgana," Macpherson stated quietly. Morgana rose then to fill his glass again with the single malt and tea for herself.

"Do ye never take a wee dram yourself, Mistress?" Macpherson asked.

"Oh, aye Inspector; I do on festive occasions or sometimes for the cold of a wintry day. A day such as today is difficult for me; ye ken?" Morgana replied.

"I do ken. You have seen death now three times and have been powerless to prevent it, as have I. I ask you to hear my story, Mistress Morgana as I know ye will keep it safe. We are kin are we not; both born of the Highlands? Ye told me yer family walked from the Highlands, Mistress. I rode from the Highlands when I left because there was a price on my family's head. My grandfather was taken down in chains for his support of the rightful King James after the rising of '45. He would not let my father see his shame and sent my father from the Highlands, first to Edinburgh and later with passage to America. We came to Alexandria, as there are many Scots there with the same tale," Macpherson stated quietly. "The families there are part of the tobacco trade of Northern Virginia. It was not a life for me, as I was expected to be a soldier from birth," Macpherson said earnestly.

He returned then to the crime scene and to the evidence found. "Mistress Morgana; ye said the crumb that you found appeared to be part of a biscuit or perhaps a piece of bread. Is it possible that someone else has heard the confession of these victims; someone who would not be willing to keep silent at the sins that they heard?" Macpherson stated.

"Ye suspect the new priest then, Inspector?" Morgana asked horrified.

"I suspect everyone, mistress except you and the Sheriff of course. I still worry about yer safety here. Ye have your dirk and your sgian dubh I ken; but would you consider moving closer to town until this sorry business is over?" Macpherson asked worriedly.

34

"If the new priest is the culprit, I am safe for now, as I have no sins to confess and no contact with the man," Morgana stated smiling, "Besides without a horse, I have not even met the new priest. The master is nearby here and well . . . some of the families of my patients visit with him when their family members are with me. They would not think it proper to come to me alone, but then; when they have secrets to impart . . . well, they ask to be with me only. I was thinking; the new priest . . . would not the Sheriff have some information on him. I believe he too came from Alexandria. Would your kin in Alexandria have information that they could share or ken one who might possess that information?" Morgana asked.

"Yes, perhaps Mistress Morgana; perhaps," he said pondering the thought. The Inspector blinked multiple times again wearily, the unmistakable look of the headache again upon him.

"Inspector; the headache is upon you again; is it not?" Morgana asked.

"Aye, Mistress Morgana; the change in the weather this time I fear," he said smiling weakly.

"May I help ye then, Inspector; may I help ye with the pain?" Morgana asked quietly.

The Inspector looked up then and met Morgana's eyes. "Aye lass; ye have healing hands. I appreciate the offer, but I do not wish to impose on your talents and skills more than I have done already," he said wearily.

"Nay, Inspector; I have told ye there are those now beyond my help. There now are three who are beyond my ministrations, but when there is a person in need of my skills, I wish to heal if I may be allowed," Morgana replied quietly.

"Of course, lass; I ken it is hard to see death and to be unable to stop it. I have seen it many times on battlefields and at the hands of mad men. To see it and be powerless to stop it is a dreadful thing. I am sorry that ye have had to watch this, Morgana and especially to see it now three times

35

over. I ken it has been a hard thing. Yer help has been invaluable to me and to the Sheriff, but I worry about the cost to ye," the Inspector said anxiously.

She came behind him again, placing her hands at his temples. She placed some of her lavender scented lotion on her hands and began the massage. Her hands travelled down the sides of his face to his ears, behind the ears, and around the base of the neck and down to the shoulders. This time she reached around and gently undid his neck cloth. She saw for the first time the scar of the saber blade on the left side of his neck. She touched it gently, not wishing to cause him more discomfort. The fire cackled and there was no other sound in the small cottage as Morgana worked quietly and efficiently to relieve the pain. Once she had removed the neck cloth, she used more of the lotion of her own creation to work the area of the neck and the saber scar that by rights should have ended his life.

"You have a guardian angel, Inspector to have lived through this wound," Morgana said quietly.

"And I have angel hands ministering to my pain," Inspector Macpherson said with his eyes closed. He placed his hand over Morgana's then and gently squeezed it.

Once again she removed the laces from his queue and relieved the pressure thorough the scalp as well. She continued with the lavender oil infused lotion at the temples, and massaged above the eyes briefly when she had concluded her treatment. When she had completed her ministrations, she moved to her seat to see the results to determine if the pain was gone. His smile told her all that she needed to know. The pain was gone and the relief was apparent as well in the relaxed smile.

"Do ye have relief then, Inspector? Your face tells me so, but I would hear it from your own lips," Morgana asked.

"Aye, mistress; relief again and I thank you for it. Ye have the healing touch for sure and it would be a lucky man to win your hand for many reasons," Inspector Macpherson said watching Morgana intently.

"Ye are kind, Inspector," Morgana said shyly.

"I think it time that ye call me by my Christian name of James," the Inspector replied.

"You are named for *Himself* then, Inspector?" Morgana asked.

"Aye, Morgana; named for our true King James Stuart," the Inspector replied.

"Were ye ever called, Jamie as you grew?" Morgana asked with the smile back in her eyes.

"Oh aye, Morgana; my mam and da called me Jamie," the Inspector replied. "I would be pleased if ye were to call me Jamie as well," Inspector Macpherson stated.

*****

That evening on his return to his rented rooms, the Inspector took out the hankie he had collected at the death scene of Edward Murphy and spread it out on the table before him. It was to him very like a favor of a lady for her knight errant. The hankie was embroidered with the two letter MMs closely aligned in the corner of the laced material. She won't need to change her initials, Jamie thought looking down at the hankie. When I take her home as my bride, her initials will remain the same. Morgana is my own sweet lass with the angel hands and the special sight. He spread it out on a table before him and smiled down at it. It was as lovely and delicate as Morgana herself. She is as rare as the sight that she holds and I must be sure to keep her safe. Her talents could so easily be her own undoing, he thought frowning. In the wrong hands, her talents could be abused. I will keep her safe with my life, he thought fiercely. He placed the folded hankie with the sprig of now dried heather on the mantle of his rented rooms. He undressed, lay on the cot and inhaled the light lavender lotion that Morgana had used to relieve him of his headache. He felt her strong, small hands on his neck and shoulders and sighed at the memory of the touch. Soon, I will take ye from this place and bring ye to my home, Morgana Mackenzie and then, we shall begin the life we were meant to have far from these shores.

CHAPTER SIX

On his next daily check in with Morgana, Jamie decided to surprise her with a personal visit that involved nothing related to the case. He did not bring tales of his interviews and the many leads followed to little avail. Today the weather was unseasonably warm and he decided that Duncan and he would set out with a basket of treats to tempt Morgana to the top of the wee mountain behind her cottage. It was his intent to gradually convey to her that she was not just a help to his ongoing investigation of the now three murders, but to Jamie the man. He had found in Morgana a person that he could talk to after so many years of keeping the stories of the Highlands bottled inside him. When she spoke, he was carried back to his upbringing and her story was so much intertwined with his own experiences. The fact that she was a healer and one with the sight made her a treasure of infinite value. Had the traditions of his youth continued, such a healer would have sat at the right hand of the laird. Such a healer had advised his own grandfather of the disaster that awaited the rising of 1745 and the outcome which was the destruction of the Highland way of life. He knew that Morgana's gifts would only grow stronger with each year of her life. He knew and understood if others did not, the special nature of her talents and how they could be used for good and must be protected against misuse.

When he arrived at the cottage on that given day, Morgana expected the customary update on the ongoing work of the murder investigations. She was surprised to find out that the Inspector was not there for talk of business, but instead to invite her on a picnic to the top of the wee mountain, visible from her cottage. She gathered a cut apple again for Duncan and her cloak and off they proceeded. "I was surprised, Jamie that ye would take a day from your investigation. I have not known ye to do so before," Morgana said as he legged her onto the back of his mount.

"It is Sunday, lass and even inspectors should have the Sabbath rest. I have been curious about this wee mountain since the first day that Duncan and I came to yer cottage. We got into our heads that this was the day to go explore it. Are ye of a mind then to go exploring with us, as I have brought a picnic lunch? Ye have entertained me more than once, Morgana. I think I am long overdue in returning the favor," Jamie said smiling.

"Aye, Jamie when would a Highlander decline an invitation to explore a wee mountain?" Morgana said with mischief in her eyes.

Off they proceeded climbing ever higher to the top of North Mountain. The day was warm for October, but a good breeze met them as they climbed to the peak of the mountain. The view before them showed the beautiful foliage of the autumn and a view of the valley spread out before them as if a rich multi-colored carpet at their very feet. Jamie found a good location for them to spread the plaid and hold their picnic. He helped Morgana down from his horse, spread the plaid out and set out the treats that he had brought with him for the day. Morgana provided Jamie with Duncan's apple so that he would not be left out of the festivities. Morgana arranged the picnic items while Jamie gave the treat to Duncan and then set him free to explore. He took off his great coat and made himself comfortable on the plaid. "So your family would have left the Highlands sometime after 1746, Morgana?"

"Aye, Jamie; our laird was killed at Culloden and his son was but a wee lad at the time. The redcoats came then as they did throughout the Highlands and everyone was turned off. We were told that the land was to be given to one of the redcoat lords for his support of the king during the rising. My grandfather said that it was time for us to walk from the Highlands, never to return. Mother understood and said that we could use the money that she had saved for the passage. Although my grandfather knew there was nothing left behind for us, he could not live with the loss of his entire way of life. He heard tell of great mountains here in Virginia, farther to the west. My family came here from Alexandria in search of the mountains, but his health started to fail. We thought if we could get him to those great mountains, he might think himself home again. We made it this far and my Mother started with her healing services to the community. She taught me all that she knew. Even though she knew that I had the sight from childhood, she was scared to teach me more about it, as she was not sure how it would be accepted in this new land. It hasn't been that long ago, Jamie that women with the sight were burned as witches, even in the Highlands; if not in service to the laird. We did readings of the leaves and palms as they seemed simple enough, but even my Mother would not offer the service of the sight to the law here. When I came to know the Sheriff, we worked together and he gained my trust. Gradually and very carefully I told him of my other gifts and that they would be available to him if helpful. I have helped him ever since with medical needs and with the other special skills when they are called upon," Morgana replied.

"My story is much the same. My grandfather lived through the rising of 1745, but within a year, the way of life that he had built and sustained was gone. We were to be turned out of our homes and my grandfather of course was to be taken away in chains as an example of his support to Bonnie Prince Charlie. My Grandfather could not bear for my father to see that, so we set off first to Edinburgh and then with passage to the new lands. It is well to be among the Highlanders again; ye ken. We can wear the plaid and speak Gaelic, wear and use our arms as we did in the old country and hear the pipes; but as you say, it is not the same. Many in Alexandria are involved in the tobacco trade as I have told ye. It was not a trade for me, as I have been trained as a soldier since birth. My calling was to be either the military or the law and I have done them both since coming to this new land," Jamie said.

"Do ye have any family left in the Highlands?" Morgana asked.

"Aye, there would be cousins left, but as ye know, the estates were scattered and land came to the English lords who had supported the king. When the clans were scattered, the people followed and many have come here to this new land, many more are farther south in North Carolina and after the American Revolution, some went as far afield as Canada. There are those who will be happy in this new land. Will ye be happy here, Morgana without yer family around ye?" Jamie asked tentatively.

"I do not ken, Jamie. I am happy in my cottage. It came to me as a grace and favor gift for a life that I saved of the master who owns the property. That is why I left town when mam died. I have my garden and I can make my medicines and tinctures and lotions. I have not thought of my whole life here, Jamie. Once you have lost yer roots, does it matter where you stay? I don't know that I have given myself a chance to think on it. Now with these cases before us . . . do ye think that this mad man will kill again, Jamie?" Morgana asked anxiously.

"Aye, lass; I do think he will. Once the taste of blood is upon a mad man and he continues to get away with his crime, he comes to think that he will never be caught. Hopefully he will make a mistake or a lead will take us to where we need to go to bring him to justice," he replied frowning.

"I ken that ye need your garden around ye, Morgana; the Sheriff shared that with me; but have ye given more thought to coming to town to stay just until this matter is sorted?" Jamie asked worriedly.

"I promise that if I am in serious danger I will do just that, Jamie. Ye and the Sheriff have both been kind in worrying about me. Ye know that the Highlander is better able than most at taking care of himself or herself; ye ken?" Morgana said with mischief in her eyes.

"Aye I know that well, lass and I know that ye ken how to handle the dirk and the sgian-dubh, but I also ken that ye are a wee thing and someone my size . . . well . . . we could get that dirk away from ye easily and ye would be defenseless. Ye must think on that, Morgana. I tell ye not to scare ye, but to make you think about things that are not so pleasant maybe, but must be faced nevertheless," Jamie responded.

"Do ye worry about me then, Jamie?" Morgana said smiling shyly.

"Aye, Morgana; I worry about ye and I think on ye often," he replied covering her own small hand with his large hand. "Have ye ever consulted the sight for yourself, Morgana? Have ye ever seen into yer own future?" Jamie asked watching her intently.

"Oh aye, Jamie; I have looked for the signs and I have seen . . . things in my own life . . . before they came to pass. I saw yer coming, Jamie. I saw a Highlander coming into my life. It had been foretold by my mam before she passed," Morgana said quietly.

"And was that a happy sight then, Morgana?" Jamie asked again watching her intently.

"Oh aye; that was a happy sight indeed. No one else could quite understand; could they, what we miss every day. The world of the clan, the knowledge that there was always someone there looking out for ye and for yer neighbors. The bairns always having someone to watch over them; the gatherings when they came, the games, even the mist and the rain; no one else could understand, Jamie what we miss each and every day. I ken we can't look back, but it helps to talk to someone who kens that other world and understands," Morgana said with tearful eyes.

"Aye, lass; it helps a great deal. We look for the same faces that we left behind and we listen for the same voices; the sounds, the food. Ah the haggis, my wee, Morgana; the gift of the Gods it was and the single malt the pure nectar. Aye, it helps quite a bit to be with one who understands," Jamie said thoughtfully. "Ye must think on it Morgana as I cannot think of ye alone without worry," Jamie said anxiously.

"I will think on it, Jamie. My patients need me, but I ken that I need to think forward also. I need to think of where I will spend my life and how. I promise to do so . . . between developments in our investigation of course," Morgana replied smiling.

"So it is our investigation now, is it? Aye, Morgana; that is all that I ask, lass; think on it and think of what will happen next in your life. Think also of your safety, as that is uppermost in my mind at the present time," Jamie replied. They spent the remainder of the glorious afternoon together taking in the sights and sounds of the wee mountain and talking of things known only to Highlanders. From their vantage point, they could look over the valley and dream of a time when the valleys spread before them for miles and miles in the distance; a time of the Highlander, forged by struggle and loss, that had sadly passed and of this new land where they now attempted to forge a new life in lands that brought their minds back to a home now lost forever.

CHAPTER SEVEN

The next day the Inspector wrote to his sources in Alexandria regarding the priest only recently arrived in Martinsburg. He asked for all information that could be provided regarding him; his education, where he had been posted before coming to the western part of the state and a physical description and age of the man. As he had told Morgana, he suspected everyone but she and the Sheriff, of course and must now go about the pain staking work of determining the motive for the murders and the possible suspects that could be identified. To date, the stories were so diverse; a man who was having an adulterous relationship with a woman not his wife; a man who visited ladies of questionable virtue and a man who was a convicted felon in the old country. The one thing that they all had in common was that they were seen outwardly as pillars of the community, but they each held deep secrets that had they been exposed, would have shamed them and perhaps forced them to leave the community. The obvious first choice would be a blackmailer, but there had been no evidence of blackmail known by the families or it would have been relayed to the Sheriff or to the Inspector at the time of the death of each victim. The next choice, however horrified Morgana might be at the prospect; was that someone else who knew their innermost secrets had decided to punish the victims for their sins. Jamie made a list of possible suspects and began the methodical work of interviewing each and everyone as the Sheriff introduced him to them and eliminated them from his inquiries.

By the end of each day's labors, he knew that he always had the visit to Morgana's cottage to look forward to. It would almost be worthwhile to arrive with the headache if Morgana would offer her ministrations to his pain. He tried to take along treats to her now as well, especially after the Sheriff let slip the real source of her fine kettle and larder.

"You know, Inspector that many of her patients have no funds to pay for her medicines. They bring her items for the kettle, the larder or for the soup pot. You know there is not much in the way of silver to be had, but they bring her chickens or ham or other things for her larder. She is a bonny cook, along with her other skills, so she is of the Highland way to always have food for her guests. Morgana could probably feed folks for a living as well as look after their scrapes and disorders. She is a bonny cook and has all of the old dishes at her disposal. Of course you would enjoy them, but maybe not all in this new land. The black pudding, Inspector . . . the haggis which you have tried, auld reekie, bannocks, bread and butter pudding, drunken crumble; she can make them all and has shared them with my wife and me. That is how I know the favorites from your homeland. My wife is a bonny cook; but no one could touch Morgana when it comes to her skills in the kitchen," Sheriff Holter said smiling.

"She had not told me that, Sheriff. It is good to know. I reckon that is yet another reason she would not leave her wee cottage; her patients and the things that they bring for her larder. Ye have given me more to think about today, Sheriff. I thank ye for the information," Jamie said thoughtfully.

Upon telling the Inspector this information the Sheriff felt guilty for revealing one more secret about Morgana, but also thought it in the best long term interest of the girl, as the more the Inspector knew about Morgana, the better it would be. He had watched the two closely as they went about the painstaking work at each crime scene and he had seen the signs. Unless he was wrong, the usually stern and always grim Inspector was much less so when in the company of Morgana. She must have brought back the Highlands to him. He knew that the Inspector would accept his confidences in the best possible light and perhaps a match was in the making, he thought warmly.

*****

On his next visit to Morgana on the following night, he found her in an agitated state that he had never seen before. She was always so tranquil and was the calm center at each murder scene that they had investigated thus far. He was anxious to find the source of the agitation as he made himself comfortable in her front room. "What ails you, lass? Ye are not yourself for sure. Has something happened that I need to know about?" Jamie asked anxiously.

"Nay, Jamie it is not me that I worry about. I have had a vision, Jamie and it worries me that another murder may be in the planning. Ye told me that a mad man who has killed before will have no hesitation in killing again; if he continues to go unpunished and has the taste for it. Have ye had word yet from yer kin in Alexandria about the new priest?" Morgana said worriedly.

"Nay, lass; no information has been received to date. Tell me about yer vision and we will try to sort it out," Jamie said patiently.

"I saw a person kneeling and I saw them speaking in hushed tones. It was as if in a confessional, Jamie. I saw the same person dead and dead in the same way, the mark of the poison upon them. It was not any of the victims that we have seen before. I knew all three of them, but I did not know this one, Jamie so I could not warn the person if I knew. Is there any way that we could follow the new priest to see where he goes and whom he sees?" Morgana asked worriedly.

"Aye, lass; I will set the Sheriff and myself to the task. We may need others who can help us on the days of confession just to see if there is a lead there. I know ye were horrified at my suggestion, Morgana; but I have sent for word about this man with a good reason. If he is not the true priest sent to minister to the community, but an imposter instead; . . . well we will only know when the information comes to us. Have ye had visions like this before, Morgana?" Jamie asked anxiously.

"None so vivid, Jamie; it was like a dream, but in waking. It was so very real that I cried out for he who would join the other three victims," Morgana continued shaken by the vision.

"I told ye that the sight will only become stronger, Morgana. I have seen it many times. I am truly sorry that ye have been brought into this whole sordid business. Ye are a healer and not meant to have to see such things," Jamie replied worriedly.

"I told ye, Jamie; I have held the hands of those who are about to pass over. There are times that my skills are not enough to keep someone in this world. I could be with them and give them peace at the end. Sometimes that is all that I can give. This Jamie is like nothing that I have ever experienced before. To know that someone is marked for death and not be able to stop it is a hard thing. I know you have seen it many times and I don't know how you can bear it," Morgana said crying softly.

Jamie came to her side then. He pulled his chair next to hers and held her hand. "Sometimes the only thing we can do, lass; is to talk it through. Like a bad dream, ye need to talk it through so that ye can get the vision behind ye. Ye know the Sheriff and I will do all that we can to try to sort out this mystery," Jamie said tenderly.

Morgana raised her eyes to him then, still filled with tears from the vision that she had experienced. "Thank you so much, Jamie. It does help to talk. I ken ye have seen horrible things in your work and I ken ye understand when the vision is of something that ye cannot prevent," she said quietly.

CHAPTER EIGHT

Within one week's time, Jamie had the information that he had sought from his sources in Alexandria. The information was conclusive and his suspicions were confirmed. The description of the priest did not match the man who had arrived in Martinsburg. Although he was now armed with private information about the actual priest sent from the church in Alexandra, it was incumbent that he catch this imposter in a lie about his own background. He sought out the Sheriff so that they could develop a plan to visit the imposter and catch him in one of several lies about his past.

"I have the information that I sought from my contacts in Alexandria, Sheriff. It is as I feared. The description of the man provided does not even come close to describing the man who is here. The age, the height, weight, hair and eye coloring are all wrong. Unless I miss my guess, Sheriff, this man has taken the place of the rightful priest. I can only guess at his motives, but given the fact that the murders began shortly after his arrival, I fear the worse," the Inspector said gravely.

"Holy Mother, Inspector; this description is nothing like the man who arrived here," the Sheriff said reading the material provided. "Do you propose that we go together and question the man?" the Sheriff asked worriedly.

"My thought is for us to go together so that we can both serve as a witness to our findings. I believe that the imposter will give himself away as we ask our series of non-threatening questions. It is important that we approach him in a manner that will not throw him to the scent of our plans, Sheriff. If I may take the lead, you can record any responses given and we can go very slowly in processing our investigation. I do not want him to become suspicious and perhaps flee in advance of our making our case. It is imperative that we end this man's murder spree because if we do not, he will but take it to another community and the trail of murder will begin again in another city," the Inspector replied worriedly. The two made their arrangements to visit the church in the morning and to in turn, question the alleged imposter.

The Inspector and Sheriff walked inside the church and approached the man who referred to himself as the new priest. "May we speak with you privately for a moment, Father?" Inspector Macpherson asked calmly. The priest inclined his head and led them to his private office for a chat.

Once the Inspector and Sheriff had taken their seats, the Inspector took the lead with a series of non-threatening questions to take the imposter off the scent of the true reason for their visit. "You are new to the area; are you not, Father?" Inspector Macpherson said smiling.

"I am, Inspector; only newly arrived from Alexandra," the imposter stated smiling.

"And before Alexandra, Father; where were you born?" Jamie continued pleasantly.

"My family moved here and there; I have no real home or fixed address; I go only where the Holy Spirit and the church send me," he replied nonchalantly.

"I see; of course, a priest must go where his services are needed. We are here, as I am sure you can appreciate; on the matter of the murder spree that has afflicted this community. It is a frightful business that the Sheriff and I have been tasked to investigate, as we ken it touches upon the entire community. Were any of the recent victims members of the local congregation here?" the Inspector continued.

"They were all members of my flock, Inspector. My deepest sympathies rest of course with their families. They are so innocent in this dreadful business and yet they must suffer for the sins of others," the priest replied.

"The sins of the murderer; I am sure that you mean," Inspector Macpherson continued.

"Well, of course, Inspector. We cannot blame the victims as they knew not what they did, I am sure, to precipitate such an ending," the priest continued. He smiled then briefly, but with a horrible smile to Jamie's mind. He had seen it before; the smile of one who harbors information regarding a crime and yet withholds it as its release would only implicate themselves or worse still, the murderer holds the information to himself viewing himself as more clever than the inspector sent to handle the case. Jamie saw the smile, however fleeting; and thought he knew the source of the murders and the reason for the murders as well. The victims had been punished, not by God; but by a man impersonating a priest. Had the actual priest been murdered as well, on his way to Berkeley County? So many questions filled Jamie's mind, yet it was imperative that he remain calm as he quietly interviewed the chief suspect.

"You will let us know if any information is provided to you that may aid in the capture of the murderer who is responsible for this reign of terror?" Jamie continued calmly.

"But of course, Inspector; any information that I would receive will be conveyed to you instantly; unless of course it is told to me as part of the confessional. Were that the case, I would be duty bound to retain the secret of the confessional as I am sure you understand. Only God then could punish the source of the evil which I am told," the imposter continued. Only you would then punish the person who had told you of his deepest secrets and sins, Jamie thought worriedly.

"We will leave you to it then, Father and wish you only the best in your work here. If you will be so kind to inform us of any information that you may see or hear that is germane to our cases, we will be most appreciative. Thank you again, Father for yer time," the Inspector stated upon leaving.

Once outside, the Sheriff and Inspector walked down the street towards the Sheriff's offices. As they entered the offices, the Sheriff offered the Inspector a dram of whiskey. He drank it down in one gulp and then his face set into the frown that the Sheriff had seen many times during the course of the investigation. "What are your thoughts, then Inspector?" the Sheriff asked worriedly.

"I think we have our man, Sheriff; we just now need to prove it. He is clearly not the man sent here from Alexandria, but is posing as him," Jamie replied. He took out the information sent to him from the home church in Alexandra. "Father Emmanuel is the name of the man who left Alexandra, two months ago. Emmanuel begins with the letter *E* and that is the very letter that Mistress Mackenzie saw in her vision. *E*, the clue was the letter *E*; we just have to prove it and make it stick to this imposter," Jamie said fiercely.

"Did you ken the look that the priest had when I asked about the victims and the secrets of the confessional? It was very slight, but I have seen that look before, you ken? I have seen it on the face of murderers who I have interviewed after they had been taken into custody. It is the look of a man who knows vital information and yet withholds; either because it will implicate him or because he plays a dangerous game and knows that he holds the cards. Either way, I need more information," Jamie said frowning and pacing. "My thought is this; you ken his whereabouts and his weekly schedule; do you not?" Jamie asked

"Aye, I am familiar as I have made myself so with the comings and goings of all since this terrible wave of murders came upon us," the Sheriff replied.

"Good then; I propose that you keep the new priest occupied during one of his daily outings and I will in turn take myself into his rectory looking for any clues that may help us further to catch him in his own game. Are you up for that then, Sheriff?" Jamie asked.

"But it would be dangerous for you, Inspector; what if he were to return before you were clear and find you in the act of searching the rectory?" the Sheriff asked worriedly.

"That is where you come in, Sheriff. If you can but act as lookout for me, you can perhaps lengthen his visit away until I am clear of the rectory. It is a goodly size house; I believe I could make myself scarce until I could be clear of it. I need to have some means of knowing where next he might strike and his pattern, if he has recorded one. Any clue that will help us going forward may very well save another life," Jamie said fiercely.

"Aye then; the day to set to work will be tomorrow. He goes out to visit the sick of the parish on that day. He will be gone most of the day, but just in case, as you say; I will position myself as lookout. I will make sure that I delay him before he can gain the house again and catch you at it," the Sheriff added excitedly.

"Good then; tomorrow is the day and could not come faster if we are to prevent yet another murder and preserve another life," Jamie said darkly.

He returned to his rooms then and reviewed the plan for the next day. He would be ready and he would do what was needed to prevent yet another death and catch a murderer in the process.

*****

The next morning, Jamie and the Sheriff set off from his office as if on a usual daily stroll and inspection of the town. The Sheriff had advised Jamie of the back entrance to the rectory and how he could gain the house after the false priest's departure. They waited in the shadow of trees down the street from the rectory and set off as soon as they saw him leave the house. The Sheriff had observed and been told that the priest was typically gone most of the morning of his visitation day. They would hope only that their luck held.

The Sheriff positioned himself near the front door so to intercept their man should he arrive back early and Jamie set himself the task of entering the rectory by the back door. He found it unlocked, as the Sheriff had advised and gained the house via that back entrance. He moved from room to room, using the floor plan that the Sheriff had drawn for him last night. He gained the study used by the priest and found the door unlocked. Once inside, he locked the door and set to review the materials on the desk and in the drawers of the desk.

Files were principally marked with the titles of sermons. He noticed that the sermons were in a different hand than the letters on the top of the desk. He surmised that the imposter was using the sermons of previous men of the cloth who had served this parish, covering for the parishioners the lack of knowledge by the man they believed to be their true priest.

He moved the lap drawer in preparation for inspecting the contents and found it locked. He said a brief curse in Gaelic under his breath, and pulling his sgian dubh from its usual hiding place in his stocking, gently twisted the lock of the drawer until he heard the distinctive click that told him he had unlocked it successfully. In the lap drawer of the desk, Jamie took out a small bound book. In it, he noted the entries made in the same hand as the letters found on the top of the desk. There were initials on one page that coincided with the initials of the three victims. Beside the initials, were confessions that had been given by the victims to the imposter priest. Instead of receiving the comfort of forgiveness that they had sought, they had received punishment for their sins by a man who was not a man of the cloth as the community believed, but a mad man as Jamie had feared.

Jamie took out a piece of paper and copied out the notes in the book. This was crucial evidence that Jamie could use to convict the man, the problem became if he were to take the book with him and then unwittingly inform the madman that Jamie and the Sheriff were on his scent. He could leave in the middle of the night, only to go to another community and continue his reign of terror. No, it was imperative that Jamie take this evidence down but replace this book where it had been found. It was essential that he set a trap himself; the type of trap that the imposter would not be able to turn down. Jamie had his man, but he now needed to catch him in the act.

He noticed a second small bound book in the desk drawer. The wording on the cover was in Latin. He had just enough of his childhood Latin committed to memory to make out some of the words. It appeared to be a recipe book for various compounds, similar to the one that Morgana had told him about that had instructed her mother back in Scotland. He quickly thumbed through the book and found a page turned down. Scouring the ingredients quickly he saw several of the items that Morgana had referenced as the source materials for the poison that they now believed had killed all three victims. That provided motive; the confessions of the victims, opportunity; one to one interactions with the imposter and means, the necessary knowledge to prepare the suspected poison.

Jamie was shaken out of his mental focus by the sound of voices coming to him from outside on the sidewalk. He placed the books back in its hiding place, gently pushed the lap drawer back into place until hearing the distinctive locking click and then checked the desk for all drawers returned to their correct places. He deftly left the study through the door in which he had entered. He moved stealthily down the steps, through the living quarters and to the back entrance of the house. As he closed the door, he heard the imposter coming through the front door, the voice of the Sheriff delaying his approach by the mere seconds needed to permit Jamie's escape. Jamie stood at the side of the rectory and waited until the door had again closed and then walked down the sidewalk in the direction of the Sheriff's office. The Sheriff had seen his escape and followed behind at a casual gait, not wishing to create suspicion on the part of onlookers.

Jamie stood at the front door and waited for the Sheriff's arrival. They went in together then, pulled the blinds and began to discuss the contents of Jamie's investigation.

"Aye that was a close one. My heart was in my mouth when I saw him turn the corner. He is never back that soon. Did you find anything of use, Inspector?" the Sheriff asked excitedly.

"Aye, I did for sure, Sheriff. In the lap drawer of his desk, I found a black, bound book. The contents showed a list of confessions that the imposter had received; the initials of the men who gave them and they correspond with the initials of the men who have been our victims. Beside each initial was a small check as if to signify that the punishment had been mete out to the perpetrator of the sin. Second, I found a small bound book with recipes in the Latin for compounds and poisons such as the one that has been administered to our victims. We have our man, Sheriff; I feel it in our bones," Jamie replied fiercely.

"Did you bring the book with you then?" the Sheriff asked.

"Nay, I did not wish to tip off the man that we have him in our sights. I know in my heart that he is the guilty party. I now need to prove it by catching him in the act. I will ponder on how that may be best accomplished. Until then, we keep the information close and we keep the suspect on a short leash until we can close in and make the arrest," Jamie replied fiercely.

*****

Jamie came to the cottage that afternoon to share the information that he and the Sheriff had gleaned from their detective work today. They were close, painfully close to both another murder and to the arrest of the most logical suspect. He paced forcefully in front of Morgana's hearth to search for an answer to the final piece of the puzzle and the best means of catching the man in the act without placing another innocent at risk.

"The book ye spoke of is just like the one my Mam was taught her compounding. I have a similar one that I have marked in Gaelic and English because I do not ken the Latin as did my Mam. Oh we have him, Jamie; we have him. He must ken enough Latin to understand the book and to read the sermons that ye told me about; if only enough from his early schooling like yerself," Morgana said excitedly

"Jamie, we ken that another murder is due to occur. I do not know the identity of the intended victim. I have had a thought though as to how we may be able to bring this to a close. You say that we must find a way to catch him in the act and we do not know who his next victim will be. If I were to place myself as the bait for the trap, we would have the evidence that we need to end this spree of murder," Morgana offered.

"Morgana; it is out of the question," Jamie said fiercely. "Come with me please. I need air and I need to move in order to think properly," Jamie stated anxiously.

Once outside the cottage, Jamie legged up Morgana onto Duncan's back and pulled himself into the saddle. Off they went again to the top of North Mountain, to the place of their prior picnic. Jamie needed the fresh air to think and to plan their next move and he needed badly to move as he did both.

"Morgana; when last we were here, I asked ye how it was with ye and yer thoughts about yer life here and whether ye would spend all of yer days here in this beautiful place," Jamie stated staring at the vista before them.

"Aye, Jamie; I remember well," Morgana replied softly.

"And have ye thought on it, Morgana as I asked?" Jamie continued staring again at the vista before them.

"I have, Jamie; I have thought of little else, besides the case of course," Morgana said glancing at the vista and sneaking a sideways glance at his puzzled frown.

"And what have ye concluded?" he said shifting his feet and yet remaining erect, his eyes only on the vista before him.

"That a life spent alone is no life at all, Jamie," Morgana said turning to him. "I need to know one thing though. Do ye wish to be with me only to protect me? If so, that is no basis for a life spent together," Morgana replied earnestly.

"Is that what ye think, lass? That I wish to be with ye only to protect ye?" Jamie replied fiercely. "If I wanted to protect ye only I would put ye on Duncan's back and carry ye to the Sheriff's house and have done with it," Jamie replied heatedly.

"Jamie, I do not ask ye these things to make ye cross. I ask only because ye have never given me the words, Jamie. It is different here, as I know ye ken. They do not wed here because it is arranged or because they are told who and where they will marry. There is no contract as there was at home. They wed because they want to and because they love the other person. I do not know what is in yer heart as ye have never shared those feelings with me," Morgana said quietly.

"Ye ask me what is in my heart. Morgana, when I walked into yer wee cottage, I felt like I was home for the first time since my people left the Highlands," he said turning to face her for the first time.

"Was it because of the cottage, Jamie or because of me?" Morgana asked confused.

"I am making a muddle of this, lass. I have not the words to tell ye correctly what I feel and what is in my heart," Jamie said anxiously. "I am not a poet, Morgana; but a soldier. I have not the words to tell ye in a flowery fashion," he said blushing.

"Tell me only what is in yer heart then, Jamie," Morgana continued again quietly, but forcibly.

He sighed audibly then and shifted his feet again awkwardly. "Since we came from the Highlands all those years ago, my heart and my soul have never left there. I am here in body, aye and in mind; but my heart and soul are there. With ye lass, for the first time I can have joy in what came before, but for the first time, I can see what life can be here in this new country. We have the same story, Morgana; you and me and ye are the only one I have ever told other than those closest to us in Alexandria. Ye know my history and ye keep it safe, just as ye have kept the secrets of so many others that ye have tended through the years. I can see a life here now, lass because I see ye beside me. That is what is in my heart, Morgana," Jamie said earnestly.

Morgana took his hands then and smiled up into his blue eyes. "I will be proud to be yer wife, Jamie if that is what ye wish to hear. I will be proud to make a new life with ye in this new country as we honor the lives that we left behind in the old land," Morgana said smiling.

"Aye, that is exactly what I wish to hear with all of my heart and soul. We canna be married here in the church as the man is not a true priest, as ye ken well," Jamie stated worriedly.

"The clerk can do a civil marriage, Jamie," Morgana stated smiling.

"Aye, aye; proved the real sacrament is to follow. Is that agreeable to you, Morgana?" Jamie said grasping her hands.

"Oh, aye Jamie; that is how it should be," she said looking up at him with shining eyes. He took her hand then and kissed it fervently. Morgana moved closer to him then and placed her head on his chest. He placed his arm around her then and kissed the top of her head. They had a plan for the present and a hope for the future to come.

Leaving North Mountain behind them, they proceeded into town to find the Sheriff and his wife to act as witnesses.

Jamie explained what would occur and the Sheriff listened intently, his worry as always about Morgana and what was to become of her during the very real danger of the investigation and afterwards when the Inspector had returned to Alexandria. When they explained that they would be wed and Jamie present at all times to protect her, the Sheriff joined into the plans enthusiastically. He closed his office and together they sought out his wife to act as witness along with himself. Their next stop was the clerk who would marry them. The Sheriff and his wife stood dabbing their eyes as Morgana gave her vow to Jamie. When the clerk told Jamie he could kiss his bride, he turned her toward him and tenderly cupped her face in his large hands, kissing her briefly. She smiled up at him and he knew he had done a good day's work.

More was to follow, the heart of the case and the trap that would lie ahead of them and all of the details that would be necessary to keep Morgana safe through the final resolution of the case. Jamie the man and not Jamie the Inspector took a moment to relish the joy of the woman standing beside him and the life he could now lead with her by his side.

Jamie shook the hand of the clerk, the Sheriff and his wife and they set off in search of a wedding lunch. "I canna take my bride to a tavern for her wedding lunch and canna have her cook her own," Jamie said worriedly.

"It is a beautiful day, Jamie. We could take a picnic back to our wee mountain; the place that is so special to us," Morgana suggested smiling.

"Ye would not mind?" he asked smiling.

"Nay, Jamie, we will have our proper wedding breakfast with our proper wedding in Alexandria, ye ken. I suspect ye have much ye need to ponder and tell me as we plan for our meeting with the dark one," Morgana said quietly.

"Aye, love; let us get a basket and go to our special place then." They gathered a picnic basket of treats and headed back to the mountain, away from all worries and concerns in their special setting that had brought them together and sealed their relationship.

Jamie spread his plaid when they arrived and Morgana spread the picnic for them. When he sat worriedly on the plaid, she reached over and released his queue, his hair free to the wind. "How do ye always know, Morgana?" Jamie asked. "Is it the sight?" he asked watching her intently.

"It is a set to your shoulders as if ye need to be set free. I see it now and ken when it is upon ye," Morgana said smiling.

"I think ye notice everything, Morgana," Jamie said kissing her hand.

"Only for ye, mo gradh," Morgana replied.

"My Mother called my Father mo gradh," Jamie said startled at the endearment; *my love* in Gaelic.

"Do ye mind then, Jamie?" Morgana asked.

"Nay, Morgana, it feels right," Jamie replied. He reached out then and tenderly drew her to him. It was the first time that he had kissed her without witnesses and the kiss gentle at first became more intense as he melded her to his body. Morgana forgot her shyness as she responded to his embrace. He pulled away when his breath became ragged and husky. "I think our luncheon awaits us . . . mo gradh," Jamie stated smiling.

Morgana cut pieces of cheese and bread handing them to him and began feeding herself. Morgana had questions about the wedding in Alexandria and if the plaids could be worn and if all manner of custom would be as it had been in the old country. "We can wear the plaid there, Morgana and the pipes are played at each service," Jamie replied smiling.

"Do they speak the Gaelic there also, Jamie?" Morgana asked.

"My mam and da do, but nay those of our age. It is being lost as it was lost at home, as ye ken; except by the old ones," Jamie replied.

Jamie then broke the spell of this revelry by bringing them back to the present and the actions they would take tomorrow against the dark one. He would not sully his wedding day with a visitation to the monster, but tomorrow being confession day; the trap would be set into motion.

"Ye are sure that ye want to proceed in the manner that we discussed?" Jamie asked worriedly.

"Aye, Jamie; if we can stop another murder and begin our new life together; it will be well worth it," Morgana stated fiercely.

"Aye, Morgana; ye are a lion heart for sure," Jamie said proudly.

"I see the headache coming on ye, Jamie. Is it the worry about tomorrow and about me?" Morgana asked worriedly.

"Aye; ye ken before ye ask," Jamie replied.

"Come here, mo gradh and rest. I will take away yer pain, have no fear," Morgana stated quietly. She bid him lie across her lap and she massaged his temples, through the rich, reddish brown hair, across the neck and down across the shoulders. She had a thought that the true source of the pain in his back could be available to her now and not be considered indiscreet as before. He opened the blue eyes to her, relaxed from the pain and drew her down to him for a kiss. "I am a blessed man, mo chroi, *my beloved* to have ye in my life in so many ways," Jamie said tenderly. She held his head in her hands and continued stroking across his temples, his face relaxing at her ministrations.

The shadows lengthened across the valley as they later gathered their picnic supplies, mounted Duncan and headed back to Morgana's cottage for the night. Once inside, Jamie rebanked the fire against the cold that would be upon them in a few short hours. "I may not make my own wedding luncheon, but I can make my new husband a wedding supper," Morgana said smiling. "What shall I make my new husband for his dinner, then?" Morgana asked.

"Whatever ye make will be pure nectar, mo gradh," Jamie replied. The freedom to speak Gaelic again to the one person who would appreciate it the most was a gift to them both. He watched while she prepared their supper and laid out the dishes for the meal. He remembered how the Sheriff had told him that Morgana had not only the skill to heal, but could cook for folks any day. She could turn her hand to any task. As she busied herself with the dinner and the associated tasks, she would touch his hand briefly as she laid out the dishes or touch his shoulder as she came behind him to lay out the food. He kissed her hand as she laid the food before him and looked deeply in the eyes as she put out the remainder of the meal.

"So am I truly yer husband now, Morgana? I have thought on it for so long," Jamie said tenderly.

"Aye, mo chroi; *love of my heart*, ye are my husband and I am proud to be yer wife," Morgana said smiling.

"After dinner we should get ready for bed, Morgana. It will be warmer for ye to bathe in front of the fire I am thinking," Jamie said watching her closely.

"Oh, ye should take the fire, Jamie; . . . I-I . . . will bathe and change in my changing room off of the bed chamber, as always," she answered quietly. Her face flushed suddenly, down to the fichu that protected her neck and bosom.

"Lass you'll freeze away from the fire," Jamie said worriedly.

"I will be fine, Jamie. I will start to get the chamber ready after our dinner then; shall I?" Morgana said shyly.

She turned then and he grasped her hand, kissing it and drew her down to him. "Dunno worry, lass; I love ye and ye love me. All will be well, mo gradh, promise," Jamie said tenderly.

After dinner, Morgana smiled and took the basin that he had prepared for her with the warmed water for bathing. She returned to her changing room and quickly lighting candles; began to undress. She did not know what would occur between her and Jamie tonight. She had heard tales, of course; from her female patients; but she didn't credit anything until she had experienced it herself for the first time. She knew only that she loved him and wanted him so badly that it hurt. All day their intimacy had grown steadily. He had never touched her more than squeezing her hand or patting her foot or waist. Today they had kissed multiple times and each time that he kissed her, she had never wanted him to stop. Now she heard him before the fire and wondered his thoughts about the night ahead.

Jamie sat and stared into the fire for several minutes before changing and bathing. He was a man who had never expected to marry. Whatever physical pleasure he had taken in his mature life had been fleeting and in the arms of professionals. He was not proud of that fact, but was proud that he had never trifled with a maiden, as had others of his acquaintance. Now a maid waited for him in her bed chamber and he thought he may be more fearful than she. He was so fearful of hurting one so slight and one that he loved so much that it hurt. He knew only to be gentle and to try not to scare her in anyway.

He finished bathing and wrapping himself in a blanket provided by Morgana, returned to the bed chamber to await his bride. He saw the door of the changing room closed and knew that Morgana was continuing her preparation for bed. He stretched out on the bed and considered for a moment the way forward for them both. He had written to his parents and asked that they begin preparations for a wedding that would occur after he returned from this latest case. The reading of the banns would be the first step; three weeks for the reading in his home church in Alexandria. He also asked that they find him a cottage; one that would have room for a vegetable garden and an herbal garden as the Sheriff had told him would be needed by Morgana. All would be in preparation for their arrival. He knew his parents would have endless questions once they arrived in Alexandria, but he also knew that they would ken he was a man who would not be swayed once his mind was set. He fancied his mam would be pleased that he had finally found a woman who would bring her the grandchildren she craved.

Morgana would be shy when meeting all these new people, but his family would give her the respect that her place in the old world and her skills in the new world deserved. They ken from their own experience the value of a healer and a healer with the sight was doubly blessed. They would welcome her as a proud addition to the family and to the community. The church community would rally around her and soon, she would have as many patients in Alexandria as she had here in Martinsburg, mayhap more.

He heard Morgana then opening the door to join him in the bed chamber. She had left candles burning in the changing room lest he need to find his way during the night. He turned when he saw her approach and the candles both lit her way and provided a tantalizing glimpse of the shift that she wore and its tiny occupant. Jamie turned to his side, smiling at Morgana as she came towards him and to the opposite side of the bed. Jamie's blue eyes blazed in the banked fire light. Morgana sought and found his eyes as she came from the changing room. Jamie pulled back the cover and Morgana sat down and turned into Jamie's embrace. She came under the covers quickly and Jamie immediately felt the trembling as she lay down.

"Come here, mo gradh; did I not tell ye that bathing away from the fire, ye would freeze?" Jamie said. "Let me warm ye, love," he said taking her in his arms and rubbing her back until the trembling stopped. He placed her under his chin and stroked her back until he felt her warm and as she began to relax in the process. "I ken ye love me lass; do ye want me also; I mean, do ye want me here in yer bed?" Jamie asked worriedly.

"Oh aye, Jamie; I want you so badly it hurts. I do not ken what to expect though, Jamie. I have heard tales, but I do not believe in gossip. If I had heard it from my mam, ye ken; that would be different," Morgana said quietly.

"Aye, lass; all will be well then," Jamie replied smiling.

She could smell the clean, masculine smell of his soap and saw the glisten of his skin in the banked fire light. As she suspected, his broad shoulders and chest took up most of the bed. She would sleep on Jamie tonight or curled around his broad form. She smiled at the thought. "Jamie; I have naught on under my shift," Morgana said quietly, her eyes searching his for confirmation.

"Aye, mo gradh; that is as it should be," Jamie responded smiling.

"And is it right that I should take off my shift, Jamie . . . for what comes after?" Morgana asked anxiously.

"Aye love; it is right," Jamie replied. "But only when ye are comfortable and ready to do so, mo gradh. There is no hurry between us; only love," Jamie added tenderly.

She hesitated for a moment then turned and brought the shift over her head as she sat on the side of the bed. He had a tantalizing glimpse of alabaster skin before she was quickly ensconced under the covers again. She turned back to face Jamie then and they lay side by side facing one another with a space between them which seemed at the moment like a chasm to Jamie. Jamie reached out then and gently brushed her lips with his fingers. She closed her eyes and took in the gentle sensation of his touch. When he had withdrawn his hand moments later, Morgana opened her eyes and duplicated the action to him. He kissed her fingers for her trouble and he noticed the distance between the two of them had gradually begun to close ever so slightly.

Jamie then traced her neck lightly with his fingers brushing her hair away from her neck as he did so. As he expected, she repeated the gesture to him and the distance closed further between them.

The next touch would be fraught with great pleasure and expectation on his part and perhaps uncertainly and worry on hers. Consequently he reached out and pulled her towards him so that she could feel the warmth of his body and the proximity of his touch. His embrace continued down her neck and gently he took her breast in his hand, cupping it, gently embracing and caressing it. She closed her eyes again and he did the same. His breath began to come in ragged fashion as did hers. His finger gently rubbed against her nipple until it became hard with his ministrations. She reached out and touched his chest, lightly at first and then with greater strength and purpose, her fingers twining in the matted hair there and his nipples became erect with her gentle caress.

The distance between them closed completely then as he took her into his arms, kissing her deeply for the first time since she had come to bed. Her arms came around his neck then and for the first time their two bodies joined. She heard his deep groan and she sighed as if the air was being gently squeezed from her lungs, at the intensity of the feeling that his touch and kisses had created.

Jamie gently stroked her abdomen and continued on lower still to her outer thighs and bottom. She began to move restlessly against him, craving his touch and more, but the more to her at least, was still the mystery.

Gently Jamie moved Morgana to her back and just as gently, prepared her for the lovemaking that was to follow. With his hands and lips he caressed her from neck to abdomen. His control was rapidly slipping, yet he knew that he needed to be gentle and take his time. "Morgana, mo gradh; put your arms around my neck, aye?" he said huskily. He touched her intimacy then for the first time and he heard the quick intake of her breath followed by his deep groan as he came within her. Her hands tightened at his shoulders briefly, but she neither cried nor cried out. The only evidence of the pain that she was experiencing was the tightening of her hands at his neck and the tensing of her body. He whispered words of endearment to her and felt her begin to

DEBORAH E. HAMMOND

gradually relax against him. She looked up at him then and taking his face in her hands drew him down to her in a deep kiss. Her hands came around his waist afterwards and she drew him to her. He responded then by moving gently within her, his best efforts at self control lost at that moment. As he neared his climax he called her name and she held him tightly to her.

When he could again regain his thoughts and his breath he whispered to her, "Morgana, love; I will crush ye for sure," Jamie said tenderly.

"Nay, Jamie, let me hold ye, mo gradh," she said gently.

He relaxed against her then, his head at her neck; he braced himself so as not to crush her completely and she held him tightly. He dozed briefly then woke and pulled her into his side, her head resting beneath his chin. She brought her hand around his waist and held him gently.

When next he woke, he thought about the lovemaking and how fiercely he loved Morgana. He thought also that he had neglected to ask her if he had hurt her when they had made love. He suspected that he was too fearful of the answer. The proud and resolute Inspector, fearless in battle and against all matter of villains, had to admit his fear at hurting his wee Morgana; the lass who had stolen his heart and changed his life forever.

He placed his arm around her waist then and felt the silken skin. Had they been in the Highlands, they would have called her a selkie for her raven hair and silken skin. Even her name Morgana meant *dweller of the sea* in the English. He suspected this silken skin was the result of one of Morgana's many lotions and potions she was famed for in these parts.

She stirred then, gently at first then as if in surprise at the arm embracing her. "Shush love; it is only me. I expect it takes some getting used to; this married life," Jamie said tenderly.

She turned into his arms and he held her close to him, under his chin. The feeling was so great as to overpower him

68

with emotion. She had not been fearful of him, only surprised by his touch.

"Did I hurt ye when we made love for the first time, Morgana?" Jamie asked tentatively.

"Nay, Jamie; is there not some pain in all things new? Yesterday morning we were Jamie and Morgana apart; then we were Jamie and Morgana as one. When I give ye our first wee bairn, Jamie, there will be pain for sure, but we will have created that bairn together. Such joy, but pain with it, Jamie; that is the nature of life," Morgana replied thoughtfully.

"Aye, lass; I had not thought of it that way. I just did not want to hurt ye for any reason. Ye mean the world to me, mo gradh; ye ken that, do ye not?" Jamie asked tenderly.

"Aye and ye are like the breath in my body, Jamie," she said hugging him at the waist. "I was dreaming of ye when I felt yer touch. It was so real for a minute it startled me. Then I knew ye were here for real and certain and it was like coming home. We were walking in the meadow that my parents described to me at home and ye kissed me in the heather in my dream just as ye touched me for real here," Morgana said quietly.

"Aye, lass; I dream of it sometimes and it is so real that I think I can but reach out and touch it. I dunno wake sad and remorseful as I once did, because I ken ye are here beside me and I can reach out and touch ye and that part of my dream has come true," Jamie said.

They slept then entwined together. Thousands of miles from their own homeland, they had found each other and had begun to build a new life together in the new land. They were home for each other, as they would be home for the family they would now someday create.

Morgana thought then of their wedding night and the excitement and anticipation that she had felt for Jamie before coming to her bed. When she heard him coming to rest in her four poster bed, she thought it would not be large enough for him, although she was dwarfed by it. When she had first seen him lying on his side waiting for her, she thought that she would have to sleep on top of him as there would not be room for his shoulders and her in the same bed. The thought was not an unhappy one, but she was also wary of what was to follow. Jamie had been so gentle and tender with her that it was hard to believe such an imposing and powerful man could be so different with the one that he loved. When she had first touched him, it was as though she was coming against a wall of hardened flesh, so different from her own body and yet the other half to herself. She had not been prepared for the release of emotions that she held for Jamie; the passion and the love. It had been so overwhelming to her and yet so right at the same time. She thought back to her mother's words to her and they all meant so much to her in retrospect; a Highlander comes for you Morgana; wait for him as he is your own true love.

CHAPTER NINE

The next morning, Morgana quickly dressed and followed Jamie out of the cottage. The trap was about to be set and Morgana, unfortunately was the bait. She had entered into that agreement willingly in the hope that the murderous spree could come to an end. She had promised the Sheriff that she would help him in any way that she could. More importantly to her, she hoped to assist Jamie in bringing an end to this case so that their new life could begin together. She simply could not face the knowledge that another murder was about to happen that she could prevent this time. She had to do whatever was necessary to save one more life, even if it meant jeopardizing her own in the process.

Jamie's jaw had tightened upon their departure from the cottage. He had spread his great coat to cover Morgana and under its cover, his free hand encircled her waist. This time he did not pat the waist as he had done in the past before they were married, but held it tightly against him. Last night he had held the silken skin beneath the Mackenzie plaid. In the light of day she was more precious to him than his own life. The thought of her as bait in the hands of a mad man made him wish to choke. He rehearsed with her over and over again on their trip to town how they would proceed and where the Sheriff and he would be located during her time with the imposter priest inside the church and the confessional.

"Jamie, ye ken he will not harm me within the confessional nor the church. There are witnesses and he will not take the chance. I will walk into the church as we discussed, give confession and walk out. If as we suspect he takes the bait, he will come to the cottage. That is where I will need ye both; my knight-errant, Jamie and his squire," she said leaning against him.

71

"Careful my love; if ye lean against me I will be tempted to return to the cottage and have done with it," Jamie said bringing his free hand tighter around her waist.

"The sooner we end this, Jamie, the sooner we start our new life. Tell me again Jamie how it will be in Alexandria," Morgana asked wistfully.

"We will be married at St. Mary Parish Church in Alexandria, my chroi and I will wear my formal kilt with the formal Macpherson. Ye will be the most beautiful bride of any Highlander since the times before the troubles," Jamie said wistfully.

"Will they play the pipes, Jamie?" Morgana said hopefully.

"Aye love; they will play the pipes and ye shall wear my plaid and all of the Highlanders of Alexandria will be present," Jamie replied.

"There is only one Highlander I need present, Jamie and that is you, mo gradh," Morgana said squeezing the hand at her waist.

As they came into Martinsburg, Jamie dismounted and brought Morgana down to stand beside him. She squared her shoulders and set off then on foot heading for the Catholic Church and the baiting of the trap.

Jamie came to stand within immediate sight of the church with the Sheriff on the opposite side of the street. Even the Sheriff's good wife had been called into the plan and was within the church in case Morgana was to call out in need of assistance. She was to rouse both Jamie and the Sheriff within minutes of Morgana's cry. Would it be enough, Jamie thought worriedly? Only time would tell.

The breeze rose on this November day, but Jamie stood erect, at attention and ready to strike. The beads of perspiration rose on his back as he waited for Morgana's return from this mission to ensnare the dark one as Jamie had come to call him.

On the minutes raced, crawling for Jamie, racing for Morgana as she came face to face with their enemy. Within the church, Morgana briefly met the eyes of the Sheriff's wife and then entered the confessional to rendezvous with the imposter and the alleged murderer who had stained the small community three times with his murderous spree.

"Forgive me, Father; for I have sinned," Morgana stated as she entered the confessional. "My last confession was two months ago," Morgana continued.

"What is the nature of your sin, my child?" the false Father Emmanuel stated.

"I have had impure thoughts and have been with a man who is not my husband," Morgana stated, fingers crossed beneath the Mackenzie plaid.

"Has this been a onetime occurrence?" the imposter asked.

"Nay, Father; I love the man. It has happened Father and I fear will occur again, so deep is my love for him," Morgana said truth in her statement.

"It is not sufficient to confess your sins; you must also combat that sin by fighting against the desire to commit that sin again. Can you do that, Mistress?" he asked fiercely.

"I can but try, Father," Morgana answered gravely.

"Perhaps there is another force here that keeps you from following the path; a force of darkness, Mistress. Are you not Morgana the healer that I have heard tell of?" the dark one asked.

"Aye, I am, Father," Morgana replied quietly.

"There is power in your healing, I have been told. Perhaps that power does not come from the light, but from darkness itself. Perhaps you have sold your soul to bring you such power. I shall come to you personally then, Mistress Morgana. Personal counseling is what is required to stem this tide of sin and false pride," the false Father Emmanuel stated solemnly.

"Father, I believe your forgiveness is all that I require; along with my penance, of course," Morgana said quickly.

"I shall visit you personally; Mistress Morgana and the matter will be resolved." The confessional window slammed shut and Morgana felt the very real fear for the first time in the pit of her stomach; the fear she knew the prior victims had felt. The difference in her case was that she knew the outcome of the planned visit by the imposter and they had not. She would have her protection at the ready as they had had none. With her, the nightmare for the community as a whole would end, but her own personal nightmare had been set into place and was about to commence.

When Morgana exited the church, Jamie could see the strain on her face and the paleness. She walked to the corner as previously arranged, followed but not closely by the Sheriff. Jamie rode to the intersection, turned the corner and dismounted to leg Morgana up on Duncan's back. Once remounted, Jamie kicked Duncan's side and the two galloped through town and back to the cottage. The Sheriff's wife kissed his cheek and the Sheriff took off separately to stand in warning for Morgana and Jamie of the dark one's departure and his coming to the cottage. The trap was baited and tonight there would be resolution at last.

Morgana and Jamie rode on in silence, Jamie's hand tightly against Morgana's waist. He could feel her tremble and knew the strain of the time spent within the church across from the man who had caused such havoc in this small community. He knew he needed to get her back to the cottage so that he could hear her tale and give comfort for the visitation that she had experienced and the trial yet to come. He pulled her against him now, his hand tightly around her waist beneath the billowing great coat. He felt the trembling stop then and her hand come to rest on top of his.

As they returned to the cottage, Jamie helped Morgana down and took her hand as they entered the cottage. He sat out two glasses and filled both with a dram of whiskey. He pulled out the chairs and Morgana sat heavily. "Take this drink, lass; then tell me the tale slowly. I need to know all that he has said so that I can be prepared and so ye can unburden yerself of this trial," Jamie said gravely.

Morgana sipped the whiskey slowly and let the warmth extend to her stomach and to her extremities. After the drink had done its work and she began to calm, she told Jamie everything that had been said and how she had replied. "Jamie, I could see the evil in his eyes; I felt it as he spoke to me. I know what is to follow, Jamie, the others did not," Morgana said gravely. She relayed then each statement that she had made and the response by the imposter up to and including the closing of the confessional door.

"Aye, lass; the trap is sprung and we must see it to the end. Ye go now and change and have a wee rest. Ye have earned it, love," Jamie said tenderly.

"Will ye come also, Jamie?" Morgana asked shyly.

"Aye, love; I will come directly. I need to check my arms and determine the best locations for the Sheriff and me to station ourselves for the arrival of the dark one. Ye will not be alone, Morgana. Ye are more precious to me than my own life. When I stood outside the church, I knew for the first time the true cost of love. There is joy to love and there is cost. The joy I knew last night and I will know in the nights and years to follow; the cost is the fear for the one ye love. I would gladly walk into battle, lass and have done so many times. To have ye walk into that church on yer own was pure torture. To have ye face that monster when he comes will be worse still. I must be ready for what will occur as I will give my life to protect ye, Morgana. Now go rest, love. I will come directly," Jamie said tenderly.

Morgana went back to her changing room and changed out of her dress. In her shift, she laid down in the bed and pulled the quilt over her. The waiting was the worst part, but she would have Jamie with her. He was intent on protecting her; but as she had thought many times; she just wanted him to love her. She wanted this sordid business over so that they could be together and she could help to take the weight of his work from his shoulders. She had seen the relief she gave him when he suffered from the headaches and wanted to do whatever was necessary to keep the pain from him in the future.

She lay thinking about Jamie and the life they would lead together. She had seen her life before her in the leaves and in the palm, but had no idea that the Highlander who was coming into her life would truly change her life forever. To have someone to talk to of the old ways, but also to look forward to the life that could be led in this new land was something she had not been expecting. Alexandria from Jamie's descriptions, seemed like the best of both worlds; the community of Scots that they had been accustomed to, but the chances that the new world brought with it. Jamie and his work with the military and the law and what of her sight and how that could help him in the future? As Jamie had told her, the sight would only become stronger as she grew older and that had definitely been the case as they worked through the particulars of this series of crimes. Perhaps in Alexandria she could both do her healing work and help Jamie with his cases; only time would tell.

She heard Jamie in the front room cleaning his pistol and checking his dirk and saber. She planned on placing her own dirk and her sgian-dubh in her pockets whether Jamie knew it or not. If she had to face the evil first hand, she would have her weapons close at hand. Her Father had taught her in the use of both and she would be ready when the time approached.

Jamie came back to the sleeping chamber then. He had taken off his neck cloth, jacket and shirt and sat on the side of the bed taking off his boots. She watched his broad shoulders and back and thought as she had so many times since their meeting that he was a fine figure of a man. To see such a man in his full Highland gear would be a sight to see and one that she planned to focus on in the hours that lie ahead.

Jamie turned to lay across the bed then, his breeches still on. He took Morgana in his arms and kissed the top of her head. "Let me hold ye, lass until he comes," Jamie said tenderly.

"Jamie, let me hold ye, mo gradh," Morgana said to Jamie with equal tenderness.

Jamie touched her face then smiling. "Would wee Morgana hold me then? I would crush ye in a moment's time, lass," he said tenderly brushing her hair from her face with his fingers.

"Nay Jamie; I am stronger than I look," Morgana said earnestly.

"Aye, lass; I know that ye walk into a murderer's den with nay more protection that the cross ye wear around yer neck. Ye are stronger for sure," Jamie said earnestly. He slid down beside her then and she put up her arms and placed them gently around his neck. "I will crush ye for sure, Morgana," he said softly. She drew him down to her and he balanced himself so as not to crush her with his weight and size. He buried his head in her neck and captured the clean, sweet smell of lavender that always surrounded her. He drank in her neck and kissed her hungrily from her neck to her breast. He shifted to his side then to prevent crushing her. His hands came to her face and he kissed her deeply, his mouth slanting over and over her mouth, his tongue mating with hers. Her arms came around his waist then and she wrapped her arms around him pressing him closer to her. "Morgana, my love," he said huskily, "you are under the covers and me above. I think we need to remedy that fact, lass," Jamie said smiling. He moved the quilt away and came to rest above Morgana again. Again they embraced body to body with no quilt between. Morgana raised her hands to Jamie's face and kissed him deeply. The heat rose from her and he reveled in the feel of her body beneath him.

She pulled him to her again so that he was directly above her. "I will crush ye for sure, love," he said into her ear. She moved restlessly beneath him and he reached to undo his breeches. Within moments of that action, a hard knock came to the front door of the cottage. The shadows had begun to lengthen yet again and the dusk was surely upon them, as well as the visitor who they had both summoned to this place of final resolution.

"Damn and blast," came Jamie's angry oath.

Morgana's eyes opened widely and she looked up at Jamie. "What is it, Jamie?" Morgana said anxiously.

"It will be the Sheriff, lass warning us of the dark one's coming. Get dressed, Morgana; we haven't long," Jamie said anxiously. Morgana quickly sped to her changing room and put on her Mackenzie plaid. She placed her dirk in the deep pocket of her gown and her sgian dubh in the other pocket. She knew that Jamie and the Sheriff would be in a position to protect her, but she planned on protecting herself just as she had always said she would do.

Morgana came out into the stillroom then and picked up the two glasses and placed them in her dry sink. There would be no refreshments offered to the dark one. His stay would be a brief one, if she had anything to say about it.

Jamie went outside to consult with the Sheriff briefly. A full orange moon began to rise as they conferred in the garden. An orange moon was called by some the All Saint's Moon and by others, a harvest moon. To Jamie's reasoning on this night, it was an evil moon. It shone brightly onto the garden and brought the shadows into stark relief. The moon raised red as blood and so close that one felt they could reach out and touch it. Jamie heard Duncan's low whickering and ken that he was aware that evil was about this night and danger in the very air. Soon, good friend; Jamie thought; soon this matter will be behind us and we will be leaving this place for home and a new life.

By agreement between the two men, the Sheriff would position himself closest to Morgana as he was smaller in size and could fit with greater ease on the far side of her dry sink and cabinet. There he would be hidden from view in the lengthening shadows of dusk; the only light coming now from the fire place and the banked fire.

Once inside, Jamie grabbed Morgana by the shoulders and kissed her deeply. "I will be just inside the chamber, lass with the door ajar. I have my pistol, my dirk and my saber. The Sheriff has his pistol as well. If you but swoon, we will take him down," Jamie said fiercely.

"I love you, Jamie," Morgana replied just as fiercely.

"Aye, lass and I love you. I will nay let anything happen to you; I promise," Jamie replied.

The Sheriff hung his head not wishing to intrude upon this private moment between the two. He knew he had been correct that the two Highlanders were a match from the first day and he had been correct. He would miss Morgana, but he knew he had been correct about these two and besides; the wee Morgana could not stay in this cottage forever by herself. It was time for her to live the life that she was meant to live and this Highlander was the man she was meant to meet, marry and carve out a new life.

Morgana sat down then and tried to calm herself for the interview that was to follow. She closed her eyes, said a brief prayer and then gazed into the fire, waiting for the arrival of the man who had been the author of so much pain and so much suffering for the small community and the affected families. The knock came but a short time after. Morgana's head came up alertly. She looked in the Sheriff's direction first and then towards the bed chamber. Jamie's blue eyes blazed and he nodded his head to her.

Morgana went to the door then, her head bowed in the position of a penitent. The imposter was waiting at the door. The wind blew hard off of North Mountain, which blew his black robes about him, like the wings of a vulture, Morgana thought warily. Morgana thought then to cross herself, but deferred the action. The harvest moon now shone brightly on the landscape beyond. It was the perfect setting for a night of mayhem. This time however, the intended victim was aware and ready for what was to come.

"Mistress Morgana; a cold wind blows tonight from the west," the dark one stated gravely.

"Aye, Father; come warm yourself by the fire," Morgana replied quietly.

"The fire is the reason I am here, Mistress," the dark one replied passionately.

"Aye, Father; how so?" Morgana asked.

"You came to me at the confession and yet admitted that you would not fight your sin. The only way for you to fight your sin is to be scourged for it. I will scourge your back and you will sin no more," the dark one hissed.

In the bed chamber, Jamie's hand came sharply around the head of his dirk. If the dark one touched a hair on Morgana's head, he was a dead man, he made this vow silently.

"Nay, Father; no man nor priest shall lay hand upon me. My own Father never beat me, Father and no man shall," Morgana said fiercely.

Jamie smiled in the shadows despite himself. The dark one had never encountered a Highland lass; that was for sure. It was also instruction to her new husband not to think of striking her; not that he needed that instruction. He would cut off his own hand before thinking of striking his wee Morgana, he thought. Like the time she spent in the church, he stood thinking he would happily step into battle rather than stand powerless within this chamber watching Morgana spar with a mad man. The beads of perspiration again formed on his back and now upon his brow. Steady on, man; stay calm and stay focused until the time is right, he thought.

"You leave me no choice then, Mistress," the dark one said. He took up the bag that he had brought with him and began to lie out the elements of a communion table. He placed a stole around his neck and poured out a cup of wine and a communion wafer. Morgana could instantly smell the dreaded poison from her proximity to the dark one. She was so close to him that she knew that neither the Sheriff nor Jamie could get a clean shot safely without fear of wounding her in the process. Jamie considered roaring from his hiding place within the chamber at that moment, but hesitated fearful of what the imposter might do next to harm Morgana.

"I canna take communion, Father if ye have not given me my penance; I have nay been forgiven for my sin," Morgana said quietly.

"You will not be scourged, you will not take communion; you are possessed without doubt and I will save your soul if I cannot save your life." He grabbed her then by the throat as if to force her to drink the poison set before her. Her hand quickly found the sgian dubh hidden within her pocket and she pulled it from its hiding place and plunged it deeply into the thigh of the false priest. The hand released from her neck and both the Sheriff and Jamie sprung like cats at that opportunity. Morgana fell back when the hold on her neck was released. The dark one began to scream in agony at the sgian dubh that had been plunged deeply into his leg. He saw the Sheriff and Inspector then and began to wail.

"She is possessed, Sheriff. She is possessed for sure. She tried to kill me. You see the bleeding from my leg. I came to save her soul as I did with the others and she placed a knife in me. You must make her drink this wine and eat this wafer as I made the others. They gave their confession, but would not end their sin. I saved their souls and it is the only way that she will be saved as well," he cried madly.

Jamie looked at the Sheriff then and the look held no mercy. "Vengeance is mine, sayeth the Lord. If ye were a real priest, ye would ken yer bible and ken that only law and justice lies on this side of the grave. Hog tie him, Sheriff and if he moves, shoot him," Jamie said fiercely. He pulled the sgian dubh from the dark one's thigh and placed it on the table. He pulled the cloth from the table and wrapped it quickly around the imposter's thigh to staunch the bleeding from the wound. Morgana stared at it as she did the tableau before her with unseeing eyes. Only when Jamie proceeded to gather the evidence of the cup and wafer did she come back to life.

"Careful, Jamie; the poison is upon them both. I smelled it the moment he pulled them from his bag," she said quietly.

"Aye, lass, I will be careful. Go get your cloak now, Morgana. I will not leave ye here while we get this business sorted." The Sheriff had tied the hands of the dark one while Jamie and Morgana gathered the evidence. The Sheriff pushed the now whimpering suspect out of the door as he left the cottage with him and tossed him over his horse.

Morgana came from the bed chamber then with eyes the size of saucers. She had pulled her cloak around her and yet was still shivering from the cold wind blowing from North Mountain and the cold from the shock of the scene that had just transpired. Jamie took her hands and feeling the icy touch, warmed them between his two bear sized hands. "It will be alright now, lass. It is over, love and ye fought like the lion heart that ye are," he said kissing the top of her head. "Come now, love; I'll not leave ye here on yer own," Jamie said fiercely.

They went out into the night air then. The evil moon from earlier in the night had now cleared and a cold, white full moon shone down on them. Jamie calmed Duncan from the commotion and smell of blood in the air. "Easy now, lad; naught but a wee man, Duncan; naught to be scared of now. Your Mistress is near and we must get her somewhere safe," Jamie said in a soothing manner. Duncan calmed at his touch and speech and whickered softly in response. Jamie legged Morgana up on Duncan's back and came behind her, settling himself and pulling her to him with his free hand. He pulled the great coat around her shoulders again and kept his free hand firmly around her waist. They followed the Sheriff and the mad man now thrown across the Sheriff's horse. The rambling had stopped now and Jamie was relieved that the sound had ceased. When the dark one had grabbed Morgana around the throat, Jamie's first instinct was rage. He had always prided himself in being cool in battle and against all manner of villains. As he had found yesterday, the cost of his love for Morgana was a complete loss of reason when she was in danger. That cost was far worth the joy he felt at every moment in her company. She had saved him from a wretched life of regret and nostalgia for a life that was no more. With her for the first time since his family had left the Highlands of Scotland, he looked forward to the future and all that it would bring with Morgana by his side.

Once returned to town, the Sheriff and Jamie travelled to the magistrate's house, woke him from his sleep and explained the particulars of the case. The dark one was to be held over and conveyed for trial; a trial that would be swift and fatal in its conclusion. Morgana sat with the magistrate's wife as the particulars of the case were laid before her husband. She sat with unseeing eyes as the magistrate's wife spoke to her of the terrible events of the night; cold and unfeeling and needing Jamie's arms around her to bring her back to life.

Jamie stood in the magistrate's front parlor at parade rest listening to the Sheriff, adding points where necessary and alternately looking to the adjacent room, to see Morgana's white, frightened face. He tried to stay focused on what was being said, but wanted nothing more than to carry his wee Morgana to his rented rooms and comfort her. She looked so small and lost at that moment that it broke his heart. They had done what they vowed to do; they had brought the dark one to justice and ended his reign of terror, but at what cost to Morgana, he thought? If only he could catch her eye, smile at her, frown even, anything to bring her out of her lost and frightened place. He had been right to bring her here away from the cottage and all that had happened there; the madness of the murderer, the poison, the stabbing; all of it.

At last the magistrate finished his work and the dark one was carried away to his improvised cell in the basement of a rented building. Whether his prisoner lived or died at that moment was of no consequence to Jamie. He would not have his dearest Morgana give her healing gift to a man who would have killed her for the crime of ending the pain and suffering of others and preventing yet another murder at the hand of the imposter.

Jamie shook the hand of the Sheriff and the magistrate and taking three long steps, was quickly at Morgana's side. He thanked the magistrate's wife and taking Morgana's hand, led her from the house. At that moment, Jamie would have gladly taken Morgana in his arms and carried her to the rented rooms, had he not wished to arouse comment in the small town. His arm came around her waist again and they moved rapidly through the moon soaked streets to the building where his rented rooms were found. He opened the door and led Morgana up the stairs to his rooms. Once inside, she waited at the doorway as he lit candles and started a fire. Morgana came inside then and smiled a weak smile at Jamie. He crossed the room and took her cloak and took off his great coat. He led her to the table and placing two glasses on the table filled them with whiskey. He sat down heavily and brought Morgana down on his knee. "Hold onto me, lass, your hands are like ice," Jamie said anxiously.

"Shock, Jamie; it is shock; I will be fine shortly. I just need to get beyond this," Morgana said quietly.

"Aye, lass; drink this. I wish I had brandy as it is better for the shock, but this will have to do," Jamie replied.

Morgana drank the whiskey, sipping again slowly. Jamie thought that she had drunk more whiskey today than he had seen her drink since he knew her. She finished the glass and he quickly refilled it. He sat quietly waiting for her to speak and unburden herself of the night's events. "I told ye before, Jamie; looking at the man was like looking at the face of evil. I knew I was so close to him that ye would not be able to get a clean shot nor the Sheriff either. I had placed my dirk and my sgian dubh in my pockets. I knew how to use them. I looked into those eyes and I said to myself; Jamie looks into the eyes of evil every day, I can do this and then I thought after, I am here now to help take the weight from Jamie's shoulders so that he can face the evil every day going forward," Morgana said quietly.

"How would my wee Morgana take the weight from these shoulders, love?" Jamie said watching her intently, his hands cupping her face.

Morgana looked up at him then and placed her hands on either side of his face. She looked deeply into those blue eyes then and placed her lips on his. She kissed him deeply and as she felt him relax against her, opened her mouth and placed her tongue against his as he had done last night to her. She slanted her mouth over his, over and over until she heard the deep growl rise in his throat. She reached up then and loosened the queue and released his hair in the process. She next reached up and undid his neck cloth, kissing his throat at the base where the pulse could be felt. She saw, then felt the pulse quicken at her touch.

His hands started to rub her back and sides. She continued on, unbuttoning his shirt and kissing the exposed flesh until she reached the third button. He grabbed her hands then, his breath coming in a ragged fashion. "Ye still have on the Mackenzie plaid, love," Jamie said quietly.

"I dinna have the Macpherson plaid to replace it, Jamie," Morgana replied softly.

"Ye miss my meaning, lass; ye need be in no plaid at all, love," Jamie said huskily. He lifted her up then and turned her around to release the lacings, his hands making quick work of the layers beyond. Within moments she stood in her shift and stockings. Jamie turned her around then and took her face in his hands, pulling her up against him. She pulled his shirt from his breeches, unbuttoning his shirt as he backed her towards the bed. She stopped suddenly and bit her lip before speaking.

"Jamie, may I have a basin of water to bathe? He touched me, Jamie and I would wash . . . before I would spend the night with ye," Morgana said quietly.

"Of course, Morgana, of course, I am sorry. I will get you a warm basin and soap and towels. Morgana, ken this; no man will ever touch you again except me. Ye have my vow, lass; never again will I let ye be touched by the hand of evil," he said fiercely.

"I ken that, Jamie. I just want to bathe before I spend the night with ye, Jamie," she repeated quietly. He could see that she was beginning to come to terms with the night's events, but she was still lost in the haze of the attempted murder and of all that she had seen and experienced.

"Dinna open the door to any one, lass. I will lock it on my way out. I will be back shortly," Jamie said worriedly.

Re-buttoning his shirt and placing it back in his breeches, Jamie went downstairs to the inn's proprietor and asked for a basin of warm water, soap and towels for Morgana and a second basin which he would claim for himself shortly. "The Sheriff tells me that ye were wed yesterday, Inspector; my congratulations to you and to your wife, Mistress Mackenzie. I understand also that you have caught the murderer who has been plaguing this community. I thank ye, Inspector for all that ye have done. It is a horrible thing to see the face of such evil. I hope that your wife will be well, Inspector," the proprietor said worriedly.

"Aye it is the shock only. She will be better when she has had a good night's sleep," Jamie replied. He was amazed as always that news travelled so quickly in a small town. Still, it was good to know that the populace could sleep easier knowing that a murderer had been removed from their midst.

"I have included a bar of my wife's homemade soap for your new wife. I am sure she will like it more than the usual lye soap. You tell her that I asked about her, Inspector," the proprietor said smiling.

86

"Aye, I will for sure. I will take this up to her and come back for my own basin," Jamie said. He carried up the towels, soap and basin to Morgana and knocking softly on the door, let her know that it was him and that she could safely open the door.

Morgana opened the door and Jamie came in with the soap, towels and basin of warm water. "I will go downstairs and claim my own basin, Morgana. Ye take yer time now, lass and I will be back shortly," Jamie said worriedly. He could see the shock of the night still on her face and worried how the events would remain with her.

When Jamie left the chamber, she took a chair and sat by the fire and bathed. Her neck was sore and more tender to the touch than she had initially realized until the warm water hit it. She would ask Jamie if he had any liniment on his return to try to draw out the soreness. Without a mirror she could not tell the extent of the injury, but she knew that the dark one had her in a death grip before she plunged her sgian dubh into his thigh. She thought about the day just ended and shuddered to think how the other three victims had fared at the hands of this mad man. It had been meant to be that Jamie would be sent into their midst to bring this reign of terror to an end.

Jamie for his part was having an ale in the tavern below, trying to think of how best to help Morgana and get her beyond the fear of the night. "Will your new wife take an ale also, Inspector?" the proprietor asked cheerily.

"Nay, Master Giles, she is nay much a drinker. I will take a cider to her, unless of course you have some brandy. Brandy is always good for shock if it is at hand," Jamie replied.

"She was with ye then when ye encountered and restrained the villain?" Master Giles continued.

"Aye, she was sir; she was with us and part of the plan to bring the monster to justice. It has taken its toll on her though and I would have her get a good night's sleep to put all of this behind her," Jamie replied warily.

"Inspector, you take this cup of brandy to her. It will help her sleep and get all of this behind her, as ye said. She is a good physic for sure. We will miss her here in the community. She took care of my wife when she was ailing when no one else could get to the root of the problem. Ye are a blessed man, Inspector to have such a rare woman in yer care," Master Giles replied.

"Aye, Master Giles; I ken it well, as does the Sheriff. I believe she will be missed in this community, even if not all ken her skills as closely as those that she has helped. I will tell her that ye asked after her and I thank ye for the ale and the brandy. I think it will be just the thing that she needs right now," Jamie said worriedly. Taking the basin of warm water, he returned to his rented rooms with the cup of brandy provided by the innkeeper. He knocked again and Morgana came to the door smiling, a more relaxed look on her face.

"The innkeeper, Master Giles sent ye this cup of brandy to help ye sleep. It seems that our exploits are already known throughout the community, mo gradh. The Sheriff has been filling in the merchants that the murderer is in custody and has let it be known that ye played a role in the capture, lass. Master Giles sends his best to ye. Are ye feeling any better, Morgana?" Jamie asked worriedly.

"I am Jamie, thank ye. Do you perhaps have any liniment that I can place on my neck? I dinna have a mirror to see the injury, but it was sore when I bathed just here," Morgana said quietly, pointing to the injury.

"Come here, lass and let me take a look," Jamie said worriedly. She came to his chair and again sat on his lap as he examined the marks on her neck. The grip of the murderer was fierce and had been hidden beneath the fichu of her gown until she undressed for bed. At her throat now were the finger marks showing as bruises on her neck. Jamie reached into his bag and pulled out a small jar of liniment that his

Mam had bought for him for just such emergencies. "Mam bought this ointment for me from the local apothecary in Alexandria. She swears by it for all nature of injuries. Let me put a wee bit on your neck, Morgana and it may draw out the soreness overnight." He gently applied the ointment to her neck and finishing, looked deeply in her eyes. "Are ye truly better, Morgana?" Jamie asked worriedly.

"Aye, Jamie; I am better, I promise. Would you like me to wash yer back for ye?" she asked smiling.

Jamie nodded in agreement. Anything to keep her busy and her thoughts away from the night's events, he thought. She unbuttoned his shirt again and pulled it from his breeches. "The soap is rose scented, Jamie. Will that bother ye?" she asked.

"Nay, lass; I will be happy to bathe at all after this day. Ye are right; when ye encounter such villains ye want nothing so much as to wash the experience away. Did it help ye lass, to bathe as you said?" Jamie asked worriedly.

"Oh aye, Jamie; I bathe every night before bed, but it was especially important today. I felt like I could not get the thought of his murderous touch away from me unless I bathed it away. Is that a foolish thing to say, Jamie?" Morgana asked quietly.

"Of course not; all ye have to do is look at the marks of the man on yer neck and ye ken his intent was true enough. He meant to make ye his fourth victim, Morgana and ye were brave enough to face the man and bring this whole sorry affair to an end. Ye are a lion heart, Morgana for sure and I believe ye will be missed by this community more than ye ken. The innkeeper told me that ye had helped his wife in the past, Morgana. Ye will be missed by more than just the Sheriff, I am thinking," Jamie said. Morgana came to his side again after washing his back. "Come here lass and let me hold ye," Jamie said worriedly. He handed her the cup of brandy and she sat again on his lap, sipping the brandy as he held her to his massive chest, her head under his chin, rubbing her back.

"So are ye intending on finishing the job then, Morgana?" Jamie asked after a few moments.

"Finish what job, Jamie?" Morgana asked quietly.

"Ye washed my back did ye no? Are you planning on finishing the job?" Jamie said with mischief in his voice now.

"Oh . . . well no, Jamie; . . . I mean I will give ye yer privacy as ye gave me mine. I will just wait for ye over on the bed then, Jamie," Morgana said blushing.

He smiled then in agreement. "Aye, lass; I will make short work of it. Ye lie down and rest and I will be with ye in a moment," Jamie said smiling. He turned then to watch her move towards the bed, the firelight providing another tantalizing glimpse of his bride in her shift. He quickly undressed and finished bathing. Morgana for her part laid down on the bed on her side, her face turned to the wall. In short order Jamie had concluded bathing and blowing out the candles, he wrapped himself in a towel, banked the fire for the night and came to Morgana's side. She felt his weight on the bed as his arm came tenderly around her waist.

"Have ye never seen a naked man before, Morgana?" Jamie asked quietly.

"Oh no, Jamie . . . I mean . . . I have treated men for various ailments; maybe an arm or a leg or even their back but never . . . their . . . f-front," she said quietly.

"Aye, I expect they would go to an apothecary for such ailments," Jamie replied smiling.

"Or to a priest," Morgana offered shyly. Jamie laughed then long and hard, the relief of the day finally coming to him as well after the whiskey and ale and the soothing warm water. The bed shook with the heartiness of his laughter.

"Was that a foolish thing for me to say, Jamie?" Morgana asked worriedly.

"Nay, lass; I thought only that I dinna think a priest would have knowledge or be of much help in that particular area,"

Jamie said with the laughter still in his voice. He held her tightly in his arms now, to help her feel safe and to relax from the events of the day.

"Jamie, I was wondering . . . do men like to be kissed and caressed as ye kissed and caressed me last night?" Morgana asked shyly.

"Well I canna speak for all men of course, but I do know that I would like that verra much if ye were thinking of offering," he said smiling. She turned in his arms then and kissed him again as she had when she sat on his lap.

"I would massage your back, as I know the pain from your old injury travels up from your neck and creates the headaches. I would spare you one after such a day and night, Jamie," she said quietly. He moved to his stomach then and placed his arms beneath the pillow, giving her full access to his broad back.

Morgana knelt beside Jamie then and moved his hair to the left side of his neck, giving her full access to his right ear and the right side of his neck. She gently kissed his ear and cuddled against his neck, kissing it as she proceeded next to his shoulders. She massaged the massive shoulders as she had done to relieve his headaches in the past and from there massaged down his muscled arms. Jamie lay so quietly that she thought for a moment that he may have dozed. That fact along with the whiskey and brandy that she had consumed made her bolder in her actions. Starting at the nape of his neck, she then began to kiss down the length of his spine. She heard then the low groan deep in Jamie's throat and pulled back for only an instant before she continued kissing the full length of his spine, ending right before his hips. She stretched out then, lying across his back and folding her body into his, her head resting on his back, her arms around his waist.

Jamie's hands flexed and relaxed under the pillow as Morgana continued the exquisite torture. The feather light touches and kisses by Morgana had nearly brought his self control to an end. She had no idea of her affect on him, but

Jamie had purposely made a point of lying on his stomach. He could have not endured the exquisite torture had it been directed to his chest and lower abdomen.

Jamie turned to his side then and brought Morgana closer beside him. Then turning onto his back, he sat up and lifted her onto his lap and quickly lifted her shift over her head. His arms wrapped tightly around her waist and he settled her over his lap and began to kiss her eyes and her mouth, his hand cupping her face. His hands settled then on her hips and gently caressed her bottom and then came to cup and caress her full breasts. He heard Morgana's quiet sigh in response to that attention and lifting her, brought her down over his full arousal. Morgana called out his name, not in pain, as in the night before; but in shocked pleasure. Jamie brought his arms around her and she placed her arms around his neck, drawing him closer to her.

Jamie returned to her mouth then and kissed her intensely, mating his tongue with hers. The sensations were all so new and so intense for Morgana that she could not speak or even begin to comprehend the growing need within her. She began to move slowly against Jamie and then for the first time, she moved towards him, grabbing his arms tightly as she met her climax. She held on to Jamie as she trembled and reacted to the sensation. He met his climax shortly thereafter and shouted out her name, holding her tightly to him. He kissed her eyes, her mouth and lying down, brought her to rest on his massive chest. She lay quietly for a few moments, trying to gather her thoughts and harness her emotions. He felt the hot tears on his chest and asked worriedly if he had hurt her.

"Oh, no Jamie; ye did not hurt me it is just . . . I dinna ken how to describe it . . . it was different from last night Jamie; it was . . . I dinna ken how to describe what I just felt, Jamie," Morgana said struggling for words.

Jamie held her then, rubbing her arms and back. "I ken well what ye mean, lass. The first time that ye feel such a sensation, it is hard to describe. Remember always that I will always keep ye safe, lass and I will always love ye. Ye mean more to me than my own life, Morgana, I hope ye know that. I just don't want to hurt ye, Morgana; not ever," Jamie said fiercely. He kissed her forehead and tucked her under his chin. He pulled up the covers and continued to rub her arms and back long after he had felt her relax and fall asleep. When he had watched a mad man grab her throat on this night, he knew then that he would die to keep her safe. She was the one that he had sought his entire adult life and now that she had come into his world and he had won her hand, he would never let her go.

He lay in the same bed that he had slept in since his arrival in Berkeley County and yet in the space of twenty-four hours, his entire life had changed. He lay listening to the crackle of the fire that he had banked before taking Morgana to bed. He had thought of her throughout his mission here in this rented room and now his mission had come to an end and he would be heading home. When he headed home this time, it would be to a new life with a wife by his side who would have sat at the right hand of a laird himself in the old days. He thanked the Lord once more for the gift of his Morgana. Together they would blaze a new trail in this new land while they honored and reflected upon the days and ways of their people far from these shores.

*****

The next morning Jamie woke with remembrance of the wee Morgana wrapped around him, sleeping peacefully after the turmoil of the day before. During the night he had heard her murmur in her sleep with memory, no doubt of what had been seen and endured the night before. He had taken her in his arms then and kissed the top of her head. He rubbed her back slowly until the murmuring stopped. She had curled around him then, her arm around his waist, sleeping again peacefully with her head on his chest. He felt as he had the first night that they had spent together; the profound sense of coming home that he had experienced when first he entered her cottage. Morgana was home and so much more; his sanctuary and yet a chance at a life in their new land with someone who understood the pull and the importance of the old world and all that they had left behind.

She woke up shortly thereafter and looked up at him with her wide blue eyes. Jamie reached down and kissed her tenderly. "Mo gradh; I am going to get us some breakfast and bring it back here. Ye do not answer the door to anyone but me, ye ken?" Jamie said earnestly.

"I can go with ye, Jamie," Morgana said quietly.

"I know, love but I can be out and back in no time at all. Ye rest Morgana and I will be right back," Jamie said tenderly.

Morgana got up and put on her shift as soon as he had left and collected her clothing items to dress. She would be ready for Jamie's return. She was anxious to hear when the trial would be scheduled and whether or not Jamie would allow her to collect her things at the cottage today. She would want to thank the owner at the Bella Vista estate and introduce him to Jamie. Their new life was about to start in due course and she was both excited and anxious. She had hoped to do a reading before they left so she would have an idea of what was to come and what lie in store for her in Alexandria with Jamie and his family. She looked around the rented rooms that he had inhabited while in Berkeley County and thought of the empty life he must have lived while here. No wonder coming to the cottage felt like coming home, she mused. It was always warm, there was always something on the hearth good to eat and they had the stories of their Highland home to share.

She looked at the mantel then and saw something white that caught her eye. She lifted up on her toes and reached above her to the mantel and touched the white item. The items that she brought down were two of her hankies. She recognized the double M initials that she had embroidered. With them was the now dried piece of heather that she had placed in his lapel button so many weeks ago now. She touched the items and thought then of the fierce Highlander who had seemed so grim and resolute when she first met him, but yet was tender enough to capture and keep two hankies; one from a scene of crime and death and one from their first picnic together. Enclosed within one hankie, was the sprig of heather that she had placed in his button hole. It was now dried, but just as fragrant as the day that she had made that gesture towards the man who was now her husband. She heard the key in the lock then and turning saw Jamie come in the door with their breakfast, his large shoulders and tall frame filling the doorway as he had filled the entryway of her cottage when first they met.

He sat down their breakfast and she ran to him and put her arms around his waist, kissing him with all of her strength. "Mo gradh," Morgana said breathlessly; *my love* in Gaelic.

He looked down and saw the hankies in her hand and all became clear. "I would have captured one of your raven curls to add to that lot, had ye not thought me daft," he said with embarrassment.

"Ye should nay be embarrassed, Jamie. Ye are the romantic I always ken ye to be," she said smiling. "What is it, love; you have news?" Morgana said looking at him intently.

He looked at her then and thought at some time in their future, he would not need to say a word; she would just know; she would but look at his face and she would know that there was news to be imparted or worry to be shared. What others would find unnerving, he found very comforting.

"Sit down, love and have yer breakfast and I will tell ye all," Jamie replied.

They sat and had the warm buns and cider he had bought from the innkeeper. While there he had encountered the Sheriff. The Sheriff had advised him that the dark one had committed suicide in his cell last night. The case was closed for certain. There would be no trial, as the guilty party had taken his own life rather than waiting for a sentence of death from the law.

Morgana crossed herself as she listened gravely to Jamie's news. "Tis a mortal sin, Jamie as ye ken," Morgana said gravely.

"Aye, lass; and so are three murders we can account for and surely one murder on the road of the true priest. Then there is the one attempted murder, which was the most bothersome of all. Let me see yer neck this morning, love," Jamie said worriedly. He moved the fichu from her gown and saw the dark finger size bruises still remaining on her neck. He gently placed more ointment on the wound as he worriedly watched her response. "Does it hurt still, love?" Jamie asked worriedly.

"It is better than last night, Jamie. Thank ye for taking care of me," Morgana said smiling.

"It is my turn to take care of ye, Morgana as ye have often taken care of my headaches. Besides, I like having ye close to me," he said smiling.

"Do ye ken that we will ever find out what happened to the true priest, Jamie?" Morgana said worriedly.

He sighed so deeply as to ruffle her hair with his breath. "I think not, love. But ye must focus on what we saved and not on what we could not prevent, as he was gone before we ken there was a case to investigate," Jamie replied wistfully. "We will inform our family priest in Alexandria and he shall write to any family the man may have possessed. We will ask him to include his name in the masses so that we can pray for the poor man's soul. I reckon he was extending kindness to a stranger in the form of the dark one and died in the process," Jamie said frowning.

"But, the news this morning means that we are free to return to Alexandria when we can get ye packed up and set off. The Sheriff has asked that we stop by and bid him goodbye on our way out of town. He will truly miss ye, lass, but is happy that we have found each other," Jamie said bringing his hand over Morgana's.

"We need to bid goodbye to the master of Bella Vista also, Jamie, after we pack my things," Morgana replied.

"Will ye miss it, lass?" he asked watching her intently.

"It will be different for sure, Jamie but exciting also ye ken?" Morgana said smiling.

"If ye are ready, love, lets pack my few things and go to the cottage to get yers," Jamie said smiling.

Morgana and Jamie visited the cottage that morning to pack her items. He watched her closely to see if the events of the previous night would reflect on her face. She was stronger than even he had ever thought. She was a lion heart and the match for him. He picked up and cleaned her sgian dubh and dirk thinking of the night before. She was a Highlander through and through, her size no indication of the ferocity carefully hidden inside. He smiled at that as well and at her comment that no man would ever lay a hand on her in anger; my fierce warrior he thought smiling. The dark one had not expected that from such a small package and she had ended his reign of terror in the process and saved an unnamed and unknown fourth Berkeley County victim from the horror that the imposter had in store for him or her.

He stepped outside and taking one of Morgana's garden tools, dug up the heather that rested next to the door. He had plans for it at their next destination.

She came to the door then with her trunk packed "What are you about, Jamie Macpherson?" she said smiling.

"I was making sure that this bit of Scotland travelled with us to your new destination," he replied smiling. He had wrapped it in burlap and it stood now at the door, waiting for their departure.

"Ye think it will take then, when next it is planted?" she asked grinning.

"I ken it will bloom wherever it is planted, just as its owner will. Heather is a hearty plant; it has to be to survive a Highland winter, but then that is what makes a Highlander tough as well, aye? I have also cleaned the dirk and sgian dubh should ye wish to place them in your pockets, mo gradh," Jamie said smiling.

"Ye do not mind, Jamie?" Morgana said quietly.

"Nay lass; we are nay home in Alexandria yet. I may need yer support," Jamie said teasing.

They stopped to say goodbye to the Master of Bella Vista. Jamie was introduced to the owner by Morgana. "You take good care of her, Inspector. She is a precious gift for sure, not only to me but to the community as a whole. She will be sorely missed," the Master stated.

"Aye sir; that I will do," Jamie said fiercely.

Their next stop was to say goodbye to the Sheriff and his good wife. The Sheriff hugged Morgana and shook the Inspector's hand. "Take care of the lass, Inspector," Sheriff Holter said. "I will see that her trunk is sent along to her new home and the plant as well," the Sheriff said smiling.

"Aye, Sheriff, I thank ye for the assistance. I will protect my Morgana with my life," Jamie said fiercely.

Morgana and Jamie left Berkeley County Virginia then headed for Alexandria and the start of their new life.

BOOK TWO

ALEXANDRIA, VIRGINIA – DECEMBER 1785

DEBORAH E. HAMMOND

CHAPTER TEN

"So where do ye live in Alexandria, Jamie?" Morgana asked as they set off along the King's Highway which would bring them into Alexandria in three days time.

"I live with my parents, lass, or I did. I have had a room with them since we came from the Highlands. I will take ye there until the wedding day and stay in rented rooms," Jamie replied.

"I could stay in the rooms, Jamie so ye could stay with yer family," Morgana replied quickly.

"Nay, lass; they will want to get to know ye and besides Mam will want to prepare ye for the wedding," Jamie said smiling.

"Prepare me, Jamie? Prepare me how?" Morgana replied worriedly.

"Aye lass; dress ye and such. These things are beyond my ken, but Mam will ken what is right. I have written her and she will have all prepared," he replied smiling.

Morgana rode on in silence suddenly shy at the thought of meeting Jamie's family and all of the new faces in Alexandra. "It will be alright, lass. We will have our own house as soon as we are married. Ye mustn't be shy, Morgana. They will love ye as I do for the reasons that I do. They observe the old ways as we do. A healer with the sight is a precious thing, Morgana; they know that if others do not. But ye, mo gradh, are more precious to me than my own life," Jamie said kissing her neck, his hand firmly around her waist.

"Do they ken that we are already married, Jamie?" Morgana asked.

"Nay, lass; they are set in their ways. Only the sacrament will count for them. So, I will stay in rented rooms until we are wed proper as we planned," Jamie replied.

"Aye, Jamie; I understand," Morgana said squeezing his hand.

They rode on in silence then; each lost in their own thoughts of the life that lie ahead and the changes that would be wrought with their arrival in Alexandria.

They spent two nights on the road. Jamie watched for the best accommodations wherever they stayed. He made a point of staying in the tavern below while Morgana bathed and prepared for bed each night. He knew that she was becoming more accustomed to the growing intimacy between them, with much more to come and he tried to be sensitive to that fact. When he came to the room each night, she was sitting in the middle of the bed waiting for him, smelling of lavender and showing her love for him in every expression.

"Morgana; ye ken this will be our last night before Alexandria," Jamie said quietly as he came into the room on the second night.

"Aye, Jamie, I thought that to be the case," Morgana replied quietly.

"I do not wish ye to worry. I will see ye each day and ye will stay with my Mam and Da until we are wed again. I do not want ye to fret, lass; all will be well," Jamie said smiling. "Do you understand?" he continued.

"Should I tell them how we met, Jamie?" Morgana asked shyly.

"Oh aye; tell them all, Morgana. Ye are to be true to yourself. Ye are not only special to me, but blessed with the healing arts and the sight. They will be verra impressed with that, as was I," Jamie said earnestly.

"Do not think me foolish, Jamie but I will miss ye until we can be together again, mo gradh," Morgana said quietly. She had gotten out of bed then to help him off with his coat and loosen his neck cloth. "Would you like me to help you take off your boots, Jamie?" Morgana asked shyly.

"Did I not take off my boots before I wed ye, Morgana? I think I can take off my boots without your help," he replied grinning. She looked down at his feet then and frowned.

"I must knit you a proper pair of socks when we are in Alexandra, Jamie. Your feet will freeze without," she said worriedly.

"I like having someone who worries about me; other than my Mam of course," he replied with a wink. He got out of the chair then and started to back her up towards the bed. She looked down at him and smiled a little grin at the sight before her.

"Haven't you forgotten something, Jamie?" Morgana asked shyly.

"And what would that be, lass?" he said taking her into his arms.

"You still have on your breeches, Jamie," Morgana replied blushing.

"Ah and that would be because my new wife always blushes at the thought of me without them," Jamie said teasing her, the smile at the corners of both his eyes and his mouth. "I thought to let you use your own fine socks to help me take off these breeches. I will unbutton and you can use those fine stockings to help me take off my breeches," he said huskily. "Your feet got cold again waiting for me; do they no? I will take care of that in quick order," he said huskily. He was lying across her now as he made the comment and she looked lovingly in his eyes as she used her stockings to push the breeches off of his long legs. He stretched out over her and began to make love to her for the last time in over a month. It would be a long month, indeed until he could feel her in his arms again. She had become like breath in his body and water to a man lost in a desert. He was determined to make this night last in his memory for as long as they would be parted. "Then we will remember this night, mo gradh," Jamie said tenderly.

"Jamie, you like it when I touch and kiss you as ye touch and kiss me?" Morgana asked quietly.

"To answer yer question; aye Morgana, I verra much like to be touched and kissed as I touch and kiss ye," Jamie replied tenderly. "I told ye on our wedding night, it is right for ye to show yer love to yer husband and ye have made me a happy man, mo gradh. Come show me yer love then, Morgana," Jamie replied huskily.

Jamie pulled Morgana up on his broad chest and she looked deeply into his eyes. She put her hands on either side of his face and kissed him deeply. She kissed his neck, across his broad chest and down his abdomen. Jamie's hands clenched and unclenched at his sides as he accepted the caresses and the exquisite torture that they provided. His hands then came through her hair, stroking her neck and back. He gently moved her to her back and lifted her shift above her head. Making love to Morgana had become as important to him as anything yet in his life. She was not just his wife, but the breath in his body. She personified all that was dear to him about the old life in Scotland and all that was possible and feasible in this new land.

He made love to her gently and tenderly as he had done since their wedding night. His hands gently caressed her body and his mouth followed as he took in the silken skin and lavender scent that met him each night. Morgana for her part was unskilled in the way of love, but her passion for her husband soon came to the surface. She moved restlessly against him and he brought her closer and closer to her first climax. His hands tenderly stroked her intimacy and in so doing, he felt her come apart in his arms. She called his name and his mouth closed upon hers, to quiet and contain the effects of that release.

He entered her then and like before, placed his weight upon his forearms in an effort to not crush the tiny woman who had become his reason for being. He eased within her and felt her hands tighten around his shoulders. She raised her leg up and placed her foot flat on the bed in an effort to accommodate him further. She held him to her saying over and over, "don't leave me Jamie," as he withdrew and came crashing into her again and again.

"Never, mo gradh," he said huskily. The tension mounted between their two joined bodies until he heard her cry out yet again. "Let it out, Morgana; don't hold it in. Let it out, mo chroi *my beloved*," he said. They had scaled that mountain together and with one last surge, he met his climax and settled his body half over her and half on the side of the bed. His breath was panting as he came back within himself, recovering both mind and body in the process. He felt Morgana's tears fall on his chest and he looked down at her face flushed with passion. Never had she looked as beautiful as she did in that moment.

"Have I hurt ye, love?" Jamie asked worriedly.

"Oh no, Jamie; ye could not hurt me. It was just different this time Jamie. It was special; even more special than before," Morgana said searching for words.

"Ye dream on me, Morgana and I will dream on ye until the day of our wedding. Ye are more precious to me than my own life now, mo gradh. Never forget that. Sleep my love and tomorrow, we shall reach Alexandria and our new life," Jamie said tenderly.

*****

The next day they arrived in Alexandria. Jamie knew that there would be much adjustment for her here, but he knew also that she had spent a good portion of her life adjusting to change. He would be here to help smooth the way this time.

They arrived in front of a pleasant two story house. Jamie dismounted and helped Morgana down. He detached her small bag from the back of the horse and led her up the walkway and to the front door. When he knocked at the door, he took Morgana's hand and smiled down at her. The door was opened by a stout lady with bright blue eyes, snow white hair and a no nonsense attitude. "Jamie Macpherson; do ye knock at yer own front door now? Have ye been gone that long then?" she asked smiling up at him. She grabbed him around the shoulders and gave him a quick hug. Her attention then focused on Morgana standing quietly watching.

"And this must be the wee Morgana that we have heard tell of. Come in then both of ye before ye die of the cold," she said briskly.

They came to stand inside the house and cloaks and coats removed, they were bade to follow to a settee where Jamie sat with Morgana, still holding her hand. Jamie made the introductions then and tea was brought to warm them.

"So, Mam; have all of the arrangements been made that I have asked you to see about?" Jamie asked.

"Aye, Father will read the banns starting this Sunday. In four weeks, ye shall be wed. We will need those four weeks, Jamie as we need to have Morgana fitted and outfitted properly," Mrs. Macpherson replied.

"I can make anything that is needed, Mrs. McPherson," Morgana offered shyly.

"Nay lass; ye are marrying the Macpherson; all must be properly done," Mrs. Macpherson replied knowingly.

"Mam will have it all sorted soon, Morgana; dinna fash," Jamie replied smiling down at her.

"Ye know I have told ye and told ye that I dunno want to ken about any of your devilish cases; but how did ye come to meet?" Mrs. Macpherson asked.

"Morgana helped the Sheriff and me on our case, Mam. Morgana is a healer and verra knowledgeable about the good and bad that herbs can do," Jamie replied proudly.

"Is she now; is she?" Mrs. Macpherson asked surprised.

"Aye Mam; her Mother was healer to the Mackenzie back in Scotland and her grandmother and on and on and back and back into that clan's history," Jamie continued.

"Well and I saw the plaid when ye came in. Do ye have the sight also then, lass?" Mrs. Macpherson asked eagerly.

"Aye, Mistress; I have had it since birth," Morgana replied.

"Are your parents still with ye, lass?" Mrs. Macpherson asked.

"Nay, my grandparents passed when we came into Berkeley County and my Da as well. My Mam has been gone these two years since. I have lived in a grace and favor cottage courtesy of the master. I saved him from a serious illness and he rewarded me with my wee cottage. It is there that Jamie found me when he came to do his work on the murders at my former county home," Morgana said smiling.

"Well, Jamie and how did ye find one so special in yer travels, I dunno. We are glad to welcome ye, Morgana. We hope that we can now be the family that ye have lost or try to be anyhow. There is much to be done in the next four weeks. There will be the fittings and the counseling with Father and Da here has found what ye asked for, Jamie. Ye need only to see and approve," Mrs. Macpherson said cryptically.

Morgana looked from one to the other faces drinking in the changes that were about to explode in her life. She noticed that Jamie had not let go of her hand and she was thankful of the support. She sat quietly taking it all in, hearing the accents of her parents and feeling well and truly at home yet again, though in a strange place.

"Jamie, why don't ye and Da go check out what ye asked about and I will get Morgana settled," Mrs. Macpherson stated.

"Aye, Mam I will carry Morgana's bag to her room and ye can get her comfortable. There will be a trunk that arrives from the Sheriff and a wee plant as well," he said smiling down at Morgana.

"Come with me, lass. We will get luncheon started. Do ye know how to cook?" Mrs. Macpherson asked.

"Does she know how to cook, Mam? She served me the finest haggis I have had since the family left the Highlands the first day I met her," Jamie said smiling at the memory.

"Well then, that is something that is always useful. Ye ken I canna keep a good cook for my life, Jamie," Mrs. Macpherson replied shaking her head.

"Aye, Mam; let Morgana loose in the kitchen and we will all eat well," Jamie said laughing.

Morgana followed Mrs. Macpherson to her kitchen while the men went about their mission. Morgana did not ask, as she assumed Jamie would tell her later. By the time they had returned, Morgana had a wonderful stew going and had put fresh bread in the oven. Mrs. Macpherson watched her at her tasks and thought Jamie right; she knew her way around a kitchen. When the men returned they headed straight for the kitchen, following the heavenly smells which emanated; courtesy of Morgana.

"I said to Jamie, this canna be my house as what are those good smells coming from the kitchen? Says he; oh wee Morgana has been let loose, ye ken. Says I; ye are a happy man then, Jamie Macpherson. Says he; aye Da, a happy man indeed. Even Duncan misses the wee Mistress; eh Jamie?" Da said chuckling.

"Aye, still she will take him an apple directly after luncheon. Wee Morgana knows her way to a man's heart," Jamie said laughing.

Morgana looked up; smiling and blushing and generally keeping her own counsel. Mam thought she had never seen Jamie happier and even his great beast Duncan was charmed by the new addition to the family. She was a wonder for sure, Mrs. Macpherson thought sagely.

Morgana laid the dishes as she had at her cottage and touched Jamie's shoulder and hand as she did so. She laid out the stew and hot bread next and Jamie and Da breathed in the heavenly scent. She was a happy addition to the family and only just arrived this very day. They joined hands for the blessing and then Jamie and Da enthusiastically dove into the luncheon. Mrs. Macpherson sat quietly until she had her first taste then nodded to Jamie. "Ye are a blessed man, Jamie

Macpherson and I credit ye with sense to bring home a treasure like Morgana. Why these lasses here think only of dresses and balls and not the real things of life. Morgana; yer Mam taught ye well," Mrs. Macpherson stated firmly.

"Thank ye, Mistress," Morgana said shyly. She met Jamie's eye then and he squeezed her hand. The first test had been passed.

"Ye must call me Mam, lass; just as Jamie does. I will not replace yer mother, but I will welcome ye as my own," Mrs. Macpherson said smiling.

As promised after the luncheon was cleared, Morgana cut an apple for Duncan and wrapping it in her hankie, gathered her cloak and took it out to the stable. Jamie had gone out to give him a brushing and she thought they could have some time together to talk in private.

He looked up when he saw her coming. "So love; have there been a thousand questions yet?" Jamie asked smiling.

"Not yet, mo gradh; I expect after supper," she said smiling and feeding Duncan.

"Ye know, ye are not only the most beautiful bride to come out of the Highlands, but the most treasured; such praise from Mam is rare indeed," Jamie said smiling. "Tomorrow we will start instruction with the priest and then the first banns will be read. Four weeks only, my love and we will be together again," Jamie said smiling. "It will be a long four weeks, mo gradh but I have memories to keep me warm," Jamie said kissing the top of her head.

Morgana smiled then and thought the same. She would not have told him for fear that he would find her wanton, but it would be a very long four weeks indeed. His touch had become the most important part of the day for her and to sleep alone again for four whole weeks seemed suddenly like a punishment. She sighed and thought again of the lovely few days that they had spent together and to the day when they would spend each day together for the rest of their lives.

They went back inside then as Mam was keeping watch. "Jamie Macpherson; Morgana will be a bride in four weeks and has come a long way. She needs a rest and ye need to get to the projects before ye. Get ye gone and we shall see ye at supper," Mrs. Macpherson said firmly.

"Aye, Mam; I expect so. Rest well, mo gradh," Jamie said kissing Morgana's hand. He winked at her when he bent over her hand and she smiled her shy smile; four weeks indeed.

Mrs. Macpherson took Morgana upstairs then to Jamie's old room. It was still filled with the essence of him and was a comfort to her for the time of their separation. "Jamie's things will not be here long, Morgana. He will clear them out over the next four weeks. Until then, ye will see the Jamie of the Highlands and of this new America. He has told ye his story then, lass?" Mrs. Macpherson asked watching her intently.

"Aye, Mam; he has told me all. Our stories are much the same; my family walked out of the Highlands and ye rode out as he told me. Our shared story brought us together. We hold close the memories and the traditions of the past and now we can both look to the future, in this new land," Morgana said smiling. It was the most she had said since she stepped in the door and Mrs. Macpherson knew then as she had said at luncheon, here was a treasure worthy of James Macpherson, the Macpherson himself, laird of the clan, though known by only a few in this new land.

When Mam left and closed the door, Morgana stood for a few minutes before undressing for her nap. She looked about the room and suddenly she could hear her mother and father's voices in her head. The Scotland that they had left behind was broken, bleeding and starving after the Rising of '45. The blood stained flag that Jamie had on the wall beneath glass was testament to those awful times.

The men who had survived the Battle of Culloden who were still ambulatory; had snuck away, like the mist that surrounded the moors on that awful April day. They had gone to mountain passes and to remote areas of the Highlands, sending messages through kith and kin that they were alive and where to meet to escape the wrath that was to follow the defeat. The Highland clearances were to begin and all traditions of the clans were to be wiped from the earth. The plaids that they wore to hunt and fish had camouflaged them from their prey and from their enemies and were now outlawed. Jamie's plaid lay across a chair in his room. She recognized it as the hunting plaid, subdued in colors to permit quiet tracks through the woods of their native land to hunt the abundant game and fish.

She gazed up at the Clayborne and the broadsword, as well as the shield called a targe used by the Highland warrior. These were weapons that her father and grandfather had wielded, but were now also outlawed after the defeat of the Scots. The dirk and sgian dubh she knew from experience Jamie wore upon his person every day. They were as indispensable and as silent a weapon as any in the Scot's extensive war chest.

She knew by heart how Jamie's family had ridden out of the Highlands. Her family had walked out until they could meet small vessels on the outward islands that would take them to the American colonies; here to begin a new life far from the starvation and misery of the old land. She heard her mother's voice as she stared at the bloodstained flag; the bonny blue that her mother had likened to Morgana's own eyes and the white cross that stood for St. Andrew, the patron saint of Scotland. She heard her mother talking of the gatherings and the competitions of the Highland games. A fiercer group of warriors the world had never seen since the days of the long ago Vikings who were the ancestors of her own kin. Jamie, she thought; who was the current incarnation of the Highland warrior; all of these thoughts filled her mind until weary from the past days on the road, she undressed and went to the bed that she knew was Jamie's bed.

Undressed and wearing only her shift and stockings, she lay under the covers. She knew the bed linen was fresh as she was looking for the scent of Jamie and could not find it. He always smelled of the outdoors and of the soap that he used to bathe. She knew he was happiest when he was free; hair to the breeze, galloping with Duncan as they had to North Mountain so many times in the past. She looked around his room again studying his broadsword now banned for use by Highlanders in Scotland; the Macpherson plaid and so many other reminders for Jamie of the life he had left behind. These were all things that had been hidden after Culloden and the death of the Stuart dream back in Scotland. It was good for him to start over and in a new place. He said they would live on their own after the second marriage ceremony and she looked forward to that for both of them. Resting finally, she dreamed of heather covered meadows and walking them with Jamie at her side.

When she awoke from the long nap, she got dressed and went back downstairs. Dinner would not make itself and she started to explore the larder to see what she could make for her new family. She found fixings for a bread pudding that she would finish with a whiskey sauce, and a Shepherd's pie. That would put a smile on Jamie's face and unless she was wrong; on Da's face as well. She wondered then why Mrs. Macpherson could not keep a cook. She would have to ask Jamie when next they were alone. She started blushing then as she thought of the next time that they could be alone. It was not a thing she had thought of until Jamie's arrival and now she thought with a little smile, she thought of little else. It was good they were starting instruction tomorrow and all of the plans for the wedding would start on Monday.

She could hear the house coming back to life with Mam and Da's footsteps on the stair and she hoped Jamie would be back in short order. She wondered about his mysterious mission and the project that Mrs. Macpherson had alluded to.

All in good time Morgana; let the man have his secrets until ye are wed again, she thought smiling.

Mam and Da were back again at the hearth, surprised that she was up and had the dinner underway. Da was exclaiming over good smells coming from his kitchen again and Mam fussing over the fact that she was a guest and shouldn't be working so.

"I always had a kettle on and a stew pot going at the cottage in Berkeley County. It is the Highland way as ye ken. I am happy to help," Morgana said smiling at her new in-laws.

"Jamie is a blessed man and I shall remind him of that every day," Mam said firmly. As if summoned by magic, Morgana heard the front door open and Jamie was at the doorway again filling it as always with his height and broad shoulders and chest, his blue eyes crinkling at the corners in one of his now routine smiles.

"Did the smell of cooking lure ye here, Jamie?" Da asked grinning.

"Morgana is loose again in the kitchen and the dinner already underway before we were up from our naps," Mam added. "Ye are a blessed man, Jamie Macpherson; without a doubt and I shall remind ye of that fact," she continued.

"Aye, Mam; I am a blessed man for sure. I ken it well and I have since the first day that I met her. Haggis it was that first day and single malt like the true nectar of the Gods. Wee Morgana knows her way about a kitchen, but not just that; she is a healer, as I mentioned and has helped many in her former community," Jamie said smiling at Morgana.

As was the case with the luncheon, the dinner was enjoyed by all. Morgana cleared up from the meal and they all sat again in the parlor, asking questions of Jamie about his cases. Morgana wondered if they would be permitted any time alone. The answer was apparently no, as Mam again set curfew and sent Jamie to his rented rooms. Morgana went to the door with him and he kissed her hand again, winking as he did so. "Soon love," were his last words to her before leaving for the night.

*****

The next day they would all be headed for church and the first reading of the banns. Morgana fretted if her dress would be acceptable here. It was handmade, but well made and tidy as its occupant. She would wait to see how the ladies dressed at church and could keep on her cloak if not acceptable to her way of thinking. Jamie was coming and they would all walk together to church. That in itself was something to look forward to and the instructions after and maybe a few minutes of private time on the way back from church.

She had started the lunch so it would be ready for their return. Mam and Pa would have their luncheon while Jamie and Morgana took instruction. When the door knock came, she was the first to the door to welcome Jamie. He smiled then and she thought about the first day he had come to the cottage in Berkeley County; filling her doorway with his broad shoulders; tall and imposing he was then and now as she had teased, only tall.

"Well, Jamie; put on her cloak for her and let us be off," Mam stated. Morgana could never recover from the fact that his mother treated *Himself* in this manner, but thought it only natural that a Mother treated her son like a small boy his whole life, even if he was a foot taller and wider at the shoulder.

Morgana took Jamie's arm then and they led the way to church, with Mam and Da bringing up the rear. As she suspected when they arrived, the occupants were all well dressed in the latest fashion. Her tidy plaid would not measure up in her mind, so she kept her cloak on and at Jamie's side, took their place in the family pew, Mam on her other side. When the banns were read, the church applauded for Jamie and turned to stare at the young lass who would be his bride. She smiled shyly and held Jamie's hand throughout the process.

The instruction later was very comfortable in that the priest was from Scotland also. He knew the true important issues in marriage and these two had them; similar backgrounds, faith and perhaps most important of all; family approval. Father McDaniel knew these two would be fine. They would go through instructions and the reading of the banns, but it was all a formality. He had seen the set of the shoulders and the stern look on the face of the Macpherson; marriage was a certainty and the Highland lass beside him was such a throw back to his own youth that he saw in her face the faces, the sounds and the words of so many he knew before, now all gone, dead, starving or relocated to other parts of the world as the three of them sitting here had relocated to Virginia in this new country of America.

Morgana and Jamie walked back to the house after the instructions, content in each other's company. If he had not feared comment, he would have kissed her on the street. As he told her before; they had only four weeks to wait, but the time was closer now with each passing day.

*****

The next day Morgana and Mrs. Macpherson set off for the market. Jamie and Da had decided that with such an excellent cook in residence, the larder should be filled with abundance. Both had baskets in hand and anything that could not be carried would be delivered. Arriving at the market, Morgana was struck by the abundance and selected items for Mrs. Macpherson's purchase.

Her attention was quickly taken by a bent, coughing figure not twenty yards from their present location. She saw the tall, bent figure with broad shoulders, wearing a great coat and the uniform of an Inspector. Her first thought was that it was Jamie and that he was choking.

Morgana dropped her basket and took off in a dead run. Mrs. Macpherson saw only Morgana's raven curls bouncing and her cloak flying out behind her and the petticoats billowing as she ran to the side of the man in distress.

Coming alongside she saw with relief that the figure was not Jamie. She motioned with her hand at her throat and he nodded that he was indeed choking. She calmly asked for a stool and sat the tall gentleman down. A crowd was starting to gather, but no other help was being provided. She motioned for him to raise his arms but to no avail. He was turning beet red and heavily perspiring now. Thinking quickly, she unloosened his great coat, came behind him as though in an embrace and pressed hard, dislodging the offending cherry pit to the amazement of the victim and the applause of the crowd alike.

Morgana then asked the stall proprietor for a mug of water and asked the victim to slowly drink. She took her hankie and daintily wiped his brow. The surrounding crowd applauded as if they had witnessed a magic trick and by this time, Mrs. Macpherson had caught up with her and saw with amazement that Morgana was the heroine of the moment.

The flustered victim had by this time regained the capacity for speech. He took Morgana's hand and pressed it gently. "Mistress, you have saved my life. Please tell me your name, as I am in your eternal debt," the Inspector stated.

"Morgana Mackenzie, sir," Morgana stated dropping a brief curtsey.

"Your quick thinking has saved my life and I cannot thank you enough," the Inspector continued.

By this time, Mrs. Macpherson having come abreast of Morgana was introduced to the Inspector as well. "Again Mistress; I wish to offer a thousand thanks for your quick thinking and work. I shall not forget this," the Inspector stated.

Mrs. Macpherson returned Morgana's basket to her and they resumed shopping. Morgana told her the whole story as they shopped. Mrs. Macpherson was again amazed at Morgana and the fact she could undertake any task with ease; even saving the life of an Inspector in an open market before witnesses who were watching him die.

That evening when Jamie arrived, he was beaming from ear to ear. Mam did not have to tell him the story; he already knew all of the details from work.

"So the Commander returns from his rounds and says his life was saved in the market. All are amazed as his story continues. I was choking to death, says he and a crowd surrounding me to watch me die. Out of nowhere comes a slight lass, making a sign to confirm that I was indeed choking, sitting me down, dislodging the cherry pit as pretty as ye please, then giving me a drink of water and wiping my brow like an angel of mercy," Jamie said smiling.

"Did she have raven hair; says I? Yes, says he. Did she have blue eyes says I, as blue as a Highland loch? Yes, says he amazed at my powers of deduction," Jamie continued smiling. "Was her name Morgana Mackenzie, says I? Yes, says he. How do you know all this Macpherson? Because the lady is my intended, says I. The Commander is speechless at this point and asks if he can provide the drink for the wedding. Ye can cross it off yer list, Mam; the Commander will provide for all of the guests," Jamie concluded with the great storytelling panache only a Scot could provide.

All eyes turned to Morgana then who had remained silent throughout the telling of the tale. "When I saw the great coat and the uniform on the tall back, I thought it was Jamie. That is why I took off running from Mam's side. It was not until I was beside him that I saw the hair color was wrong and that it was nay Jamie. I would have done it for anyone," Morgana said quietly.

"A treasure for sure, Jamie Macpherson," Mrs. Macpherson exclaimed proudly. "Have I not told you so from the first, James Macpherson? You mind that you treat this lass with the respect that she deserves," Mrs. Macpherson said firmly.

"And me now the favorite lad of the Commander and drink for the wedding provided in the bargain. Add two more guests to your list, Mam; the Commander and his wife," Jamie said laughing and squeezing Morgana's hand.

*****

Wedding preparation continued the next day with a visit to the local seamstress. Mrs. Macpherson would brook no interference that Morgana was to be suitably outfitted for the wedding. The girl was not marrying just anyone, she argued; but the Macpherson after all. Mrs. Macpherson described what she wanted and Morgana was directed to a changing room to be measured. She was told to remove her outer clothes so that the correct measurements could be taken. Clad only in her shift and stockings, the seamstress arrived to take measurements and bring fabrics to be draped and approved by the mother of the groom and by the bride as well. Mrs. Macpherson ensconced herself in a chair in the fitting room to give nodding approval to each item brought for inspection; a new shift, silk hose and garters, a new corset, underskirts; each piece was meticulously added until a dress was brought for consideration of design.

Morgana transformed before their eyes, from the young, Scots country lass who had first walked into the Macpherson house, to a sophisticated young woman; the equal of any lass in the St. Mary congregation of Alexandria. The seamstress then put up her hair and tied a choker at her neck. If Morgana had not watched the progress, she would not have believed

118

her own eyes and the transformation before her. Her main concern was the deep décolletage created by the corset and the wide expanse created by the underskirts and structure. She was not sure of Jamie's response to this much exposed skin.

"There is more of me out than in," Morgana exclaimed with dismay as she saw herself in the offered glass.

The seamstress clucked her tongue to diminish the concern. "This ensemble is all the latest style, Mistress. The Mistress has the most beautiful skin I have ever seen. What is your secret, my dear?" the seamstress asked.

"It is a lotion of my own making, Madam with goat's milk," Morgana replied.

Mam then interjected, "Morgana can bring ye some in exchange for the blue fabric I saw in your showroom window. It will match her eyes perfectly," Mrs. Macpherson said approvingly.

"Done, Madam and shall I add up the pieces shown today as well?" the seamstress asked anxious to conclude the transaction.

"Done, Madam," Mrs. Macpherson replied. Morgana bit her lip and looked again at her reflection. If Mam thought it acceptable, it must be alright. The final piece chosen was a pale gray cloak that would obscure the dress on the big day and a pair of matching gloves. Morgana hoped the cloak would prevent the chest cold she feared was in her future.

That night Mam relayed the story of their wedding finery to Jamie and Da. "She will be the most beautiful bride in Alexandria, Jamie. And here was the seamstress wanting Morgana's lotion also and the secrets to her beautiful skin," Mrs. Macpherson stated.

"Her lotion, Mam?" Jamie asked curious.

"Aye, she said Morgana had the most beautiful skin that she had ever seen and wanted to know her secret. I traded two containers for more fabric for Morgana. We will need goat's milk, Jamie so best see to it," Mrs. Macpherson stated matter of factly.

"And where pray am I to get goat's milk, Mam?" Jamie asked with exasperation.

"Ask yer Commander, Jamie. Ye are his favorite lad, so ye said. He will ken where to find it," Mrs. Macpherson replied, with a shake of her head.

"She does have beautiful skin though, aye," Jamie replied lovingly "and so soft; like silk," Jamie continued wistfully.

Mrs. Macpherson's eyes flew to Jamie's face at that comment. "On her hands and face, Mam. What did ye think I meant?" Jamie replied heatedly. Morgana looked from one to the other and said nothing and thought to herself, four more weeks; only four more weeks until we can be alone again.

*****

As had been their practice since their arrival, Jamie and Morgana found they were not to be left alone throughout the four week period for a moment. By the end of the first week, Jamie's patience was severely strained. He decided to have a discussion with Da and bring the enforced separation to an end. He was a grown man, a battle tested warrior sitting with the love of his life who was being treated like a bird in a gilded cage, protected from his sight and touch. Had he known the four weeks would be like this he would have admitted they were already married and had done with it, he thought bitterly.

The conversation with Da bore fruit, as that Saturday night, for the first time, they were again alone; Mam and Da retired to their room after dinner. Jamie and Morgana sat strangely nervous at the fact that they were on their own for the first time since their arrival. Jamie took Morgana's hand and kissed it tenderly then turned it over and kissed the palm and the wrist. He felt the quickening of the pulse at his touch and smiled again at her, taking her in his arms and kissing her passionately for the first time since their last night on the road to Alexandria.

Jamie kissed her over and over, his mouth slanting hungrily. He felt his self control begin to slip and knew he needed to stop, as he would not compromise Morgana under his parent's roof and with them only a few feet away on the second floor.

He stopped then and took her small hands in his, He saw her face, blushed and her lips red from his kisses and noted that her breath was as ragged as his own. He was pleased at that fact and smiled at her, his head resting on her forehead. "I dinna ken it would be this difficult for us, Morgana. Had I never touched ye before we were wed, I would have never known what my life would be like with ye in it. I find it difficult to be with ye and not touch ye when we are alone again like this, Morgana," Jamie said regaining his composure.

Morgana smiled also and traced the back of Jamie's hands with her fingers. "I have dreamt of ye, Jamie as ye said, but it only makes it harder somehow," she said quietly.

"I ken it well, love," Jamie replied whispering.

"Jamie; can ye tell me about yer cases; the ones you have taken on since your return to Alexandria? That will pass the time, nay and give us something else to put our mind to?" Morgana said anxiously.

"Aye, the more blood curdling the case the better; aye love?" Jamie said laughing.

"Aye Jamie; the bloodier the better in the telling, I am thinking. Mayhap I can help you with some of them, Jamie?" Morgana said eyes bright.

"Miss it do ye, lass?" Jamie said with a wink.

"Almost as much as I miss ye," Morgan said with mischief in her eyes.

"Oh, not that much surely," Jamie replied with a grin.

Jamie began to relay one of his most gruesome cases in exquisite detail. Morgana listened rapt with attention, taking in each element. She made a suggestion which Jamie considered and made a mental note to check. They were Jamie and Morgana again; sharing everything or nearly so. Mam found them so two hours later; still chatting and discussing the outstanding cases and the particulars that he had laid before her.

"Jamie lad; Morgana needs her rest for church in the morning. We will see you tomorrow, eh?," Mam said tenderly.

Jamie rose then and kissed Morgana's hand, touched Mam's shoulder and left into the night.

"Dinna fash; lass; it will not be long now. I ken ye love him something fierce. All will be well," Mrs. Macpherson stated tenderly.

"Aye, Mam; I love him so much it hurts," Morgana said quietly with a sigh.

"All will be well, lass," Mrs. Macpherson stated. "All will be well," she said assuredly.

*****

The next day coming into Morgana's room as she dressed for church, Mam asked about Jamie's retelling of his cases the previous night. "Does it bother ye lass when he tells ye such blood curdling stories as those that he relayed to ye last night?" Mrs. McGregor asked worriedly.

"Nay, Mam; I am happy to help him in any way that I can. If nothing else, it takes the weight off his shoulders, ye ken; and is that nay a wife's duty?" Morgana asked smiling.

"Aye, it is lass; but do they not prey on yer mind and haunt yer rest?" Mam asked worriedly.

"I think that Jamie looks into the eyes of evil, Mam and all nature of villains. I reckon I can look there also or at least take the weight from his mind when he must. I can help him sometimes also or the power of the sight can least ways," Morgana replied.

"He is a blessed man, Morgana to have you in his life," Mam replied tenderly.

"And I am blessed to have him and a family again for the first time in a long time," Morgana replied hugging Mam.

When Jamie arrived to walk with them to church, Mam saw them both in a new light and found she felt comfort to leave them alone together after dinner from that point forward, just as Da had requested. Jamie had found his other half and she would be his helpmate in so many ways from this time forward.

CHAPTER ELEVEN

At last the great day dawned. For Morgana it was exciting because it meant that the marriage would begin again at last. The wedding would be special of course, but more important was the fact that she and Jamie could be together again unencumbered by chaperones and they could start the life together that they had planned as they first wed back in Berkeley County.

Mam was in Morgana's room first thing waking her up and handing her oatmeal to start the day. "Ye nay are cooking today, Morgana. Today ye are waited on hand and foot. Eat the porridge as I will nay have you swoon at the altar. Do ye need help bathing, child?" Mrs. Macpherson asked.

"Nay, Mam; I can manage," Morgana said shyly. A hip bath was brought in then and filled with hot water for bathing in front of the fire. Breakfast done, Morgana bathed and placed on her new silk stockings and garters and her new shift.

Mrs. Macpherson was at the door again, coaxing her to another room so that the preparation could begin in earnest. They started with her hair, then following that; piece by piece assembled the wedding finery; corset, hip structure, petticoat under skirts and the dress itself; royal blue to compliment the Macpherson plaid, held at the waist and across the neck bound by a pin with the Macpherson motto which read *Touch Not the Cat But a Glove* at the shoulder. The motto had referenced the fierce nature of the Macpherson clan; both in the new land where members of the clan had fought in the American Revolution and in the old country where the clan had sided with the Jacobite cause. No one in the wedding party today would forget the land that had brought them forth and what they owed to that benighted place of happy memory. Last was the choker at the neck and her heels. Morgana looked in the mirror again, startled at the transformation. She still worried about the deep décolletage and Jamie's reaction to it, but if Mam approved; it must be fine. The light gray cloak was placed above all and gray gloves finished the attire. All was ready.

A carriage would take them to the church today rather than their customary walking. Morgana was relieved at that fact; as the chest cold she feared developing over the extreme décolletage and the untried shoes were both worries of the bride. Mam and Da would ride with her to the church. Jamie would of course arrive first and be in place before the service which was to begin at 11:00.

Morgana cautiously navigated the steps in her new heels and waited in the foyer for Mam and Da. She looked in the mirror again, so unsure was she of her own reflection that she looked one last time to make sure it was indeed her. She thought then of her Mother and remembered her stories of the Gatherings, and the fact that she dressed so fine for the recognition of the entire clan. Those who attended that last Gathering would have thought they saw a ghost when they looked in this glass and saw Morgana's likeness. Would her own Mother believe that today her daughter married the Macpherson himself, if not in the Highlands, then in this new land? Her Mother had repeatedly advised her to wait for the Highlander to come. Had she foreseen this day as well? Morgana hoped that she had seen the happiness in her daughter's eyes, even if she would not be here in person to witness the marriage.

Mam and Da joined her then and she quickly left the ghosts of the mirror and smiled at the here and now. Waiting at the church was the Macpherson. He had been amazingly patient for a man already married, trying to do a thing only to please his Mother. Over the past four weeks he must have questioned his own sanity, but today it would be done and they could return to the life they started in Berkeley County and resumed again now in Alexandria.

They went into the cold December day and Morgana was glad of the gray gloves and cloak and the carriage that would carry them to St. Mary's Catholic Church.

Mam had her hankie at the ready and was already blinking away tears. Morgana was the daughter she had always wanted and Jamie the son that she had loved and nurtured since his arrival into this world. On this day, just as Morgana had seen ghosts, Mrs. Macpherson saw the ghosts of all the Macpherson clan gone before them; dead or scattered to the four winds. Her Jamie, the Macpherson himself and this beautiful lass; who was as close to the Highland lasses of her youth as Jamie was bound to find in this new land, would be joined today in marriage. And what of the children these two would have? They would be bonny for sure; smart and gifted as these two young people she had been given as surely as if she had borne them both.

They arrived at St. Mary's Church and Morgana was helped out of the carriage by Da. He escorted both Mam and Morgana up the steps and into the narthex. There Mam removed Morgana's pale gray cloak and gloves and the bride stood looking every bit the beautiful woman that Mam knew she would be on this happy day.

Mam and Da told her to stand to the side as they entered the church and took their seats in the front row. Their seating was the sign for the piper to begin his work. The doors were opened wide and a bouquet of heather was handed to Morgana. She looked at it for a moment and smiled. Her mother had brought heather from their home when they had fled after the Rising of '45. Jamie's mother had done the same when they arrived in Alexandria. Here, thousands of miles away, the heather brought them back to the place where it had all begun for both families. Her heather had been preserved in the garden of the wee cottage in Berkeley County and his mother's in their home here. Heather had found its way into this ceremony as well; the old mixed with the new. She stood for just a moment, eyes closed; saying a

126

prayer to her parents for bringing her here. She kent that their spirits were nearby today; and not only in her thoughts. When she had heard the piper began, she felt the music in her blood and in her bone; she felt it at the base of her stomach and it was as if her people's memory had ignited within her like a flame. She felt that music as if she had kent it for her entire life; for the memories of her parents on many winter nights had made it so.

She opened her eyes and set off down the aisle, searching in the distance for Jamie. She was not disappointed in her search. He stood at the rail in his full formal Macpherson kit; jacket, plaid, kilt, sporran, boots, sword, dirk and his hair pulled back neatly and tied with a black silk ribbon. He smiled at her as she came down the aisle, a surprised look at first as if he could not quite believe that his wee Morgana was the same beautiful woman who now walked towards him. His face transformed before her and he gained a look of arrogance and pride; replacing the surprise as if to say; aye; here is the bride worthy of the Macpherson. Morgana was surely that in all aspects. Had her parents been present, they would have thought the same. It was a day of ghosts for all concerned, but they all pushed those painful thoughts aside in the joy before them and the joining of these two beloved family members.

When Morgana met Jamie at the rail he took her hand, kissed it and that was the signal for the priest to begin the service. The ring that Jamie brought from his sporran was his grandmother's ring. The ghosts of Highland weddings before them were here in this Virginia church, just as sure as the heather bouquet that Morgana held and the pipes that had called the service. The priest stated at the conclusion of the service that Jamie could kiss his bride and kiss her he did; not a small, brief kiss, but a kiss that held with it all of the separation of the past four weeks and the longing of years of loneliness and need. She placed her hand at his neck and suddenly they were the only two people in the church. They could have been alone in the world for all of the care that they gave to the onlookers.

Morgana smiled up at him with mischief as he released her and their foreheads joined for a brief moment before he took her arm and turning her; led her back down the aisle.

At the end of the aisle, he turned to go into the parish hall where he created a receiving line with himself at the lead, Morgana next, followed by Mam and Da. Whenever Jamie did not know a person, Mam would know and Morgana was introduced to every Scot in Alexandria and of course, the Commander and his wife; the man already known by the encounter in the market, and the thankful wife who followed behind; giving her good wishes and her thanks for Morgana's quick actions.

At the conclusion of the line, Jamie led Morgana to the head table where they were joined by Mam and Da. The piper played the Scots reels in earnest and food was served to the many guests. Morgana learned that Jamie did not dance; the laird never did in the days before in the Highlands of Scotland, but instead sat taking in the joy of the day and accepting the well wishes of the repatriated Scots. Jamie in turns held Morgana's hand and kissed it, particularly when he saw she was not eating. "Are ye not well, mo gradh?" Jamie asked worriedly.

"Whalebone Jamie; I understand now why Mother never ate at the Gatherings," Morgana replied smiling.

"We will wrap it for later, mo gradh," Jamie replied smiling.

As the reels exploded after the meal was over, Morgana let her mind return to the stories of the Gatherings of old and the tales that she had been told as a child. She could very nearly feel the stone walls of the laird's home and the faces of the smiling guests present. It was not the same certainly, but as close as they would come in this new land. Morgana would not let the ghosts of the past intrude upon her wedding day, however. After today she and Jamie would carve out their new life in this new land and she would let no nostalgia interfere with that joy.

Morgana and Jamie made a turn around the room thanking everyone for coming. Silver teaspoons and gifts of cash were given to the bride and groom. The spoon represented the fact that the bride would never go hungry and was an old Scots tradition. Those members of the bridal party who had lived through the time of the troubles in the Highlands knew firsthand the significance of that tradition as they kent the many who had died of starvation after being turned off their land. The cash was money to start the new couple on their way in this new land. The day's events were capped off by the traditional sword dance performed by men of the congregation.

At last the time had arrived for the bride and groom to depart from the reception. Morgana hugged Mam and Pa and thanked them for all they had done to make this day possible. The happy couple boarded the carriage for their wedding night. The destination was a surprise to Morgana, but not to Jamie.

The carriage brought them to a quiet, residential street, not far from the home of Mam and Da and they stopped in front of a medium sized cottage with a narrow opening to the back yard area. Jamie exited the carriage and handed Morgana down. He took her hand as they entered the gate and the walkway up to the cottage door. Jamie opened the door and asked Morgana to wait in the foyer until he lit candles and started a fire.

"Keep yer eyes closed now, mo gradh; I have a surprise for ye," Jamie called out. She patiently waited in the foyer until the candles were lit and the fire started. Jamie came to her side then and took off her cloak and gloves.

"Can I open my eyes now, Jamie?" Morgana asked.

"Yes, love; take my hand," Jamie said tenderly.

"Where are we, Jamie?" Morgana asked.

"Yer new home, mo gradh," Jamie replied smiling.

"This is our home, Jamie?" Morgana asked with wide eyes.

"It is, mo chroi. Do ye remember Mam sending out Da and me to approve of something and the mission she had for me on the first day of our arrival? This was it; approving the house and having in the men to paint and freshen everything for our arrival," Jamie said beaming.

He took her hand then and led her room by room. "This can be yer stillroom where ye can see patients until the babies come of course and then it can be a nursery also and this is the changing room right off of it," Jamie stated giving the tour as they proceeded.

"This is the great room to entertain the family when they visit," he continued excitedly. "And this is the kitchen and dining room connected," Jamie continued.

"It is a palace, Jamie," Morgana said smiling.

"If I live here with ye then aye; it is a palace," Jamie said capturing her face in his hands and kissing her for the first time since they had entered the house.

"And this then is the master room and a changing room beyond," Jamie said bringing her into the bed chamber.

"The garden in the back can be for all of yer herbs and such and for a vegetable garden as well. That is what the Sheriff told me ye would need. We have no wee mountain, Morgana; but I hope ye will be happy here, mo gradh," Jamie said kissing her hands.

"What is a wee mountain, Jamie when I have ye beside me?" Morgana said smiling.

Jamie shook his head and moving into the room, took off his sword, dirk, plaid, jacket and sporran and his boots. He sat on the bed and pulled Morgana to him.

"This is a braw bed, Jamie. Did I ever tell ye, when first we wed, of the first night that we spent in the wee cottage? I came from my changing room and I saw ye on my bed. Do ye remember? I said to myself, Morgana; ye will sleep either on top of the man or beneath, as we will not fit side by side," Morgana said giggling.

"And was it a happy thought, mo gradh; to sleep above or below?" Jamie said grinning.

"I was so afraid, Jamie; but I ken that you had never hurt me and that ye never would. I did not ken what would happen or what I was to do, but I ken that I would do it with ye, Jamie and I was so happy that we would be together. I had dreamt on ye from the very first, never believing that ye would be mine, despite what all the signs had told me," Morgana replied quietly.

"Aye, ye ken all because the sight had told ye. I had no prior sight to guide me, only that I ken from the first day ye would be the answer to so many prayers and so ye have. Mam asked me if she should come by to undress ye this evening. I told her that she had the honor to dress ye this morning and I would do the honors to undress ye tonight," Jamie said quietly.

"There are many layers, Jamie," Morgana replied shyly.

"Aye, I expect so. We will take our time mo gradh and ye can tell me about the day and what ye liked best," Jamie said smiling. He reached up then to take the pins from her hair and bring it down long around her shoulders as he was accustomed to seeing it worn.

"Did ye like my hair, Jamie? Mam fixed it special this morning," Morgana asked shyly.

"Oh, aye love; I thought when first I saw ye; I canna call her my wee Morgana anymore because she is a beautiful woman now for all to see," Jamie said wistfully.

"I am always wee Morgana to ye, Jamie," Morgana replied.

"Aye, I expect so," he responded quietly. He turned her around then and took off her choker and gently kissed her neck and shoulders. He unpinned the plaid from her shoulder and untied it from her waist; lying it aside with the rest of the clothes.

"Did ye like my dress, Jamie? I worried that there was more of me out then in, but Mam said it was proper and the Madam did say that it was all the style," Morgana asked tentatively.

"When I first saw ye, I was so surprised because I had never seen ye so adorned. Then I was the proudest man in the room to marry such a bride. Then I reached for my dirk in case I had to fight my way out of the room with such a prize," Jamie said laughing. "Then I thought; when I have her alone, I will show her what I think of the dress." He pulled her to him then and gently kissed the deep décolletage created by the dress and the whalebone corset within. His breath became ragged then and Morgana's the same. Morgana reached behind him and undid his queue, letting his hair fall free and ran her hands through the thick, dark russet strands.

The pace of the process accelerated from that point forward. Jamie reached in and removed the stomacher and undid the outer laces, freeing Morgana from the dress. He pulled it over her head and placed it with the other clothes at the base of the bed.

"Ye did not lie Morgana when ye said there were many layers. No wonder ye could not eat; I am surprised ye could breathe," Jamie said smiling.

The next layers consisted of the under structure, underskirts and corset of whalebone. Jamie undid layer after layer laughing as the pieces came away. At last the stays to the whalebone corset fell away and Morgana could at last take a deep breath again. The only pieces remaining were her shift, stockings and garters.

"Did ye see my stockings, Jamie? Silk stockings they are and these garters. Have ye ever seen anything so fine?" Morgana asked proudly.

"Aye love; they are verra fine indeed. We will take them off last," Jamie said huskily.

He reached for the hem of her shift then and his fingers traced the length of her body lovingly as he brought it up and over her head. "Ye are the most beautiful woman I have ever seen, Morgana," Jamie said with a sigh.

"And ye have on a great many clothes still, Jamie," Morgana said smiling shyly.

"Nay, lass; I am dressed today as a Highlander." He pulled off his shirt over his head, unbuckled his belt and his kilt fell to the floor as he pulled Morgana to him and on to his chest and down to the bed behind him.

Morgana's hair fell to either side of his face, creating a waterfall of dark silk that enfolded them both. He kissed her deeply as he pressed her to his chest. His mouth hungrily found hers; mating his tongue with hers as his hands caressed her back and bottom, making lazy circles and relaxing the muscles held tightly by the whalebone corset and stays throughout the course of the long day.

She heard the deep groan in his throat and broke away to kiss his throat at the location of the pulse. He placed his hands on either side of her face again and kissed her again deeply.

"I have missed ye so much, mo gradh; I did not think it possible to miss ye so much," Jamie said quietly. He positioned her then straddling his body and proceeded to show her just how much he had missed and wanted her. His hands came to caress her breasts and to enfold her tightly to his chest. He couldn't get enough of her and from her strained breathing, she felt the same. He wanted to be gentle, he wanted to take his time, but for this time at least; he kent that neither would be possible. Next time, he thought with the last of his mental capacity; next time I will be slow.

He entered her quickly and she cried out in his arms. He held her slim hips, establishing the rhythm that he wanted her to follow. She moved slowly against him and then quicker and quicker until she found herself at the edge of her first climax. He called out her name and thrust inside of her one last time, assuring his own release. She collapsed against his chest and they both lay collecting their breath and their thoughts.

"Mo gradh;" he said breathlessly, "I have missed ye so much it hurt. I will never part from ye again; as God is my witness," Jamie said quietly.

Morgana rose up and took his face in her hands. "And I will never let ye, Jamie; never again," Morgana said fiercely.

*****

The next morning, Morgana felt the gentle embrace at the base of her abdomen. She had felt it the first morning that they had woken together and was startled by it then. This morning she knew the source and turned into Jamie's arms. "I was dreaming of ye, mo gradh," Morgana said sleepily.

"And me trying to wake ye for nearly an hour," Jamie replied laughing. "I tried taking the covers and ye held on for dear life. I remembered holding ye the first time we woke together. Do ye ken? I startled ye then. This morning ye turn in my arms as if you have always been here," Jamie said kissing the top of her forehead.

Morgana opened her eyes then and saw the daylight at the windows. "Jamie I must get up and get yer breakfast," Morgana said worriedly.

"Nay, love; stay still. The Commander gave me another day to spend with my bride. I will go nowhere today, Morgana except to the hearth to eat with ye and then back to bed," Jamie said smiling.

"I should make yer breakfast just the same," Morgana replied worriedly.

"Nay, love; I have cheese and ham and all good things from yesterday's feast laid by so my bride does not have to cook and can spend the entire day with her new husband," Jamie said kissing the top of her forehead again.

"The whole day, Jamie?" she asked surprised.

"The whole day, my love; we will not leave this bed, except to eat to keep up our strength," Jamie said laughing. "Besides ye did not eat much yesterday. Ye may take a bite of me by accident. I will not mind if ye do," Jamie said capturing her for a deep kiss.

He pulled her then onto his broad chest and she kissed his throat at the pulse location again, across his chest and continued down to the base of his abdomen. "Jamie, ye should have woken me earlier," she said giggling. She had only just realized that Jamie was fully aroused and ready for her love and attention.

"I did try, Morgana. Are ye laughing at me, lass because if ye are; I would remind ye that ye are in a very dangerous situation," he said laughing and tightening his hold around her waist.

"Aye, as are ye," Morgana continued giggling.

"Ye shall be sorry for that, lass," Jamie said turning her to her back. He kissed her deeply then; mating his tongue with hers and moving his embrace to her breasts which he caressed and then suckled until Morgana arched her back and cried out in response. She had ached for his touch for those four long weeks. Having never known it would have been far better that to know it and lose it yet again. She heard his deep moan and added her own. In short order, he entered her quickly yet again and gently made love to her, easing within and then withdrawing and repeating the movement until he brought her to her climax, followed shortly after by his own. He moved slightly then as if to roll to his side, but she grasped him around the neck and he balanced himself trying not to crush her. He buried his head in her fragrant neck and chest.

"Let me hold ye, Jamie. I have missed holding ye, mo gradh," Morgana said quietly.

"Aye and have I nay told ye before I will crush ye for sure," Jamie said tenderly.

"Aye and I care no more than I did on our first wedding night," Morgana said quietly.

"My fierce Morgana, who does not come to my shoulder," Jamie said smiling.

"I may be your wee Morgana, but I am fierce as ye ken well," Morgana said smiling with her eyes closed.

"Are ye sleeping again, wee Morgana," Jamie said laughing.

"Nay, mo gradh; I am only so happy to spend the day with my new husband," Morgana said smiling. "Does Mam know that ye have today off from work? She will not visit and find us so?" Morgana asked worriedly.

"We are married love; remember? Not once but twice now, Morgana. If there is a knock at the door I shall put on my kilt and look fierce and tell all visitors that today is not the day for visitation; today is the day for love," Jamie said laughing.

"Aye, tall and imposing ye were, but now only tall," Morgana said giggling.

"So ye wake up giggling and will laugh the whole day, aye?" Jamie said laughing.

"I am just happy, Jamie and starving," she said quietly.

"Aye, ye must eat then. Let me find yer shift in our mass of clothes," Jamie said rousing.

"Jamie, I have no other clothes but my wedding finery," Morgana said worriedly.

"Yer shift will be all ye need today, mo gradh," Jamie replied. "I promise ye that," he said with a wink.

"Can ye find my shoes also, Jamie?" Morgana asked.

"Why do ye need yer shoes, my love?" Jamie asked curious.

"To protect my new silk stockings, ye ken?" Morgana replied smiling as she pulled on her shift.

"Aye, I ken; the stockings were to come off last. Ah well, after we eat then," he said laughing again. "Come here, wee Morgana, I will carry ye to the hearth to protect those fine stockings of yers," Jamie said laughing. He gathered up her plaid also to drape across her shoulders.

Jamie carried her to the hearth then and sat her down in one of the chairs in front of the banked fire. He started in on the fire to bring it to life. "Does it remind ye of yer old hearth at the cottage then, lass?" Jamie said watching her intently.

"Oh, aye, Jamie; but it is so much larger than the cottage; I can cook a feast on this hearth," Morgana said eyes widening.

"Aye, love; as Mam says, I am a blessed man; in so many ways," he said winking at her. "Such praise from Mam is rare indeed," Jamie said earnestly. He gathered a plate for them both to eat as they talked.

"Your Mam is strict, Jamie," Morgana offered.

"Aye, well, when we came from the Highlands, I was God's wee angry bairn, ye ken; mad at the world, mad at God, mad at everyone and everything, home sick and heart sick. She soon put me to rights, letting me know how blessed I was to be in a new land where we could live free and not look behind every tree expecting to find a redcoat to place us in jail or to kill us on a gibbet. The time is long ago, now; but the pain remains, I reckon and it always will," Jamie said wistfully.

"Was she always so strict on ye, Jamie?" Morgana asked.

"Oh aye, she said I may be the Macpherson in Scotland, but I would not dishonor her nor Da either. Nay, I would mind her or know the strap," Jamie said smiling.

"And did she beat ye then, Jamie?" Morgana asked wide eyed.

"Aye, beat the sense into me. I may be the Macpherson in the Highlands, but here, I was Jamie, no more or no less," Jamie said staring into the fire.

"She loves ye so, Jamie. Ye can see it in all that she does; even if she does treat ye still like wee Jamie," Morgana replied grinning.

"Wee Jamie, eh? Ye ken she treats me like wee Jamie, my wee Morgana?" Jamie asked picking her up from her chair and bringing her to rest on his lap. "Wee Jamie is it? I have not been wee Jamie since I was a wean of five years old, lass," he said smiling. "And why is it that ye were never afraid of the tall and imposing, Inspector eh? Did I not do my best to be tall and imposing to all when I first came to your wee cottage? Did I not do my best with my frowns to make ye fear me?" Jamie asked smiling.

"Aye, Jamie; ye tried hard, but I could see the creases of smiles at your eyes and mouth. I could see the stern Inspector on the outside and Jamie the man inside the great coat and uniform and the rigid stance; Jamie the soldier and Jamie the man, ye ken," Morgana said emphatically.

"Aye, I canna hide the Jamie ye see even if no one else does. The sight ye ken? But more than that, ye see what others do not. The sight of Morgana's eyes is a fierce thing to behold," Jamie said kissing her tenderly. "And now, back to the honeymoon, I think. Silk stockings were last to go; eh?" Jamie said picking her up and gently carrying her back to their bed.

He carried her to the master bedroom again and lay her down carefully. "I promised myself I would be gentle and be slow as I made love to ye," Jamie said tenderly. "I have been neither," he said worriedly. "Mam said to me last night; be gentle Jamie with our Morgana, she loves you so," he said wistfully.

"And what did ye say, Jamie; to that?" Morgana asked.

"I told her that I loved ye with all my heart and mind and soul. I told her that the Church of England had one thing right when they said in their sacrament; with my body I thee worship," Jamie said quietly.

"And what did she say to that, Jamie?" Morgana asked wide eyed.

"She said that she had prayed for me to find a lass for as long as she could remember. She thanked God for sending ye, even if I have forgotten to be tender in my desire to worship ye," he said smiling.

"But ye were, Jamie. Ye were so kind and gentle when first we were wed; do ye not remember?" she asked anxiously. "Jamie, ye said last night that I was the most beautiful woman ye had ever seen. Have there been many other women . . . in your life . . . before we met?" she asked worriedly.

Jamie took her in his arms then and held her tightly. "Do ye hate me, Morgana for not waiting for ye as ye have waited for me?"

"Nay, Jamie; I could never hate ye for any reason. But have there been many and did ye love them as ye love me?" she asked again worriedly.

"Nay, Morgana; never as I feel for ye. Do ye remember the murders and how ye felt when ye came from the scene of death each time? I watched ye and ye went directly to Duncan and ye stood with him, petted him and let him give ye some of his strength. Ye held him and talked to him; ye sought comfort from another living thing. That is what I sought, Morgana; comfort and comfort only; nay love. I knew what ye sought and I would have taken ye in my arms and given that comfort, but I could not and have the Sheriff think I dishonored ye. I never expected to find ye, Morgana or anyone that could bring back the life I kent and the joy of that other life. But ye did, Morgana and so much more," Jamie said earnestly.

"Jamie," Morgana said looking at him intently, "I will see to the needs of the Macpherson from now on; all of the needs of the Macpherson and no one else," she said fiercely.

"Aye, lass; that ye will; that ye will. Do ye do so because ye think ye must or because ye truly want me?" Jamie asked worriedly.

"Ye will not think me wanton if I am honest?" she asked worriedly.

"This has been a day of truths has it not? Ye tell me true," Jamie said watching her intently.

"I like it verra fine, Jamie," Morgana said quietly, her hands on either side of his face, she blushed with the words.

"Aye, lass," he said kissing her intently. "Aye lass, I like it fine also and I love ye and always will," he said touching his forehead to hers.

*****

Later that afternoon, Jamie dressed to go to Mam and Da's house to collect Morgana's trunk and small bag. Should Mam and Da come to visit tomorrow, Morgana's only clothing would be her wedding gown. He knew she would not greet them in a shift and plaid.

While he was gone, Morgana lit candles, found basins for bathing, put out Jamie's uniform and brushed it for work and put away all of the wedding finery from the day before. She straightened the bed then gathered her own bath water and returned to the changing room. Her only item of available clothing until Jamie's return was her shift. She smiled then thinking of the day that they had spent together and how much they had shared of their life, their love for each other and their secrets from childhood.

Jamie's return to his childhood home was met with the usual multiple questions. "Why did ye not come earlier for her chest, Jamie? She had naught but her wedding gown at the new house," Mam asked.

Jamie's eyebrows rose in his usual unspoken manner. "It was our wedding night, Mam and our honeymoon today. How many clothes were needed?" Jamie replied smiling. Mam was for once speechless.

"I will get the bag and chest together then; shall I?" Mam responded at last walking upstairs to Jamie's old room. Da sat on the love seat smiling and shaking his head as usual.

On Jamie's return to their new house, he found his way lit by candles. He went first to the hearth and found his uniform brushed and ready for the morning and a basin ready for his bathing and water heated in the kettle. He returned to the bed chamber and found all of the wedding clothes put away and the bed smoothed and ready for sleep. Wee Morgana kept a tidy house for sure and a well organized one, as he knew from the cottage. He saw the changing room door closed and knew she was preparing for the night.

He set down her chest and bag and returned to the hearth to bathe and change for the night. She would be cold from bathing away from the fire, but he knew he could not sway her. She was his one and only Morgana; as unique as any woman he had ever encountered; shy, but passionate, calm and yet fierce; a mixture of contradictions that made her his own Morgana, as distinctive as her special skills and the sight she had had since birth; the power of the sight that would only increase with each passing year.

*****

The next morning as Morgana walked about her new house, she stepped out of the back door briefly and into the garden that she knew must be nearby to see the depth of the yard and the space that she would have to plant come spring. Jamie had mentioned a garden, as he knew that she had need of one for the ingredients of her many tinctures and tisanes, lotions and potions of her own creation. It had been laid out neatly into sections which would permit a kitchen garden and a garden where she would grow her herbs for all of her concoctions. She walked among the bed areas, thinking of what she would plant in the spring and what she would need in the interval. In the kitchen garden near the house, she found the small heather plant. She knew since the rest of the garden was not yet planted that Jamie had brought it here for her and had planted it upon its arrival. She thought of their exchange at her wee cottage in Berkeley County and of his confirmation that his mother had done as hers and brought heather from the old country. She bent over and cut a branch to place in water for the dinner table. She might be in a new place with a new family, friends and husband; but the smell of the heather and the touch by her hands told her that she was home. This new place with all of the foreign people and customs, dress and food was nevertheless home because of Jamie and because of the heather brought from their other home far across the sea and a world away from this place of freedom and plenty.

*****

That weekend, Morgana and Jamie took a walk after church and their steps led them to the Masonic lodge of Alexandria. Men were seen leaving the building and when they saw Jamie, they stopped to converse.

"Madam, it is my honor to wish you well on the occasion of your wedding. We think very highly of your husband and consider him a true asset to our lodge. I am your most humble servant, Madam," the tall gentleman stated.

"Morgana, this was the lodge of President George Washington. He was a fellow member of my lodge before he led our country in the rebellion against the British and our country afterward," Jamie said smiling. "This is the lodge which he attended for all of his years near Alexandria," Jamie said proudly.

"There is much to recommend here, Jamie and a fine new life. I will never stop thanking ye for bringing me to yer home. Here we will find a new life as we respect the history and tradition of the lives that went before us. Here we will be at home, Jamie and here we will find happiness," Morgana said smiling. "My cottage is just what I have dreamt of and wherever I stay, if I am with you; I am home, mo gradh," she said smiling.

CHAPTER TWELVE

It did not take Morgana long to settle into her new life in Alexandria. Through the contacts that she made at church, her business was soon bustling with those who sought her out for her famed lotions and potions. The ladies of the congregation in particular found it more comforting to seek out Morgana's assistance concerning a woman's condition then to speak to the local apothecary. Some who were familiar with the old ways sought her out privately for a reading and she shared with them all that she had learned from her consultations. Whether for medicinal visits or for consultations that related to their future, Morgana soon became a favorite in the community and in the church.

Morgana also partnered with the local midwife so that she could offer assistance to both new mothers and to their babies. Her special tinctures aided both when they were ailing or cutting teeth. The midwife shared cuttings from her garden to start Morgana's kitchen and herbal garden. This relationship would prove especially advantageous, because Morgana planned on starting a family as soon as nature cooperated.

Jamie and Morgana quickly were aware that they would soon be visited by a blessed event. Because the child would be the first grandchild of Mam and Da, the news was greeted with great joy and wonder. Morgana was in good health and continued working throughout her confinement as she continued to build her business and build her place in the new community. She had made it clear that she was not to be coddled while she carried their first child and continued in good spirits and bloom until the day that the baby was to make his appearance.

Morgana woke to the first stirrings that told her today was the day; her son would be born today. She didn't want to alarm Jamie; so she kept the knowledge to herself. It was

Sunday so he would be with her. The time would bide; they needed no outside help for the foreseeable future.

Jamie woke and began rubbing her lower back without a request on the part of Morgana. He had begun doing so when he saw her stretch her back early in her pregnancy and it brought her relief throughout her confinement. She didn't want to alarm him now, because she didn't want the house to fill with people just yet. She wanted it to be her and Jamie until the contractions were close enough that help was needed. She would just have to convince Jamie of that plan now, however.

She rolled to her back and smiled up at Jamie. He placed his hand on her belly and rubbed slowly. "He has gone quiet, lass after kicking ye for so long," Jamie said smiling.

"Aye, Jamie; they go quiet right before they come into the world," Morgana replied smiling.

Jamie's eyes grew wide at the comment, "The baby is coming then, mo gradh? The baby is coming today?" his voice rose as did his look of worry as he asked the question.

"Aye, Jamie; I think so, but ye must not be alarmed; it will not be for some time yet," Morgana replied calmly.

"Ye are too calm, Morgana. Ye do not plan on delivering the baby yourself?" he asked anxiously.

"Nay, Jamie; but neither do I want the house filled with people until they are needed. It will be sometime for a first baby, Jamie. I want to be able to walk and stay clear of the bed until I need to," Morgana replied softly.

"What can I do to help ye, lass? Tell me and I will do it," Jamie replied earnestly. He held her hand so tightly that she had to take her other hand and slip it gently from his grasp.

"I will need to walk, Jamie so ye can walk with me if ye will and when the time comes nearer, we will call for the midwife and Mam and Da of course; but not just yet. I don't want them to have to sit and wait and worry." Morgana replied smiling.

She was far too calm for his liking and he thought to tell her so, but reconsidered then and thought better of it. Right then, if I can look evil in the eye and root it out, he thought; I can surely help a wee lassie in her time of delivery. He got up and dressed in his open shirt and kilt. He would greet the day in comfort and meet his son as a true Scot would do.

"I shall go tell the neighbor that we shall not be in church this day so that Mam and Da will not worry. Dinna move Morgana until my return," Jamie stated authoritatively.

Morgana lay in bed rubbing her belly, happy in the knowledge that her son would arrive today and that they would have peace in the house for at least a few more hours. On Jamie's return she saw the worry on his face and hoped to relieve it.

"Will ye be wanting yer breakfast, Jamie?" Morgana asked calmly.

"I will not have ye make me breakfast while ye deliver my son, mo gradh. Here is yer plaid, lass, let me help ye to yer feet and we'll walk to the hearth. I will get a good fire going to keep ye warm. Can ye eat do ye think? Ye should keep up yer strength for what lies ahead," Jamie said anxiously.

"I will have some cider and maybe a bannock and we will see what's what," Morgana replied. Jamie's strong arm came around her as he helped her get to her feet and walk to the hearth. He would have carried her except for the fact that she had told him she needed to walk and she would know what to do; this much he knew for sure.

"There now, let me get the fire blazing for ye and some cider and a bannock. Ye just baked yesterday, lass. Did ye know then that the bairn would come today?" Jamie asked watching her intently.

"I cleaned yesterday and baked. They do say ye ken when the birth is near and that we nest by making sure the house is clean and all ready in advance, just like a Hogmanay preparation, ye ken. That is maybe the case. At least we will have food in Jamie," she replied smiling. She was gripped by a contraction then, but slowly breathed through it. Jamie watched her anxiously, helpless to know what to do next. Moments later she smiled up at him again. "It is alright, Jamie. It has passed; I will be fine," Morgana replied cheerfully.

He felt himself breathe again and thought for not the first or last time that he would rather face battle than watch Morgana in pain or in danger of any sort. Memories of her walk into the church in Martinsburg and her wrestling with the imposter came readily to mind. She was so brave and so calm though and tried so hard to put him to ease.

After breakfast they started in walking in earnest and he watched the hall clock to time the space between contractions. Morgana kept her spirits up and his by telling him how excited she was and how she could not wait to see their boy after so many months of waiting.

By lunch the contractions had moved closer together and Jamie knew that Mam and Da would soon come after church. "Shall I send for the midwife yet, mo gradh?" Jamie asked after a particularly long contraction.

"Not just yet, Jamie; but soon," was the calm reply.

Mam and Da arrived after church as expected and Mam tried to coax Morgana into bed. She would have none of it and stood her ground, Jamie standing it with her. Mam and Da retired to the hearth and Jamie continued walking with Morgana until her water broke and things started to progress more quickly. Da was dispatched for the midwife and Morgana positioned in the birthing chair as she had chosen.

The midwife's arrival relegated Jamie to a minor role outside the birthing chamber, so he took up residence with Da in front of the hearth and the still blazing fire.

"All will be well, son. She is a strong, healthy lass and ye will hold yer son soon enough. Will ye name him James then?" Da asked.

"Aye, Morgana; would have it so. She is so strong Da for such a wee lassie. I was more frightened for her than she was of the birth," Jamie said staring into the flames.

"Aye, lad; I ken it well. Still, ye got to spend more time with her than most Das. She was right to keep the fuss until the end. She wanted a calm birth and so she will have it," Da said smiling.

There was no sound from the birthing chamber, although the door was closed. Jamie knew that Morgana had not cried out all morning and knowing her for the stoic that she was, would probably refuse to cry out. Da watched Jamie's face and saw the anxiety there.

"She will be fine, lad. It will not be long now. Have ye got the single malt to welcome the lad to the world? Ye canna welcome a Highlander into the world without single malt," he said cheerfully.

"Aye, Da; I am ready for all that is needed," Jamie replied still staring at the fire. He had never been around births before and had no idea what to expect. He just kent he wanted Morgana safe and he wanted to hold his son for the first time more than he had ever wanted anything, except Morgana herself.

After what seemed like an eternity to Jamie, but what was in reality no more than two hours; Mam came to the hearth, cap sideways, face flushed and hair escaping from the always neat bun. "She has done it, lad. He is born and Morgana is fine. Let us get her settled and then ye can come and see them both," Mam said with tear stained eyes.

Jamie stood then and grasped Da by the hand and then around the shoulders. A short time later the midwife came to get Da and Jamie and led them into the chamber. They found a tired, but radiant Morgana lying in the bed with a tiny bundle in her arms. She looked up at Jamie then and he came to her side and kissed her forehead, staring down at his new son. He had russet colored hair and blue eyes and stared up at his Da as if seeing his double for the first time. "He is a fine lad, Morgana," Jamie replied smiling.

"Aye, Jamie; he is that. He is small, but he has the whole world to grow in. He will be as big as ye some day," Morgana replied smiling.

"Thank heaven he didn't come that size," the midwife replied shaking her head. "Ye would not have wanted to leave it much longer, lass or ye would have delivered the babe yerself," the midwife continued laughing.

"Aye, she is a wonder is our Morgana," Jamie said again wide eyed. He kept kissing the top of her head and staring at his new son.

"Would ye like to hold him, Jamie?" Morgana asked quietly.

"I would be afraid to lass," Jamie replied.

"He leads men into battle and faces down villains and is afraid to hold a wee bairn?" Mam said smiling.

"I will get the way of it I reckon, Mam. Let me ease into it, aye?' Jamie replied to the barb.

Morgana smiled up at them all. Nothing and no one would take away her joy today. She had the two greatest loves of her life around her; Jamie and their new son.

"Let's give them some time together, eh Mam? We will be at the hearth, son; celebrating the birth in true Highland fashion," Da said smiling. The door closed and Jamie made himself comfortable behind Morgana, bringing her back to rest against his chest, supporting her back and his son in the process.

"It is all worth it today, mo gradh," Jamie said wistfully. "My family came here so that our family would live on and today my grandsire lives on in his grandson. I would give anything to have him see the wee Jamie," Jamie said smiling.

"I am sure he sees Jamie; as does yer grandmam and my parents," Morgana said with shining eyes.

"I always thought; I am a soldier; it is no life for a lass or a wee bairn. When I met ye, it was the only thing I thought of; a wife, and sons to carry on what my family dreamt of far away in Scotland where the world was coming apart over our heads. To think that we could live to see this day and a free land to raise our son, is quite a thing, Morgana," Jamie said smiling.

Baby Jamie yawned widely then as he looked up at his Mam and Da. "Being born is hard work, eh wee Jamie?" Morgana replied smiling.

"No harder than giving birth I reckon," Jamie replied. "How does it then, lass? Are ye alright? Ye have been so brave all day. I dinna hear a sound and I was listening hard. Ye are a lion heart, mo gradh as I have told ye many times before," Jamie said kissing the top of her head.

"I wanted only to stay calm and not have a lot of fuss and bother, Jamie. All was well, as I knew it would be and we have our first boy, Jamie," Morgana said smiling.

"Did ye ken all would be well, beforehand I mean?" Jamie asked.

"I have attended enough births Jamie to ken when something is amiss. I would have asked for help if I needed it, but all was going well, the baby was in the right position and I just wanted the house calm and quiet and not have a lot of fuss. I wanted to keep walking also and have ye near me Jamie. Ye ken ye are my strength; whether ye know it or not. With ye close by, I knew I would be fine. I did not mean to scare ye, Jamie; but he is yer son and well, it was only fair ye not be shipped off to drink whiskey in another room while he made his way into the world," Morgana replied firmly.

"Ye are much braver than I when it comes to such things. Can ye show me how to hold him, mo gradh?" Jamie asked worriedly.

"Of course, Jamie; just mind his head and neck when I pass him to ye. It must be supported when he is brand new to the world. He will sleep now; until he is hungry again of course," Morgana stated.

"Then ye must rest also while he does. Shall I leave ye alone, mo gradh?" Jamie asked anxiously.

"Oh, no Jamie, if ye will; stay with me and we will rest together," Morgana stated.

"I will let Mam and Da know and be back shortly," Jamie replied. He carried his new son to the hearth to let his parents know that they would rest while the baby rested.

"Slainte mhath, lad; to the next generation of the clan Macpherson, as fierce as his Da I am thinking," Da said grinning. Da drank *to your very good health*; the traditional toast over a dram of whiskey, and he and Mam promised to be back with the dinner for all of them. Mam kissed Jamie then and patted the head of her new grandson who she had helped bring into the world.

Jamie came back to the chamber and saw Morgana's eyes begin to flutter. He placed his new son in the cradle and stretched out on the bed next to Morgana, kissing the top of her head. She moved to his shoulder and placed her arm around his waist. He held her as she slept, thinking again of his family and the many sacrifices they had made for Jamie so that this new grandson would be born in a new land, far from the misery of their homeland. He hoped then that he could be as brave as his family had been if the time came for sacrifices on his part.

They slept the better part of the afternoon into early evening. Baby Jamie made his presence known by crying lustily for his dinner. Jamie got up and gingerly picked up his son from the cradle and brought him to the bed for Morgana. She rose sleepily and Jamie handed her the baby and placed pillows behind her back and stationed himself to give her back support. Morgana untied her shift and young Jamie was soon lustily having his next meal, Morgana relaxed happily on the pillows. Jamie picked upon one closed fist and the baby circled his Da's finger within his tiny fist. "He has a strong grip, mo gradh; he is a braw lad for sure." Jamie said proudly.

DEBORAH E. HAMMOND

"He has not learned to release yet, Jamie, so he holds onto ye. I suspect he is strong though; as he will take after his Da," she said seeing the disappointment in Jamie's eyes. "He is braw; he looks just like ye down to the hair and eye color. And the strong grip of course," Morgana said. She smiled up at him and he kissed her on the top of her head again.

A short while later, Mam and Da arrived with the supper. Mam had a cook that was staying with them this time and the supper was a good one. Mam made them both promise that they would eat well for the sake of the baby. The wee one rested in Morgana's arms as if he was a permanent fixture and not less than a day old.

Mam and Da watched Morgana's radiant face and Jamie's eyes that never left her. They both thought of spirits that were around them today, just like the ghosts that surrounded them on the day of Jamie and Morgana's wedding. They all knew the sacrifices that had been made for this new baby to be born into an environment of warmth and love, versus starvation and misery in their homeland. No one spoke of it, but only the joy of the day and of the happy and healthy birth.

"Will ye take off from work tomorrow, Jamie or shall I come over to stay with Morgana?" Mam asked.

"I will stay with her tomorrow, Mam; but I would appreciate the help to her. She will not ask for the help, but I will for sure," Jamie replied smiling.

Morgana smiled shyly, her attention solely on the bundle in her arms. She blew softly on his face and his little eyes fluttered and then closed and remained closed. Jamie watched her; amazed that she already knew how to handle this mysterious new creature that had come into their hearts and their home.

The baby slept through the night and Jamie ever watchful, was instantly out of bed to bring the sleeping lad to his Mam in the morning.

152

"Morgana; will ye teach me all that ye ken about the baby? I watched ye last night and yesterday. Ye had no fear, lass. Ye took to him and he to ye like a duck to water. I want to learn, mo gradh not only to help ye but, well; . . . I do not want to be left out. Ye were kind to not exclude me yesterday. I want to learn, lass. I had no idea how badly until he arrived and Mam was right, I was fearful to pick him up until ye showed me how. I canna have it, mo gradh; I canna be fearful of a wee lad not a day old. I must ken how to do things," Jamie said anxiously.

Morgana listened carefully to Jamie's request. "Of course, Jamie; I am so pleased that ye want to be a part of the baby's life and not just after he learns to ride and shoot and to be a swordsman. I ken ye would have had those to take care of the bairns in the old land, but here it will be just us and Mam and Da of course," she said softly.

"Mam will want to have Jamie as soon as she can. She loves bairns, even though she is strict, as ye ken," Jamie said.

"I ken, Jamie. I think there were a number of spirits around us yesterday; yer grandparents and mine, my parents and the lads that they could have brought into the world had they lived were all there too," Morgana replied.

"It will be fine, Jamie," she continued. "I will show ye all and some ye may not wish to know and others like picking him up ye most definitely will need to know. If he cries, ye will want to ken why. He may be hungry or sleepy or he may need his tiny clout changed or he may just be fussy and cries because he frets and needs to be comforted. My Mam could tell what was wrong by the sound of the cry, but that comes with time and practice. Our lad is healthy and will have the whole world to grow in," Morgana replied smiling.

As planned, Jamie stayed home with Morgana to spend the day and learn about the baby's care. Jamie picked him up and brought him to Morgana. He was now comfortable in picking up the baby, holding his head carefully and passing him carefully to Morgana for nursing.

She showed him how to change his wee clout and they gave him a bath before the fire. She showed him how she checked the temperature of the water with her elbow and laid out all that she would need for dressing him after the bath in advance of setting him in the water. She held him delicately as he had his first bath and Jamie watched her and the baby, so fragile in the hands of his Mother. She showed him how she swaddled him and placed him in his Father's arms where he sleepily looked up at his Da.

Jamie rocked him in the hearthside chair. He would not be awake for long, based on his sweet, yawning face. Jamie beamed at his son and Morgana looked from one face to another, the wee Jamie the mirror image of his warrior Father.

By the time Mam and Da came with dinner, Jamie was comfortable in holding his new son and sat looking worshipfully at the wee Jamie. Mam said nothing, but looked at Da shaking her head. Jamie's life had changed for the better the moment he had met Morgana in faraway Berkeley County. It had only improved with each passing day and now they had their new baby and the whole world had changed yet again. They were in a new land where they would be safe and where generations of their ancestors looked down on them and the happiness that God had brought to them in this new country.

CHAPTER THIRTEEN

It was a hard morning as Jamie rose to go to work the next day. He wanted nothing so much as to remain with Morgana and his son as he had the day before. He kissed Morgana goodbye and told her he would come by at lunch to check on them both.

Mam arrived shortly thereafter to provide the unrequested, but still welcome assistance. Mam commented on the scene from the prior night. "I never thought to see Jamie Macpherson so in love with a wee bairn, Morgana. Ye can see it on his face; he idolizes ye both," Mam said with tear stained eyes.

"He is a good man for sure and his son will be a good man as well. We will raise him in the old ways, Mam; ye can be sure of that," Morgana replied smiling.

Jamie was true as his word and checked in on them at his lunch hour. Wee Jamie was sound asleep, but at least his father could check in on him and Morgana as always and see the two faces that had come to mean more to him than anything else in his life.

*****

Seamus Mac Seamus; James, son of James in the Gaelic, was christened six weeks later at St. Mary's Church where his parents had been married nearly a year prior. Alternating yawns and smiles, he was perfectly quiet until the cold waters of the baptismal font came over his head. He left out a lusty cry then which was quickly dispatched by his Mother's comforting embrace and by her little finger in his mouth. He was christened James Alexander Macpherson, III after his Father and grandfather and ghosts of the Highlands circled around the happy couple once again, as they had on this couple's wedding day and on the birthday of the wee Jamie.

The day was remarkably warm for November and Mam and Da said they would take the baby home for a nap so that Jamie and Morgana could have a walk on their own; this being the first day Morgana had been out since her confinement. Their steps took them to the heart of the town referred to as the Scot's walk and on to the Masonic Lodge to which Jamie belonged. Members of the Lodge were on the sidewalk after a meeting. They greeted Jamie warmly. Jamie introduced Morgana to the members.

"We understand double congratulations are in order Madam; on your marriage last year and the healthy delivery of your first son. Congratulations on both fronts Mrs. Macpherson," Mr. McKay stated.

Morgana thought back to the first time that she had been to the Lodge and had heard that here George Washington, Commander of the American forces in the Revolutionary War had attended lodge and did so still today. It made her proud yet again of her husband and his acceptance in this new country. She was proud also of the community that she had made her own over the past year and the way in which she had been accepted. It seemed that her lonely life was far behind her now, just as her mother had foreseen long ago.

*****

In the summer after the crops were planted, Jamie took Morgana, the baby and Mam and Da to the closest Highland games in a community near Alexandria. He had not participated in several years, but this year, he felt a new purpose to reintroduce his wife and child to the larger Scots community in Virginia and to also reconnect with those things that had given him larger purpose when he grew to manhood in America.

Due to his strength and fitness, he had been a crowd favorite of many of the events in the past. Da and he had practiced for a few months to get him back to where he needed to be from a strength standpoint, as many of the events in which he participated in were strength driven.

Jamie rode on Duncan's back the entire way and the rest of the family in the wagon; with Da driving and Mam on the front seat; Morgana and baby Jamie were made comfortable in the back of the wagon. The food that Morgana had prepared a week in advance was all tied to one side of the wagon, with the tents that they would erect upon arrival. The other side of the wagon was comfortably outfitted with blankets that Jamie swore would make Morgana snug as a bug in a rug. A cover was added to the wagon for the first time in the event of rain. Nothing was too good for the wife and the son and heir of the laird at their first official trip to a Highland game.

This morning, the cover to the wagon was left off so that Morgana and baby Jamie could enjoy the beautiful sunshine and to watch Jamie as he rode his faithful horse Duncan beside them. Jamie had held the baby carefully while Da helped Morgana into the back of the wagon. He handed off their precious son to his wife once she was settled and the caravan headed off for an extended weekend of Highland hospitality and good natured competition among the men.

They arrived at the competition grounds some four hours later. Tents were scattered across the great meadow, as Scots throughout Virginia came to this spot to meet, greet, exchange gossip and for competitive sport. Some of the arrivals had travelled long and hard across the mountain from Monterey, Virginia. The location was changed each year so that the travel time could be shared between those of the Northern Neck of the state and those of the mountain areas. The participants settled in and all were engaged in putting up tents, setting a pot on the boil and finding relatives and friends who had not been seen for a year. It felt good to hear the Gaelic freely spoken again and to see the plaids worn again as they had been in a Scotland long ago and far away, as well as the pipes which were heard day and night throughout the duration of the gathering.

The first night, music was offered by some of the gathering members. A true ceilidh occurred, with the Scot's music, dancing and storytelling well known in the Highlands of Scotland. The story tellers marked certain members of the group as the old tales were told. Da was referred to by the storytellers as Seamus Macpherson to differentiate him from young Jamie and still wee Jamie. The young people danced and the young married couples brought babies to be admired and to be jostled while the drums beat the time and the pipes played for all. It brought back many memories to the older members of the gathering who could still recall the events of old held in their youth and the stories memorialized in the songs. Stories were shared and memories stored up for the long period between gatherings.

In the morning, Jamie was up early to participate in his first event. Morgana and Mam were adamant that he have a braw breakfast to prepare him for the day before him. The cool temperatures of the night coupled with the agenda of the day convinced him that they had the right of it.

His first event was the caber toss. It was the first of the so called heavy events which included the caber throwing, the hammer tossing, shot put and the tug of war. Only the strongest among them would participate in this event which involved the toss of a wooden log the size and height of a tree the furthest down the field. The log was traditionally made of Scot's pine which was replaced with loblolly or other American pine in this gathering. A good deal of meadowland was needed to permit this event to be held and only the strongest participants would be whittled down to the precious few who would carry away honors for the day.

Stripped down to his kilt, shirt, stockings and boots, Jamie stood at the line to begin the competition. The other ladies gathered to watch the event quickly looked towards Morgana when Jamie was revealed in all his muscled glory. She smiled shyly and instructed baby Jamie to watch his father. His toss was the longest of the morning and the obvious one to beat. Despite the best efforts of his fellow participants, Jamie's toss had won the day. Donning his plaid, Jamie came to the main seating area to receive his award for the first event of the day. Morgana's eyes shone with her pride at her strong, healthy husband and Mam and Da shook their heads with the knowledge that their son had once again made them proud.

The next event of the day was also one that Jamie excelled in; the hammer toss. A weighted hammer, twenty-two pounds or more in weight, attached to a wooden pole or handle, made from a metal ball, was required to be tossed as far as possible. The successful competitor needed to have the strength to throw the hammer. Few would have the strength or agility needed to perform the task. For Jamie, it was again all in a day's work. He stripped down again to his shirt, kilt, stockings and boots and his muscular back and shoulders were revealed yet again for all to see. He stood at the line and threw the weighted hammer. His first attempt was the one to beat yet again. Although numerous competitors tried to best his effort, none could do so. Jamie again was in the winning circle for his second event of the day.

By that time, lunch was called for and Jamie met his family on the sidelines, taking up baby Jamie on his wide shoulders as they returned to the line of the family tents. Jamie and Morgana had their own tent, with a boxed cradle for baby Jamie to sleep in. Mam and Da were next door in their own tent. The soup kettle stood between both tents and was kept full with stew and other good and nourishing food to complement the baked goods that Morgana had spent the past week preparing. Not just the immediate family enjoyed the largesse of that kettle. In true Highlander fashion, hospitality was the order of the day. As Morgana had fed her neighbors in far away Berkeley County, so now did the Macpherson family feed any who came to visit and to congratulate Jamie on his two wins in the events completed during the morning schedule.

The next event after luncheon was the shot put. In this event, a large stone which weighed between twenty to twenty-six pounds was thrown as far as possible by the participants. Jamie had excelled at this event since he was a young lad and today was no exception. Jamie's throws were always the ones to beat and today was no exception. His appearance in the winner's circle was again no surprise for those who regularly attended the Virginia Highland Games.

The next event involved teams of eight members with a ninth member who shouted both encouragement and instructions. The Alexandria team was an odds on favorite with the addition of James Macpherson. Jamie stood at the very end of the line and was the anchorman who brought his team to victory. Again Jamie was in the winner's circle with his eight team mates and Da acting as coach. It had been a wonderful day for the family and a great day to be a Scot in Virginia. Tonight would be the highlight of the games schedule with Scot's dancing featured and more music.

The late afternoon brought a rousing competition between pipers. In the old country, lairds would have brought their own clan pipers to compete. In the new land, the pipes were a worthy bit of nostalgia and the echoes of those beautiful instruments brought a tear to the eye of any who had been born and reared in Scotland and knew the history of the fabled land. In 1746 with the failure of the rising of Bonnie Prince Charlie and the Stuart cause, all of this tradition had been lost in their home country; outlawed by the conquering British. Here in the new world, the games brought back the spirit of friendly competition and reminders to those in the crowd of all that had been left behind in the fabled land of their forebears and for some, of their lost youth.

Again, Morgana experienced the same feeling that she had on her wedding day. When she heard the pipes, the music seemed to go through her, into her blood and bone. She felt the music as much as she heard it. All of the stories handed down from her parents were there before her and she could see and feel the pipes which had been used for both societal reasons of gathering and to invoke a call to participants in clan events and to call warriors to battle back in Scotland. She felt the spirits of her parents around her yet again and would not have been surprised to see their shadow before her as she listened to the competition. It was a comforting thought to ken that thousands of miles away and an ocean apart, the Scots of the scattered clans could still gather and hold dear to their traditions and the ways of their forebears.

That night alone in the tent, Morgana lie in the arms of the victor of the Virginia games. "Ye were braw, Jamie; I was so proud of you and me having all of the women looking my way when you stood in your shirt and kilt for all to see. Ye are a beautiful man, James Macpherson and a fierce one as well. I reckon any villain would think twice to be chased by the likes of ye," Morgana said softly. She was both trying to speak quietly so as to not wake the baby and to shelter her voice within the confines of their tented space.

"Any man could be a victor with such a wife cheering him on. Someday, yon wee Jamie will take his Da's place in the games. Oh he will be a braw lad, Morgana; this I know for sure. He will make us proud," Jamie said smiling into the darkness.

"I expect the next one will make us proud as well," Morgana said grinning.

"The next one, lass; you mean there is another on the way, then?" Jamie asked wide eyed. He had captured her face in his hands as he searched out her eyes in the darkness.

"Not yet, Jamie; but soon. If we have another boy, they can both compete in the games and you can teach them to be winners like yourself. If we have a girl . . . well, I will be happy either way; so long as the baby is healthy," Morgana said smiling.

"Aye, love; healthy and happy is all that we can wish for. Do you ken when this next bairn will make his or her appearance?" Jamie said tenderly.

"I do not ken exactly Jamie, but I ken it will be soon. I feel it as I have felt many other things that have come to pass between us," Morgana replied.

"Aye, Morgana; this is news better to my ears than any award that I might have won this day. It is news that will make Mam and Da happy as well. Thank ye, Morgana for making me a happy man many times each and every day," Jamie said as he kissed her forehead.

CHAPTER FOURTEEN

In October of that same year, Jamie was dispatched for yet another investigation. He could not take Morgana and Jamie along for this trip, as he was investigating yet another murder. Morgana told him that she would be with him in her heart and that she would do a reading and send him whatever she had learned from that in her letter to him confirming his safe arrival. He kissed his first born and his wife and placed his hand above her abdomen. She had not yet even begun to show, but he knew the secret treasure that lie beneath the Macpherson plaid; the second born of the laird of the Macpherson clan and the woman who was his seer, his healer and the love of his life. Morgana had confirmed for him the vision that she had given him during the summer at the Highland Games. A second bairn was on the way.

*****

Jamie set off with a heavy heart, but with a grim determination to solve the mystery of this murder and to return home to his growing family. The time away at the gathering this summer had been good for them all. Da and Mam had the joy of reuniting with friends that they had not seen since the last such event. Morgana had met many Scots and had been admired for her skills in healing as well as the sight. Baby Jamie had his first exposure to the world that he would grow up in. Jamie planned on providing him the same training that he himself had received, nearly from the time that he was able to walk. When the time came, baby Jamie would take his father's place in the heavy events, just as Jamie had taken Da's place. Today in this new world, it was a mark of pride. Back in the old world, the skills had saved a man's life and still today, Jamie had the necessary knowledge to protect himself in his chosen profession of peacekeeping.

The murder that he had been sent to investigate had occurred during the annual training for the Virginia State Militia. This year it had been held in Richmond and Jamie traveled there to solve the case and to quickly return to the woman and small bairn who held his heart.

Morgana went about her usual morning's events, trying as much as possible to set about her daily routine and keep Jamie's departure in the back of her mind. Since they had first met in Berkeley County, they had not been apart for a day. Morgana knew in her heart that the day would come when he would be sent along on another special mission, as he had been to Berkeley County; she just didn't know how she would handle it. She had baby Jamie to keep her company first thing in the morning as she bathed and changed him as she normally did. She would have her customers as soon as the normal hours began. They would all help keep her mind off of Jamie's mission and of his absence. The nights were her biggest concern and she dreaded already the night ahead that would be spent without Jamie. She planned to bring baby Jamie into the master chamber tonight in the hopes that his presence would keep her fear at bay. It was times like these that she feared her gift. What if she was to have visions of Jamie in danger or worse yet injured or killed? She put the painful thoughts to the back of her mind and carried on her morning routine.

Soon the day's customers arrived with aches, pains and mental malaise and she was the healer yet again; a woman with the skills to aid bodily harm and illness and with the patience and forbearance to listen and provide comfort to those who grieved or held a personal story that plagued their days and interrupted their sleep at night.

Mam and Da were to come over that evening to visit and to spend time with the baby. She knew that their visit was also tailored to help fill the empty night that stretched before her. After the departure of her first customer for the morning, she tidied the house as she did each day, put Jamie to bed for his nap and then sat down at her stillroom table to do a reading and to look for assistance that could help her Jamie in the work that he pursued and to provide comfort to herself that she was helping in some way to bring him home safely.

*****

Upon Jamie's arrival at camp the next day, he had gone directly to the Commander and introduced himself. Together they visited the scene of the crime. A soldier stood at attention at the tent that had been the location of the murder. The body was lain out for the Inspector's review prior to burial. "The death would have been almost instantaneous, Commander. This wound to the neck has been done with almost surgical accuracy. Has there been any accounting of the possessions of the deceased?" Jamie asked frowning.

"I posted a guard at the tent entrance as soon as Sgt. Marshall failed to arrive for morning roll call. Nothing has been permitted to be touched since that time," the Commander replied.

"Excellent then, I shall start my work by going through the personal effects of Sgt. Marshall. You can prepare the burial detail for the deceased now, sir. I assume that his pockets were all turned out at the time he was found?" Jamie asked.

"We have kept everything exactly as it was found, other than washing the body, of course. That was carried out by our surgeon. Nothing else has been touched in the tent in the interval," the Commander stated.

"Very good, sir; I am going to take the liberty of checking his uniform pockets and then I will go through item by item of the personal effects of the deceased. I will be making an inventory and looking for any clues that would have explained his murder. I would also request that his personal records be requested from the military headquarters. I would know his story and how he came to be here and in this particular militia unit. He looks a bit older than the usual recruit. Anything that we can determine may be of assistance in the long term investigation," Jamie replied.

"I will leave you to it, Inspector. Please let me know if there is anything that you could possibly need," the Commander replied in leaving. "I will leave the guard on duty as well, round the clock," the Commander added.

Jamie sat down on the cot next to the body and began to check each of the pockets. He suddenly thought of his experiences with Morgana when together they solved the murders in Berkeley County. That investigation had brought them together and he sorely missed her and her intuitions about murder investigations and about all things related to the human body. She is a marvel, he thought; as beautiful as a spring day and as bright as a new penny. What he wouldn't give to have her here today, by his side as he tossed out theories and tried to reach the truth. "What do you have to tell me, Sgt. Marshall, eh? Who in this camp hated or feared you enough to end your life?" Jamie asked as he continued his inspection.

*****

The first hours had passed uneventfully since Jamie's departure. He had promised to write to let them all know that he had arrived safely. Morgana planned to keep busy both with her garden, baby Jamie's care and her patients. The morning had passed in perfect order until she sat down to take her first reading. She read the leaves and when she did so, she began to receive a vision; a vision of such horror that she closed her eyes against it. Had she been sleeping, she would have thought it a dream, but as it continued on, she knew in her heart that she had been visited by one of her visions; the gift of the sight that Jamie had told her would only grow stronger with each passing year was again telling her of impending danger.

In the vision, she saw Jamie in a bed in a room that she did not recognize. He was thrashing in the bed in pain and in a fever. The worst part of the dream was when she saw Jamie's wound, the leg had been removed from the knee down. Jamie was tossing and turning as he cried out at the pain of it and of the horror experienced of losing a limb. A man who was without equal in the heavy events of a gathering of the Highland Games would now be reduced to a crutch and a wooden limb. She came away with a start from the first vision; she moved with a determination by the second such sighting.

Moving quietly in the house, she packed her case and a small one for baby Jamie and prepared for a trip with Da. She knew if the events had not yet occurred, she must arrive at the militia camp in Richmond in time to prevent them from happening. She packed her most important medical instruments and the teas, tinctures, salves and bandages needed for a siege in a sick room.

She dressed the baby after he woke from his nap and brought herself along to Mam and Da's house a short distance away, her packed cases in one hand and the baby in the other. She knocked on the door and waited for Da to answer it. She did not have long to wait. He looked at her worried face and waited for the verdict of her uncustomary arrival.

"I must travel to find Jamie, Da; he is in trouble and needs me. Will you take me to him in the wagon?" she asked worriedly.

"Ye have had a vision then of Jamie and that is what brings ye here?" Da asked worriedly. "Come in then, lass and let me change and pack a bag. I will take ye to him, Morgana; have no fear. I know what you see to be true, as Jamie has told me of your knowledge many times. The wee lad will stay here with Mam if it is agreeable to you, lass. We can travel faster and ye can concentrate your skills on Jamie's care when we arrive," Da said worriedly.

By this time, Mam had also come downstairs from her nap in her night rail to determine what had happened. "Did ye have a vision, Morgana? Ye look as if ye have seen a ghost and I see your cases packed and wee Jamie on your hip. It is Jamie that ye have seen in yer dream?" she asked worriedly.

"Aye, Mam; I had what I thought to be a visitation, but it kept reoccurring. Two times I saw the same sight and I must travel to prevent it. I began packing on the second such vision. Da says he will take me and that it would be best for wee Jamie to stay with ye here. Is it alright then, Mam?" Morgana asked worriedly.

"Ye go and do what ye must, Morgana. Bring our Jamie home and in one piece; that is all that I ask of ye. I will look after the wee bairn until yer return. Go now, like the wind as soon as Da is ready," Mam said in hushed tones.

Da came down the stairs then, dressed and packed for their journey. He hitched the wagon, packed their bags and a dinner for the two of them and they set off on the king's highway towards Richmond. They must find Jamie and they must prevent the tragedy that awaited him.

*****

As they travelled, the normally taciturn Da told Morgana stories of his youth in Scotland. He told her the story of his brother, the laird who had remained in Scotland. He had married, but had remained childless. All the while he continued to write to his brother in America to tell him that his son, James must take the place of the laird when the time came. Da had instructed Jamie in all of the old ways, building his body and his mind as he must to take the reins of the clan, now scattered to the four winds in this new land of America and further north into Canada.

Jamie had been his heart and his soul and no father could be more proud of the man that he had become, he said. When he had come home from Berkeley County with Morgana, it felt somehow as if the circle was now complete. Morgana and James had had their wee bairn and a new generation had been born in this new country; free to live as they would, to dress as they saw fit and to honor the old ways in this new land.

Morgana had not yet shared with Da and Mam that she was expecting yet again. She felt somehow that Da and Mam would not have approved of this journey had they known that she was with child and she knew also that she must make the trip if she was to bring Jamie home safe and whole, as Mam had commissioned her to do.

*****

The entire first day of Jamie's investigation, he had spent in the tent, going methodically through each item in the sergeant's quarters and reading every document that could be found. The documents he organized and provided to the Commander at the end of the day. They involved matters related to the militia; attendance rolls, training missions and the like; but nothing that could have pointed to a reason for murder. He returned to the room that had been provided to him in the Commander's temporary residence and unpacked the items that he had packed for the trip. He sat down and wrote a letter to Morgana to let her know that he had arrived safely and then laid down on the bed to think on the case and on his next steps.

As was frequently the case, ideas came to Jamie when his mind relaxed. If documents were present that would have provided a motive for murder, they could easily have been kept in a hidden location, just as the imposter priest had kept his secret correspondence in a locked drawer of his desk. He rose from his bed, put on his boots and travelled down the row of tents until he reached the tent of the deceased. The soldier on duty waved him through and he sat down to look under each piece of furniture in the outside chance that something had been missed in his preliminary evaluation. The cot was turned over and the pillow, blankets and sheets all removed to uncover any hiding place of documents or other evidence. Next was the field desk that graced one corner of the tent. Jamie went through every nook, cranny and drawer looking for something that might lead him to the answer. As was frequently the case when such inspiration hit him, he worked long into the evening and through dinner. Each piece of furniture had been thoroughly inspected, turned over and turned out and at long last, he had arrived at the one piece of furniture that remained in the tent. It was a coat tree that the sergeant had kept his uniform and weapons on to assure that it could be brushed and ready for the next morning's wearing. Jamie had used a similar piece of furniture when he himself was in the military. It had kept his clothing ship shape and Bristol fashion and had permitted him to dress quickly and in the dark.

Jamie turned that piece of furniture over and when he did so, he noted a brass fitting that disguised a hollow interior center which could, in a pinch; house documents if rolled and placed inside for hiding purposes. He brought the candle that he had lit to his side and peered into the hollow interior. As he suspected, there were documents rolled and housed within the hollow space. He took out his sgian dubh and loosened the rolled document housed within. Gingerly he pulled the document down so that it could be removed from its housing. When he finished extricating the document, a small bag followed which housed gold sovereigns like those that had been used before the Revolutionary War. Jamie's brow furrowed as he looked at both the rolled document and the bag of gold. Where would Sgt. Marshall have acquired a king's ransom and why was it kept hidden in this fashion?

Jamie's attention was on the unexpected bounty before him and kneeling as he was, he did not hear the silent assailant who was at that moment lifting the tent on the opposite side and climbing beneath from the woods side. The assailant had pierced the cloth with a small hole as he had studied the prior occupant of the tent. There, he had watched the previous murder victim as he went about his evening chores, hoping and praying that his bounty of secrets and their hiding place would be revealed. He had waited in the shadows of the trees for the opportune moment to end the life of the first victim; Sgt. Marshall.

Now, the assailant watched and waited, hoping against hope that the Inspector's ingenuity would reveal the very thing that he himself had been looking for when he had killed Sergeant Marshall. Jamie saw the shadow on the tent wall, but too late to avoid the garrote that quickly encircled his neck. He was on one knee and off balance, but his extraordinary strength enabled him to insert fingers under the garrote and loosen it sufficiently to allow him to breathe again. He reached back to grab the hands of his assailant next and tried to throw him off balance and over his head.

The two struggled and the assailant tiring of the fight, and worrying about the outcome, pulled out a pistol from his left pocket which he had kept hidden until now. He knew the camp would be roused by the shot, but he reasoned he had little time before Jamie would use his superior height and strength to throw him off balance. He pulled the pistol quickly from his pocket and being left handed; shot Jamie in the leg, hoping to stop the attack and to disappear back into the woods from whence he had come.

When the shot rang out, Jamie released his hold. The assailant grabbed the document and bag and disappeared under the tent and into the darkness of the woods again. He quickly took off the mask that he had worn and threw the mask and the pistol into a hollow log in the woods where he had also hidden the garrote that had killed Sergeant Marshall. He folded the document into fourths and placed it and the bag of coins into his deep pockets. He needed to circle round and regain his tent before the general alarm was sounded and he was roused to offer surgical assistance to his own victim. He had no fear of discovery, as it was his intention to silence the Inspector once and for all with the life saving surgery that he alone would recommend. The Inspector would die at his hands, but then men died every day from surgery such as that he planned to complete.

The soldier who had stood attention at the front of the tent had temporarily walked away in order to gain his dinner. He sprang to attention at the sound of the shot and ran down the row of tents to find the Inspector sprawled on the floor, shot in the leg. Any evidence that had been found had been taken by the masked assailant who had exited as he had come in the back of the tent and into the surrounding woods. The soldier came to Jamie's side and calling for help, picked up Jamie under the arms to enable him to hobble to one foot. His weight was placed on this man's shoulder and a second fellow soldier as he was taken to his room in the Commander's temporary headquarters. Jamie told them that the assailant had exited the tent into the woods. The woods were ordered to be searched, but the assailant was long gone, back to his tent to await the call for his services. The surgeon was called for and Jamie's boot was removed as they waited for the surgeon's verdict.

Not all had been ignorant of the surgeon's retreat, however. One had stood watch and had seen the surgeon's disappearance into the woods after the shot rang out. His suspicions were confirmed, but now; he needed to make sure the Inspector lived so that his theories could be advanced and the murder solved. A miracle was needed if the Inspector would not die at the hands of the man who had wounded him in the first place.

*****

Da and Morgana spent one night on the road between Alexandria and Richmond and arrived on the evening of their second day on the road to the grounds where the militia lay in camp. It was their annual training to protect the state of Virginia against all enemies; foreign and domestic. Da and Morgana had travelled last night longer than usual because of the presence of the full moon. Morgana looked to the sky and thought back to the evil moon that she and Jamie had witnessed when the evil one had continued his spree of murder back in Berkeley County. She prayed that she was in time to prevent the vision that she had seen before leaving Alexandria. She must get to Jamie and stop what had been predicted in her vision before it was too late.

The sentry who stood guard motioned the wagon to move forward. "Name and purpose?" the young sentry stated.

"We are here to see my son and her husband; Inspector James Macpherson. We reckon he has been here now going on a day," Da said worriedly.

"Your purpose here, sir?" the young sentry asked.

"My daughter-in-law is a healer. We heard tell that you have need of a healer here and that my son has been injured in the line of duty," Da continued.

"Just one moment, sir, ma'am," the young sentry moved to confer with a superior officer. They both stepped forward and searched the wagon and then waved them on. "Inspector Macpherson is currently residing in the Commander's residence. He has been injured this very evening and is currently receiving treatment," the young sentry stated.

As she listened, Morgana's attention was briefly taken by the rise of the full moon; blood red, just as it had been in Berkeley County on the night of the arrival of the dark one who had been the author of all of the murders there. Again an evil moon rose and her breath held at the portent when Jamie's life lay in the balance. Right then; Morgana thought squaring her shoulders; the moon is not the cause of this any more than it was in Berkeley County. Evil is afoot and my Jamie is in danger, but that is the work of men and not moons.

Morgana looked worriedly at Da as they drove on in search of the Commander's residence. They saw before them a tent city, not unlike the tents that had been arranged at the recent gathering of the Virginia Scots. Both of them thought again for a moment of the healthy and braw lad who had easily won the heavy events at the recent gathering. Were they in time? Could they save Jamie from the vision that Morgana had seen and had haunted her waking moments ever since?

Da pulled the wagon in front of the Commander's temporary brick residence, used while the camp was in place for the annual training. He helped Morgana down and she grabbed her bag laden with her instruments, tinctures, tisanes, lotions and bandages. She would need all of her skill and her treatments if they were faced with what she had witnessed each time the vision was upon her. Da knocked on the door and a young lieutenant answered. "We are here to see Inspector James Macpherson. I am his Da and this here is his wife, Morgana. The lass is a healer and we have heard tell that Jamie is in need of medical attention," Da said worriedly.

"Come in sir; the surgeon is with him now," the young lieutenant said worriedly. Da and Morgana entered the brick residence and saw a crowd gathered at the door of one of the rooms. They heard a slew of Gaelic curses which if they were not mistaken, were being uttered by Jamie himself. "He is just in here," the lieutenant said leading the way. The Commander himself stood at the door, a look of worry painted on his face. "Sir, this is the father and wife of Inspector Macpherson," the lieutenant said quietly.

"Mrs. Macpherson, you could not have come at a better moment. The surgeon is trying to explain to your husband the nature of the injury he has just sustained. He wishes to . . . well, to amputate your husband's leg, below the knee. He has been shot you see and the surgeon fears the leg will fester and that the wound will poison his entire body. I am so very sorry to tell you this horrible news as soon as you have arrived," the Commander said worriedly.

"My daughter-in-law here is a healer, Commander and the best that I have ever ken. Will ye let her take a look at the situation and determine if she agrees with the surgeon's opinion? It is only that the lad is young and fit and braw and whatever might be done to save the leg, well . . . Morgana is the lass who can do it," Da replied urgently.

"Yes, of course . . . if you think there is a chance . . . of course you must examine your husband. However did you know to visit now when things are at such a state? Let me gingerly separate your husband from the surgeon, then," the Commander stated. He moved from the doorway towards the double bed which was on the far wall. Jamie had not ended his slew of Gaelic curses which he continued to hurl at the surgeon. Fortunately, no one in the room kent the Gaelic and could not understand the mortal danger that the surgeon now found himself as he threatened Jamie with amputation of his leg.

"He will not calm until that man is sent away, Da," Morgana said quietly. "I can see from here that his instruments are filthy with blood. He must not be permitted to touch Jamie," she whispered.

"Aye, lass; we will see to it," Da replied taking her cold hand in his. He knew that Morgana had seen her share of sickrooms and places of death and he prayed with all of his strength that she did not need to stand by the bed and assist this surgeon in removing her husband's leg. They watched as the Commander spoke to the surgeon and Jamie started to calm as soon as he heard the words father and wife. His eyes moved from the surgeon's to the doorway where he saw Da and Morgana standing, waiting to be admitted. The surgeon angrily packed his instruments and frowned at his patient and at the new arrivals.

"I will not take responsibility for the outcome if you do not allow me to remove the injured portion of this leg. Let the verdict rest with you, Inspector. On your head be it," the surgeon said angrily as he strode from the room, not giving a backward glance to either Morgana, Da or to Jamie. The Commander spoke to Jamie for a moment and then moved towards the door.

"You shall have everything that you need, Mrs. Macpherson. I shall enlist my aide de camp to provide all assistance to you. Please let him know whatever we may do to assist," the Commander said. With one word, the young lieutenant was at Morgana's side.

She walked directly into the room and to Jamie's side. His eyes devoured her every step. "Ye came, mo gradh; I hoped and I prayed . . . but somehow, you knew to come," Jamie said tenderly.

"Aye, *mo chroi* and I will always know to come. Let's see what has happened to you, Jamie and then we will see what is to be done." She quickly called for hot water and taking off her cloak, rolled up her sleeves and began an examination of the wound after quickly washing her hands. Da came to the far side of the bed and watched as she worked. "It is just as I thought, Jamie; there has been no break to the bone. The bullet is lodged in the muscular part of the leg. I will remove it and though sore, you will have a leg, Jamie Macpherson and ye will participate in the Highland Games once again, mo chroi," she said smiling.

"Aye lass, if such a thing can be done, you will be the healer to do it," Jamie replied.

"I need a cot brought over to the fire so that I have the light to work by. I need good Scot's whiskey if ye have it and if not . . . any type of whiskey will do. I need help in getting Jamie to that cot. He must not put weight on the leg so that there is no more bleeding than he has already suffered and I will create from my work to save the leg," she said quickly. She tied on the white apron that she wore during the births that she assisted in and laid out her instruments to be boiled in the kettle currently before the fire. Da and the lieutenant fashioned a way of getting Jamie to the cot and he was laid before the fire so that Morgana could work most efficiently. Extra candles were brought and placed at the head and feet to give her all the light needed for her work.

She brought forth one of her tinctures and handed it to Jamie. "I need you to drink this, mo gradh as I cannot have ye move while I am probing for the bullet," she said with authority. She washed the leg and poured whiskey over the sight of the wound. Jamie called out but did not move as she did her preparations. She sat on the stool beside the cot and began to probe the sight of the bullet wound. The tincture that she had given Jamie was composed of laudanum which she used only when she needed the patient to be immobilized while she worked. She began the processing of probing for the bullet and after several minutes, brought the full bullet from the wound held in the forceps that she kept with her medical supplies. She placed it in the tray at the base of the cot. "Ye may need this bullet if ye are to discover who shot my husband. I do not think he shot himself," Morgana said to the lieutenant.

"No ma'am; the Inspector was here to determine who had killed one of our number, as I am sure you are aware. The Commander thinks he was too close to the truth when he was shot himself. Thankfully he was struggling with the assailant and he was unable to shoot him in the heart or the head. The Inspector said the man's face was covered with a mask. The assailant exited the rear of the tent and I called for a search of the woods, but with dark upon us, nothing was found. This bullet is unlike anything provided as part of our official issue, ma'am. It had to be a personal firearm and not one provided by the militia. I will have the men begin a tent by tent search for the weapon that would have fired this bullet," the lieutenant said worriedly.

"Aye then, it sounds as if Jamie had gotten the right of it as usual. I only wish the villain had not gotten off a shot at my husband in the process," she replied. As always, those around her were amazed at the level of concentration that she showed when she was about her work. She had been carefully sewing the wound as she talked, Jamie now quite peacefully asleep as she went about her work.

"Right then, we need to move him back to the bed and keep him still and warm until we see what is to become of the wound. Jamie is strong as an ox and we just need to make sure that he does not develop fever. I have tinctures to keep it at bay, but it will bear watching," Morgana said busily, as she placed her instruments in the kettle on the boil and began the bandaging of his wound and its treatment with a honey mixture that would help in the healing. Once completed, two additional men were found to move Jamie from the cot back to the bed. Morgana covered him over and stood then, stretching her back from the work just completed.

"I will stay with him on the cot that we used for the surgery if there is no other need for it," Morgana said.

"We have many others, ma'am. I will set up a room for you, Mr. Macpherson while the Inspector convalesces," the lieutenant said smiling.

Morgana fussed the covers again, watching Jamie's face for signs of pain. Thank the Lord and her gift of sight that she could foresee what was about to occur. The surgeon was no healer for sure and a butcher if the truth was known. She planned on having a word with the Commander in the morning, but for now; she planned on settling in and getting ready for the night ahead. Jamie would either sleep soundlessly by the tincture that he had been provided, or he would be tossing and turning in pain. She was ready for both eventualities.

Using the table in front of the window, Morgana laid out all that she could potentially need should Jamie take a turn for the worse during the course of the night. She took out her clothes from the bag and placed them on the peg so that they would not wrinkle and picked up each of Jamie's clothing items. She looked at the uniform breeches and saw the hole and the blood that had followed the assassin's attack. She decided to give them to the lieutenant in the event that someone assigned to laundry could get the blood out. She would try to mend them as an extra pair for use while they were in camp.

Returning to Jamie's side, she took one basin of water that she had let cool. She had two basins that she worked from. One basin held cool water, in the event that a fever came upon him during the night; one basin held warm water from the kettle and the remaining water in the kettle itself in the event that hot water was needed. She had packed plenty of bandages and had all that she needed for a lengthy medical siege should it prove necessary. She took out her sponge and using the warm water, began to bathe Jamie to make him more comfortable. She sang the lullaby that she always sang to baby Jamie as she worked.

Jamie felt the loving hands upon him. He couldn't open his eyes from the effect of the laudanum mixture, but he could feel the comforting warm water and smell the lavender that always reminded him of her, hear the voice of his beloved, singing to him as she did to baby Jamie when she bathed and changed him. He felt as helpless as a kitten and yet comforted because he knew that Morgana was nearby, nursing him, loving him and providing her miracle sight and healing. Part of him was not surprised when he had looked up from the middle of the stramash with the surgeon to see Da and Morgana standing in the doorway. She had come because she had known that he needed her, even before he knew himself. He had known from the first day that he met her of the treasure that he had in his Morgana and never more than on a day in which the fate of a limb and his life lay in the balance. Morgana had arrived in the nick of time and the butcher surgeon had been sent on his way. He knew he would have pain and he would have recuperation before him, but he knew also that because of Morgana, he would walk again and that he would participate in future Scots games and walk beside the woman that he loved once again. Morgana, heart of my heart; ye came and I am blessed once again by your love and your care, he thought as he again was captured by another wave of deep sleep.

CHAPTER FIFTEEN

Jamie slept through the night and when Morgana woke in the morning, she came to his side and felt his forehead. He was a wee bit feverish, but nothing to worry about concerning the surgery yesterday. He still slept on and Morgana would do nothing to awaken him from that slumber. She waited and would change his dressing later in the day and give him another sponge bath. She smiled at the deep slumber of her husband and the look of peace upon his face. He would soon have to face taking his first steps and recovering from that bullet wound, but at least last night and this morning, he was sleeping peacefully.

A rap came on the door and Morgana pulled her plaid around her shift and went to the door. "Mrs. Macpherson, the Commander would speak with you, ma'am; after you are up and dressed. Did the Inspector sleep well last night?" the young lieutenant asked worriedly.

"Aye, he slept well and continues so. I will get dressed and then ask Da to sit with Jamie in case he should need anything while I am with the Commander," Morgana replied. She closed the door and bathing quickly, dressed, checked on Jamie one last time and then left his room to meet with the Commander. Da was sitting in the front room playing checkers with the young lieutenant.

"Da, would you look in on Jamie while I am with the Commander?" Morgana asked.

"Aye, lass; it will be my pleasure. Did the lad sleep well last night?" he asked worriedly.

"Aye, Da; the laudanum did the trick, I reckon. He will have pain when he awakes and he will be stiff when we get him up for the first time to walk on that leg. Will ye fashion a pair of crutches for Jamie? He will need them for a while until his leg strengthens and that wound mends," Morgana said.

"That I will do, lass; you go on now and meet with the Commander and see what is what," Da said smiling.

Morgana knocked on the door of the Commander's office. He called come in and she went inside. The Commander was sitting behind his desk, a worried look upon his face. "Mrs. Macpherson, I cannot thank you enough for all that you have done for your husband. He slept comfortably through the night, I trust?" the Commander asked worriedly.

"Aye, sir; he slept well last night, but he will have pain when he awakens and when he takes his first steps. I have asked Da to sit with him while we chatted. He will be making him a pair of crutches to use also," Morgana replied smiling.

"Please sit down, Mrs. Macpherson. I have something to ask you and I hesitate to trouble you with anything further considering the fact that you came all this way to nurse your husband. The surgeon who you saw briefly yesterday is in no fit shape to attend to the men today. He called off from today's sick call and I am told that he is the worst for drink yet again. If it were not an emergency, ma'am; I would not ask it . . . but would you consider taking sick call for the camp today?" the Commander asked worriedly.

"Does the surgeon have his own tinctures and other supplies, Commander? I brought only enough to nurse Jamie, you see," Morgana said worriedly.

"Oh yes ma'am; I believe you will find everything that you could possibly need. If there is anything further that is required, I will order it for you from the nearest apothecary. Will you need a man to accompany you also?" The Commander asked.

"If possible, I would ask for the young Lieutenant Henderson. I will need someone to keep a fire going for me for the hot water and to cleanse the instruments during the day. Did you not ken, Commander how filthy the instruments of your surgeon were? I should not wish him to treat animals with such instruments," Morgana said angrily. "Please pardon my plain speech, Commander; but I cannot abide anyone who would not endeavor to do their best when they are treating human life," Morgana said emphatically.

"I value your plain speech as you call it, ma'am and I would ask you for any suggestions that you can make today as you are about your work. It is my intention to rectify the surgical care that my men receive without fail," he said smiling. "In addition, ma'am, although you have not asked it for yourself, I shall also be assigning two of my best men to control the lines of men who will be coming to see you as you administer your healing skills. There is still the possibility of a murderer among us, as I am sure you understand; and I will do nothing to jeopardize your safety and security while you do this angel's deed for us, particularly as your own husband and father-in-law would not be able to stand guard for you," the Commander said smiling.

"I do appreciate it, sir and I understand your concern. If my husband were well, he would insist on accompanying me, I am sure. He is very protective," she said smiling.

"Wonderful then, Mrs. Macpherson; I shall give my assignment to Lieutenant Henderson and to the other men who will serve as your security as you gather your instruments for the day. Should you need any additional instruments, I shall send for the materials from the surgeon's tents and they will be properly cleansed as per your instructions. I shall also send for his tinctures and other such materials for your use. You have only to ask, ma'am and I shall have delivered to you whatever is needed," the Commander said arising.

Morgana went back to Jamie's room and told Da of her assignment. "Will you stay with Jamie today, Da? I should not wish him to awaken and be in pain. I have his tincture here should he awake while I am gone. He should also be offered broth to start when he awakes and nothing but water or cider to drink. The whiskey will have to wait until the laudanum is out of his system," Morgana said emphatically.

"Aye, lass; I shall do only as you say. Ye have saved my Jamie's leg, Morgana and I am beholden to ye for life. I shall see that he receives only what you direct and we will get him up and back on his own two feet in no time," Da said smiling. "Ye get along then, lass. The Commander has seen that you will have escort for the day?" Da asked worriedly.

"Aye, Da; I am to have Lt. Henderson with me in the tent and two of the Commander's men to control the lines of men who will come on sick call, as well as to tend to my fires to keep the instruments clean. I would not allow an animal to be tended with the instruments of the surgeon such as we saw yesterday. He is in his tent dead drunk, Da if you can fathom such a thing. The man is a disgrace and would have operated on our dear Jamie," Morgana said angrily.

"Aye, but God gave ye the sight, lass and ye have used it to save our Jamie from being maimed or possibly killed. Get on with ye then lass as I hope it will bring ye back all the faster. I will mind Jamie here and will follow yer instructions to the letter; ye can count on it," Da said smiling.

Morgana left the Commander's headquarters then, setting out with Lt. Henderson by her side. He brought her to a large tent which would be her place of duty for the day. A fire was already being started in front of the tent to keep a constant supply of hot water for Morgana for the various procedures that she would complete during the course of the day. She did not expect anything that would exceed her patient's needs back home in Alexandria, but she would have to see how the day progressed. She also set the men assigned to her to find the surgeon's tinctures and his log book so that she could record each patient seen and the follow-up care that should be given after her departure. She soon saw the wisdom of that action as the men began to line up to take advantage of a true healer in the midst of camp.

Simple procedures were the order of the day, from lancing of boils to removal of splinters to feet complaints brought on by ill fitting boots and the marching required of camp drills.

AN EVIL MOON

For each patient, she sat them down in one of the chairs offered and asked them the nature of their complaint. She dutifully took notes of the patient's name, their complaint and the treatment that she had provided, as well as directions for follow-up care. She told each patient so that they could provide a reminder to the surgeon. She feared for his skills and interest in any necessary follow-up given his aborted actions the day before in removing Jamie's leg when probing and nursing were the order of the day. She was prepared to overlook the surgeon's negligence had they been in the midst of battle, but for mere treatment purposes; the man was a disgrace and she did not mind mincing words about it with the Commander.

Near the end of the morning's roll, an older soldier came through the opening of the tent. He looked to be around the age of Da and Morgana wondered why at his age, he was still soldiering. All wonder soon fled as the man began to speak to her in the Scot's Gaelic. Lt. Henderson had stayed with her faithfully throughout the morning, instructing the two soldiers outside of the tent to tend the fire going, to keep fresh water coming and to keep the men who waited for care in good order. This man purposely spoke in the Gaelic, however as he had more on his mind than a complaint to be tended by Morgana; he had information for her to impart to the Inspector once he had regained his health.

He sat down on the offered chair and instantly resorted to the Gaelic in addressing Morgana. He gave his name and then told her that in addition to the splinter that he showed her to be removed, he had information that was germane to the case. He desired that it be provided to the Inspector once he could again engage in the investigation. "My name is Lucas McCall and I came originally from the Highlands, lass. I saw the time of troubles there and nearly starved before immigrating to America. This is a wonderful country and I have been proud to serve her. I have information that will be

185

useful to yer man when he is up and about again," Mr. McCall stated confidentially.

"I shall be happy to hear yer story and to relay all to my husband, when he is well again," she replied in the Gaelic.

"The man who was killed, ma'am was an Englishman who came to Scotland with the British in '46. He remained there after Culloden in order to collect ransoms on men who had served the Prince during the Rising. He made a fortune hunting men and delivering them to the British. When the last of his unfortunates were collected, he immigrated here to America. The story did not end there, lass; as the men who had been hunted down and sent to the gallows or to prison had families who loved them and who vowed a Highlander's vengeance. Ye ken well what I speak of as I ken that both ye and the Inspector are of Scot's stock," Mr. McCall continued.

"Aye, sir; that is so and we ken of what ye speak," Morgana said as she continued to treat the wound. She knew that Lt. Henderson could not understand the Gaelic so she continued an elaborate treatment as a cover so that the conversation could continue and the information imparted.

"The families of the men who were ransomed vowed reprisal. They followed this man to America and they waited and they bided their time. The man became invisible to those in Virginia who did not ken his story. To those who followed him and have now completed their work, he was not invisible but known for his deeds. The Highlander vengeance has been completed, ma'am, and they who kent his story have continued on to North Carolina where other English have hidden who were also responsible for similar actions after the Rising. The Inspector will have no more call to follow these men, lass; as their work here is done. I will be happy to speak directly to him when the time is right and ye can tell him the same. There was no intent to hurt yer man, lass; he just got too close to the truth before this man could complete his work. He saw who wounded yer man, lass and for that he will be forever sorry, but he did not kill or maim as he kens yer husband to be a good man and the head of his clan," Mr. McCall continued.

"I will tell my husband all that ye have shared with me and I am sure when he is again well, he will wish to speak with ye direct; if you agree to do so," Morgana said as she completed her treatment.

"Aye, lass; that is as it should be. He was sent here to do a job and he needs to ken the details; the whats and wherefores must be shared in order to close the case. I thank ye for yer care today and to the care that ye have provided to the men here. We will not soon forget it. That surgeon they have given us should not treat horses, ma'am; if ye pardon my plain speaking," Mr. McCall said smiling.

"I ken it well, Mr. McCall and I have shared my opinion with the Commander of one who would amputate a leg rather than treat it," Morgana said smiling.

"Ye speak of yer husband then, lass? I ken that ye would let no other treat yer husband but yerself. Keep the surgeon from him, lass; whatever may occur and keep him from ye as well. Be mindful of this advice. God be with ye, lass and with yer good man also," Mr. McCall said standing.

"And also with ye, Mr. McCall," she replied. Morgana would have much to share with Jamie when this day ended. She wondered if he would be willing to let the truth stand as told by Mr. McCall or if he would feel compelled to follow the man or men who had assassinated the Englishmen here in camp. Morgana shivered as she thought about the long process of following a man who had ruined the lives of so many back in Scotland and the families of those men as well. Would they now rest easy in their graves knowing that they were avenged for the wrongs done to them and to their families? A Highlander Scot's vow of vengeance was to the death and they had seen justice on the man's murder that Jamie had been sent to investigate.

Morgana sat for a moment and gathered her things together. It had been a long day. The worry yesterday about

Jamie and now another long day of providing care to the sick and wounded here in camp, coupled with her own pregnancy was beginning to tell. She needed to go back to the Commander's residence and rest, unless Jamie was up and ready to talk. She hoped that she could get in a wee nap before she needed to relay all that she had learned today to Jamie.

Lt. Henderson escorted her back to the Commander's residence and a quick peek into Jamie's room showed that he was fast asleep. "I gave him a shave this morning when he woke up, lass. He was more himself, but the tincture that ye gave him knocks him out for sure. I have completed his crutches and I told him that ye would have him up and about for the first thing tomorrow. He was itching to try. He says his leg pains him, but not as much as the alternative. He ate a good portion of breakfast and then was asleep again just a few minutes ago. Ye just missed him awake," Da said.

"I think I will join him in a nap, Da. The worry about Jamie coupled with a day of sick call has left me worn out," Morgana said smiling.

"Aye lass; I expect so. Ye have a good rest now and I will wake ye when it is time for supper. Don't worry; I will see that ye are both left to yer naps," Da said smiling. He sat out the chessboard for his evening match with Lt. Henderson once the lad was finished with his duties for the day.

Morgana went inside and checked Jamie's forehead for any remaining signs of temperature. He was a bit warm, but nothing that concerned her. She checked his bandage and saw that there was only light bleeding. She would bathe and change it again after dinner. She stretched her back and then stripping down to her shift; lie down on the cot for a brief nap before supper.

She woke to a hand gently rousing her some three hours later. The sun had already gone down and Morgana would have slept through the night, but for the fact that Da wanted to make sure that she got a good dinner into her given the demands of the day. She smiled up at him and putting her plaid around her, got up to dress for dinner. Jamie was sleeping through from the latest draft that Da had given him and she would not wake him if her ministrations did not.

She came to the table to hot stew and fresh bread that had been made by Lt. Henderson and his men. The food did a good deal more to rouse her from her slumbers.

Following dinner, she took in a basin and fresh bandages and washed Jamie's wound and bandaged it. The wound was recovering nicely from her handy work the day before. Her specially made salve, complete with healing honey had done the trick yet again. She gave Jamie a sponge bath and then turned to her own comfort for the night. Lt. Henderson had mentioned that the Commander had ordered a hot bath for her in thanks for the long hours at the sick call this morning. When it arrived at the door, she warmly thanked the men for bringing the large tub and filling it with hot water; jug after jug of it arriving from the large fire outside the residence which was always tended.

The tub had sheeting that had been draped inside in deference to the female occupant who had been treated to the luxury of a hot bath. Morgana gathered her soap and a fresh shift and stripping down, sank into the hot water which restored the aching muscles from the long day of nursing.

Unbeknownst to Morgana, Jamie awoke briefly from his slumbers to watch Morgana at her bath. He blinked twice to open his eyes to determine if he was dreaming of the beautiful water nymph that had descended into the fragrant, hot water. He remembered Da telling him that Morgana had single handedly taken on the sick call for the camp this morning. He had not seen her since she performed the surgery that had saved his leg a day ago. He knew that she was near, because he felt her tending to his leg, and giving him a sponge bath with her own specially made homemade soap. It was not the same as seeing her with his own eyes, however. The firelight made her wet skin sparkle. She had put up her hair so that she could enjoy the warmth of the fragrant waters without wetting her hair. The oil that she had added was now perfuming the room as well. She was a feast for all of the senses and she had always been. My Morgana; mo chroi, *my beloved* and my home; he could not wait to hold her in his arms yet again. He fought the sleep that was capturing him once again. He sank back into the dreamless sleep that Morgana's draft brought to him. He would soon be better and stronger and able to hold the wee Morgana and tell her in person how much he appreciated all that she had done for him yet again.

Morgana dried off before the fire and then putting on her fresh shift, checked Jamie's forehead yet again and then went to her own cot, pulled up the covers and slept like a baby. She was glad that Da had taken over the duties of writing to Mam on a daily basis. The demands of Jamie's care on the first day and the sick call today had robbed her of her ability to do anything else but eat, bathe and now sleep.

*****

In the morning Jamie woke with the first gray light of dawn streaming in the shaded window. He looked to his right and saw the mass of black curls that belonged to his wee Morgana. The lass was still sound asleep after the long day handling the sick call of the camp. He had remembered waking to watch her bathe and seeing her head now, the distinctive black curls on the pillow beside the bed, he remembered that it had not been a dream. She had come here to rescue him from the butchery of the camp surgeon and to nurse him. Da had told him that she had also nursed the members of the militia who were on sick call yesterday. He had told him also that Lt. Henderson accompanied her as well as two of the camp's best men to keep her from harm.

He rolled to his side and captured one of the shiny curls of his Morgana. It seemed like an age since he had held her and longer still since he had made love to her. Watching her last night as she bathed before the fire, he knew that he was on his way to a full recovery. He had wanted Morgana like he had on their first wedding night, back in Berkeley County where they worked a case to bring a mad man to justice. He remembered his own mission here in camp and declared that today, he would begin to walk again, regain his strength and return to the completion of the mission. He had Morgana to return to and the wee Jamie, as well as the new bairn that she carried now. He reasoned that she would not have told Da about the wee bairn, in fear that he would have prevented her coming. What would have happened if she had not saved him from the butchering surgeon? It did not bear thinking about.

He gently touched her shoulder then to determine if she was already awake or still sleeping soundly. She turned to her left and her eyes were open and smiling. "Ye are awake then, my wee water nymph. I thought I but dreamed it, but it was no dream; my own Morgana was here in the flesh. Ye made me want to get up and walk again, lass and far more, if the truth be known," he said huskily.

She rolled to her side so that they could look at each other eye to eye. "I missed ye so much, love and I have so much to tell ye that has taken place since we spoke last," she said softly.

"First things first, though lass; come here and give yer man yer love because I am longing for it, Morgana," he replied huskily.

"I canna hurt yer leg, Jamie; it is only now beginning to heal well," she replied worriedly.

"Dinna fash, mo gradh; we will not hurt my leg. We will be careful and quiet as mice so that the young lieutenant and Da do not ken what we are about," he said grinning. Morgana got up and walked to the door and put a chair beneath it so that Da did not accidentally come in to wake her as he had last afternoon. She came to the side of Jamie's bed and placed her hand on his forehead. It felt cool to the touch.

"Ye are cool to the touch, Jamie," Morgana said smiling.

"Ah but not so cool to the touch, if ye ken it right," he said taking her hand and kissing it. He pulled her gently towards him so that he could gather her up and have her straddle his lap. He sat up straighter on the bed, his back against the pillows and took her face in his hands. "I have missed ye, *mo chroi*; I have missed yer touch upon me and I have missed my lips on yers," Jamie said quietly.

"Ah but I did touch ye, Jamie; though you would not have ken it," she said smiling.

"Now ye speak of me as yer patient, when ye washed me as ye would have washed our wee Jamie," he said taking her face in his hands.

"Did ye mind the lavender soap, mo gradh?" she said as he kissed her gently.

"Why would I mind, Morgana when I have smelled the lavender from the first day in yer wee cottage. I ken that you have cared for me night and day and I ken that I am all the better for it. Let me show ye how much I appreciate what ye have done for me," he said kissing her deeply. From that moment further, there were no words, only touches and sighs and the reuniting of two halves of the same whole. Jamie had not yet asked her how she kent to come, but in his heart he knew already; she would always ken when he needed her even when they were apart. There was still recovery to begin and a murderer to find, but for now; the two lovers and two sleuths needed to reconnect and to show the other just how very much he and she was loved and needed.

Jamie whisked Morgana's shift over her head and she took his shirt over his. Their bodies were joined torso to torso and soon the nearness and the touch of the other was more than either of them could ignore. Jamie lifted Morgana slightly and brought her over his arousal. She sighed into his mouth and he quieted her moan with his own deep kiss. He took her slim hips and moved them with the rhythm that he had established. There were no words, only feeling; touches and a reuniting that brought them quickly to a shattering climax, made all the more sweet by the separation that they had just experienced and the threat to Jamie's life that Morgana had personally prevented.

He continued to hold her and to stroke her back and sides as they came back into the here and now and away from their momentary departure into love and passion. He kissed her eyes, her nose and captured her face once more for a deep kiss before releasing her to carefully move to his shoulder; an accidental touch to his wound her greatest concern. He held her until she was ready again to speak of all that had occurred since they had been apart.

"Jamie, ye ken that I took the sick call yesterday when the surgeon was worse for the drink. I saw a powerful number of men, Jamie and one of them; a Scot spun a tale so fanciful that I cannot wonder but that it is true. He said that the man who was killed and whose murder ye investigate was English and had received ransoms for the Scots that he turned into the British after Culloden. He told me that these men had been hunted by the relatives of those who died on scaffolds and in British prisons since the failure of the Rising. He said that the man was followed here and that he was killed for his part in the clearing of the Highlands. He said also that the man who had done the deed is still here and is being watched. There are others who have continued onto North Carolina where they follow other such men. If this were true, Jamie; these men would be following a Highlander's vow and not committing a random murder. Would ye be compelled to chase these men all the way to North Carolina next?" Morgana asked worriedly.

"How did this man relay this information to ye, Morgana? Were you not accompanied while tending the sick by the young lieutenant?" Jamie asked worriedly. "Da told me it was so or I would not have agreed to you being in the company of one who could be responsible for the murder or the attack on me," Jamie said fiercely.

"Oh aye, Jamie; he never left my side and there were two others who the Commander assigned to tend to my fire to clean my instruments in the front of the tent and to keep the men in tidy lines until they were called. The man who I spoke of came for treatment and he spoke the entire time in the Gaelic as he told me this tale," Morgana said worriedly.

"The Gaelic, you say; well then, the young lieutenant would not have kent what was being said," Jamie said frowning.

"Aye, Jamie and the man said that he would speak with ye and tell ye the same tale so that ye would ken it was true. Do we not have records on the man who was killed so that we would ken his history before coming here?" Morgana asked.

"Aye, I asked for records upon my arrival in camp. They should be here by now. We will question the Commander when the camp is awake and when ye let me start to stand on my leg again," he said smiling. "How do I thank a woman for saving my leg as ye have done, mo gradh? I ken ye were a treasure on the first day that I met ye and yet every day, ye do even more amazing things. Why taking on the sick call as ye did and ye carrying our next child. Were ye not exhausted when it was over?" Jamie asked worriedly.

"I ken it was the reason for the offer of the hot bath last night. The warm waters felt so very good. It was my back only that minded the day. I tried to sit as much as I could while I was treating the sick. The surgeon is a disgrace, Jamie and I told the Commander the same yesterday morning. I apologized for my plain speech, but he said that he ken the same and had been told by more than one of his men that it was the case. His instruments were a disgrace, Jamie. I took one look at them and ken what I must do, even though I ken a *stramash* was in the making," Morgana said smiling.

"My wee Morgana is a lion heart as I have said from the first. Stood up to a surgeon she did and not backed down for an inch and I have my leg whole to prove it," Jamie said smiling. "I will let ye rest for a bit more and then we will get up when the camp awakes and see what we can check out of this Scot's story," Jamie said as he hugged her further.

An hour or so later, a knock came again to the door. Morgana donned her shift again and wrapped herself in her plaid to answer the door. Jamie was still sleeping she noted as she responded to the knock. "Mistress, I apologize for waking you again, but the Commander asks for your presence after you are dressed and ready," Lt. Henderson said somberly.

"Is there another sick call that he wishes me to answer?" Morgana asked.

"No, mistress; the matter will require both you and the Inspector if he is up to walking, that is. You see, there has been another unnatural death last night in camp," Lt. Henderson said nervously.

"Another murder you say? I will wake Jamie and then when I am dressed, I will ask ye and Da to help him up on his feet for the first time. He will need to be involved for sure. We will not be long, lieutenant. Thank ye for waking me," Morgana replied.

Morgana went to Jamie's side and sat on the bed. She felt his forehead and hands and could see no trace of fever. He opened his eyes at the movement. "What is it, lass? Has something else happened?" he asked worriedly.

"Aye Jamie, I will need yer help for sure. The young lieutenant has come to the door yet again. It seems that there was another murder last night in camp. They will want me to check on the body I reckon, but I told him that I will need help on his part and on Da's to get you up and walking again. I need ye to assist on this matter, Jamie. I can confirm the death and perhaps can assist in answering the cause of it, but this is beyond my ken to address," Morgana said wide eyed.

"Ye get yerself dressed and ready, love and then get Da and the young lieutenant. We will need to see what is what. I hope and pray that the scene of death has not been trampled by a hundred feet by now," Jamie said worriedly. He swung himself to the side of the bed and pulled on his nightshirt which would serve as the shirt to his uniform today. He knew he could not wear his boots over the wound, so he would need Morgana's innovation to fashion something that would cover his foot and ankle as he navigated on the crutches that Da had fashioned. As soon as Morgana was dressed, she retrieved Da to help her raise Jamie and to get him dressed. They ate breakfast quickly and then joined the Commander in his office.

"I cannot apologize enough for bothering the both of you yet again. I know you are not recovered by half, Inspector; but young Henderson tells me that you are willing to make a slow progress to the tent to assist with the murder investigation. I hesitate to request Mistress Macpherson's assistance as well, but you see the victim is the surgeon so I have no other medical expertise to draw upon," the Commander said worriedly.

"The surgeon ye say; the devil take it," Jamie swore. "We will get to the bottom of it, Commander. My progress may be slow, but I will put these crutches to good use. Morgana has fashioned a bandage for me over my foot as I canna wear my own boot for a while yet, I reckon. If ye are ready, Commander; we will make our way to the scene of death," Jamie said wearily.

Jamie, Morgana, the Commander and Lt. Henderson strolled slowly down the main aisle of the assembled tents. The Commander had had guards posted at the entrance of the tent so that nothing inside would be tampered with before the arrival of the Inspector. They entered the tent and began to take stock of all that they found. Morgana went to the victim first and took his pulse and then smelled the contents of the drink by his side. "There appears to be a sleeping draught in the cup, sir; but it is not poison. It is possible that too much was given, however and that could have given him a heart seizure or stopped his breathing, particularly if it was mixed with alcohol. The smell of the drink is strong on him still," she said with her preliminary appraisal. Jamie had been looking at the note that was on the desk, as well as a diary that was left open on the desk. The diary was in the doctor's hand, but the letter was in another hand all together. The letter was addressed to Inspector Macpherson. He sat at the desk to rest his leg and opened the letter and found that it was both addressed to him and like yesterday's statement; was written in Gaelic.

"Has the roll call reflected any men missing this morning, Commander?" Jamie asked as he read the letter.

"There was one man missing; but how did you know that, Inspector?" the Commander asked warily.

"This letter details the reason for the death of the first man as well as the death of the surgeon. Ye may recall that the death of the first man was completed with what we had called at the time surgical precision. It appears that there was a reason for that. The letter accuses the surgeon of the death and the following attack made upon me was to prevent me from getting any closer in my investigation. It seemed the surgeon would not have worried about his shot having killed me, because the amputation of my leg would have certainly done the trick. He had not counted upon the arrival of my wife and of a healer whose talents surpassed his tenfold. He says further that the woods beyond Sgt. Marshall's tent should be searched for the presence of a garrote, a black mask, and the gun that was responsible for my wound. The diary is turned to the page in which the surgeon detailed his plan. It seems our amateur sleuth knew that the surgeon took a nightly drink and laced it to permit him to do some investigation of his own. My wife was provided with some details yesterday which she accounted to me this morning. The deaths seem to be connected to a debt of honor dating

197

back to these two men's time spent in the army of the British. Have the records that I requested been received thus far, Commander?" Jamie asked.

"The record on our first victim was received yesterday, Inspector. I will need to request the records on our surgeon here as well if what you tell me could be true," the Commander said worriedly.

"This diary indicates that the first death was a means of covering the activities of these two when they were both stationed in Scotland after the Rising. It seems that they both made their share of coin by turning in men who survived Culloden and collecting the reward from the British government. The surviving families commissioned a search of all of those who worked to identify and roust out the men of Culloden. Some died in prisons, some died on the gallows, some were sent here as indentured servants and many of their families fled Scotland to the new world as a result. Both my wife and I number in that group, Commander. Anyway, it seems that the surgeon recognized our first victim on the first day of camp and needed to find a means of silencing him before he could reveal their horrible secrets to any who might have kent the story or to prevent blackmail of himself. There was such a man in camp and he is the man who has now fled into North Carolina where he searches for other such men," Jamie said as he read and translated the letter.

"So you are saying that the two deaths were connected and that the second death has now evened the score as it were on this so called debt of honor?" the Commander said frowning.

"The debt of honor is very real, Commander; especially in the Highlands of Scotland. Anyone tasked with this mission will not stop until all of those responsible are made to pay for their crimes. It does appear that our man has fled as his job is now considered done, at least as it applies to your company," Jamie continued.

"I assume that our departing militia man was operating under an assumed name?" the Commander continued.

"The letter doesna say, but I think it would be a fair bet, Commander. If we can pull records on this man as well, we may be able to connect some missing points, or perhaps not. He could have signed on using his alias in which case only a trip to Scotland would confirm the mission. I dare say we have most of the missing pieces between this letter and the surgeon's own diary and the search which must be undertaken. I will need the lieutenant here to assist me in a search of these quarters. Unless I miss my guess, the document and gold that I found in the first tent the evening that I was attacked will be found here in this tent," Jamie said.

"Gold, you say Inspector?" the Commander asked.

"Aye, the night that I was shot, I had just unearthed a rolled document that had been hidden in a piece of furniture in Sgt. Marshall's tent, as well as a bag of gold sovereigns. I did not have time to read the document fully before being besieged by the assailant, but I would surmise that it would contain information about those who were collected and turned into the British or information on those who were blackmailed for their involvement in the matter," Jamie continued.

"So you believe these documents will be found among the surgeon's papers?" the Commander asked.

"Aye, I do. With yer permission, I shall ask Morgana and Lt. Henderson to remain with me and we will search each of the surgeon's personal affects, just to make sure that nothing of interest to the case remains. She can advise me on any finds that could be related to his surgical healing work. I would ask if Lt. Henderson can assist in the process as I noted. I would think it well to also plan a funeral for the surgeon here. We will search his person to make sure that there is no other vital information on him before he is buried," Jamie said firmly.

"Thank you very much, Inspector. I shall leave you to it and shall leave Lt. Henderson to assist. I shall return to my headquarters and prepare the funeral arrangements for the surgeon here. He did not leave any information regarding next of kin which interestingly enough was also the case with our first victim. Thank you both again for your assistance," the Commander said as he left the tent.

"Lt. Henderson, we shall leave no stone untouched. If you will be so kind to bring each satchel and case to me here, I will examine it and not incur the wrath of my wife for standing on the leg before time," Jamie said grinning.

"Are ye married then, Lt. Henderson?" Jamie asked as they worked.

"I have not yet had that pleasure, sir," Lt. Henderson replied.

"Take it from one who kens such things; choose a wife who will be both a helpmate and a partner in yer life. Mistress Macpherson here answers both calls. Had I been a soldier still, she would have followed the drum and set up sick calls throughout all of Virginia. As it is, I am an Inspector and Mistress Macpherson is as good at detecting as most of the men on our force. A mighty force is our Morgana Macpherson in both healing and detecting," Jamie said grinning.

"I will remember those words, sir and shall seek to find a mate who is half as accomplished as your good wife," Lt. Henderson replied. Morgana shook her head and blushed as she continued her search.

"I have found no other wound, Jamie. I believe the sleeping draught mixed with the alcohol was the cause. I see no marks that showed where he had been held down and forced to drink either one. He gave himself too much in error or he did so on purpose to end his life. It could also be that he took the sleeping draught, but that it mixed with his alcohol intake, caused the death. If the heart slowed too much, he would stop breathing," she replied firmly.

Morgana busied herself with going through the pockets of the surgeon. It was grisly work, but she assumed that the lieutenant would find it less tasteful than assisting Jamie with his mission. The diary and the letter were bagged to be kept as evidence for the inquest that would follow Jamie's return to Alexandria.

Nothing further emerged from Morgana's search of the surgeon's person. However, in another hiding place beneath the cot on which the surgeon had laid, Jamie and the lieutenant found the document and gold bag that Jamie had unearthed the night that he was shot. When it was unrolled, it showed each man who had been turned into the British government from those hunted after the Battle of Culloden. These were men who had survived the battle itself only to be turned in after running to ground in the route by the British army. The gold sovereigns in the bag were the blood money that had been provided to Sgt. Marshall and the surgeon for their part in the grisly work of hunting down the rebels and turning them into the crown.

The document also showed the blackmail victims of the Sergeant, among them, the name of the surgeon. It seemed that Sgt. Marshall had recognized the surgeon on the first day of camp and had set off to plan his blackmail effort. The surgeon would not wish to be reminded of the grisly business that he had participated in that had paid for his medical expenses and his voyage to the new world and a new life.

After collecting all of the evidence, Jamie, Morgana and the lieutenant returned slowly back up the walkway between the row of tents to the headquarters building.

Jamie sat heavily at the table in the dining room as they returned to the headquarters. It was his first time out of bed and his first time on the crutches that Da had fashioned. He knew that recovery would take longer than he would hope, but it appeared as if his work here in camp was nearing an end. As soon as the records on the surgeon and the missing militiaman were received, Jamie would detail the information in his final report and they would be returning back to Alexandria. He had no intention of chasing the errant Highlander to North Carolina or any other port of call. What had happened here was a tragic end to one of the most tragic pages in Scotland's long and storied history. He closed his eyes for a moment against the power of the old world that pulled on him whenever such memories surfaced. It was one of those times that he had to stop and remember all that the New World had brought him; his life's work, his Morgana and wee Jamie who they would be returning to soon. The thought of Morgana and the wee Jamie could bring a smile to his face every time.

"Do ye think that yer work here will shortly be done, Jamie?" Morgana asked worriedly.

"Aye lass; I canna ken that the Commander back in Alexandria will want this lad chased down to North Carolina or beyond, depending upon where his next mission called him. If so, I ken that he will be looking for another man to complete the chase. As ye said, I will not be in my boots for at least two weeks. I am as tired as a new born babe. I dinna realize what the past two days had taken out of me, lass. The man had done his best when he shot me in the leg. It was a military type wound designed to immobilize a victim and then generally a kill shot is made to the head. He did not have the time to take his second shot, but he immobilized me for sure," Jamie said wearily.

"I will get ye some real food, Jamie and some drink. It will give ye more strength to face what needs doing. Can I do anything to help ye further today?" Morgana asked.

"Nay lass; I will just sit here and study this diary of the surgeon's as I put the last pieces of the puzzle together for my final report. I expect that the Commander may need ye to complete sick call again today after ye have had yer meal. There will be no other to do it after what happened last night. Make sure that Lt. Henderson and the other two men follow ye to yer wee tent. I want no repeat of yesterday's confessional by anyone else in this camp. Do ye hear me, mo gradh?" Jamie asked worriedly.

"Aye, Jamie; I hear ye and I will ask Lt. Henderson to confirm the very thing. I will just go and get my instruments. I will need to go into that tent again to get the man's herbals and tinctures. I hope that they have him removed by now," Morgana said frowning.

"Aye, love; it is like it was when we first met, back in Berkeley County. We work well together; do we not?" Jamie said smiling.

"Aye, we do Jamie. I will be but a minute with yer luncheon," she replied smiling.

Da came into the dining room and sat down next to Jamie. "How is the leg, son?" Da asked.

"Hurting more than I expected it to, Da; but all the same, I should rather have the pain than not have my leg. The surgeon it seems was not just disgraceful in his practices. It was he who tried to end my investigation by attacking me and he would have finished the job but for the sight of the wee Morgana. This is his diary and he makes it quite plain what his plans were. The bugger was with Cumberland in Scotland, Da and then with the men who hunted and sent Scots to the gallows, to prison and into indenture in the aftermath. The other man murdered was killed at the hands of the surgeon. He intended on making me his next victim, but for the good graces of our Morgana," Jamie said wistfully.

"The wee lass has been a blessing since the first time ye laid eyes on her, Jamie. I dunno what the camp would have done without her. I expect she will be healing yet again today?" Da asked.

"With the murder of the surgeon last night, Da; I expect she will have little choice. She will not want anyone to suffer if she has the skills to aid them. Such is the heart and soul of my beloved. We must watch her close though, Da as she is carrying again. She did not dare tell ye, because she feared ye would not bring her here to nurse me. She is a lion heart for sure; I have kent it from the first time that I met her. We must watch that she does not overdo, although she will not complain," Jamie continued.

"Aye, I will ask the young lieutenant to keep a close eye on her to make sure that she does not overdo. Are we for home soon then, lad? Morgana will be missing the wee Jamie for certain," Da said sagely.

"Aye and he her, I expect. Mam will be a happy soul for the past few days, ye ken; what with the wee bairn all to herself," Jamie said laughing.

"Aye and God willing, she will soon have two to spoil verra soon," Da replied laughing.

CHAPTER SIXTEEN

Morgana's services were needed again today, as she had
expected. Lt. Henderson was dispatched to remain with her
throughout the sick call and within the tent while the men
were treated. The same two guards were on the outside,
tending her fire for the hot water needed to clean her
instruments and to complete her treatments and to keep the
men in orderly lines until it was their chance to be seen by
the healer. Jamie had commented to Da that those on sick call
today may have heard of the wee healer from yesterday's
treatments and may have heard that she was not only the best
healer for miles around, but the most beautiful as well. He
thought he might have to take another trip down the row of
tents if the sick call dragged on past lunchtime. He was
keeping an eye on Morgana himself now that his own health
crisis was on the mend.

Morgana and Lt. Henderson returned by dinner time.
There were fewer lines today thanks to the fact that Morgana
had helped so many the day prior. The consensus of the camp
was that the loss of the surgeon was not much of a loss after
all. They hated to see anyone pass, but he had not been a
friend to the men or to his patients. Morgana had updated the
treatment book again today with the hope that she would
soon pass it along to the surgeon's replacement. She felt that
more of the men had been seen in the past two days than in
the past two weeks, based upon the treatment log. She hoped
that the next surgeon would have more conscientious skills
and a better bedside manner than the last.

Jamie was still sitting in the same place when she returned
with the young lieutenant. He had completed his review of
the surgeon's diary and had made the appropriate notes for
his report and for purposes of the final coroner's inquest
hearing. The items had been discovered in the hollowed log
of the wood beyond the tent of Sgt. Marshall, as directed by
the letter. The two murders had been connected and it would

take one greater than him to determine if the surgeon had killed himself to avoid discovery or had been helped along by the Highlander who had spoken with Morgana yesterday. He hoped that the man would not need to be chased into North Carolina. He himself would not be up to it for several weeks and by then, the man could be anywhere. Those who had committed the ultimate sin of destroying families and a way of life in the Highlands of Scotland had been avenged. It was time to go home now and await the birth of the newest Macpherson family member.

"Will we be going home then, Jamie?" Morgana asked that night, as if echoing his thoughts.

"Aye lass; the Commander will be sending me a copy of the records that I requested upon their arrival. I will need them for my final report and for the coroner's inquest that will be completed on the two men. I believe that the details have been wrapped up to everyone's satisfaction. If the Commander in Alexandria wants the Highlander followed, he will need to send another man out to do so; at least for the next several weeks. It shames me to say that I will be riding in the back of Da's wagon when we leave here. Duncan will have to be content to be tied to the back of the wagon as we make our way home," Jamie replied smiling.

"I canna wait to see wee Jamie. It seems like an age since we saw him last, although it has only been a few days," Morgana replied.

"And soon we will have yet another wee bairn to join the wee Jamie. All this, Morgana has come about because of ye and yer kind heart and soul. Ye had no fear of coming here, love and preventing what the sight told ye was about to occur. Ye came again into the den of a murderer, Morgana and ye had no fear of doing so," Jamie said with admiration.

"I should walk into the den of a great beast, Jamie if it was to save ye or wee Jamie. Ye ken I would do anything for either of ye," Morgana said with tear stained eyes.

"And the past several days have been too much for ye, lass; despite yer grand heart ye are still wee Morgana and carrying our next child to boot. Tonight, I will look after ye, my love and ye must rest after two days of a lengthy sick call," Jamie said worriedly.

"I dinna mind, Jamie; as I would have no one suffer if I could but take their pain and illness away. The surgeon, God rest him; was a disgrace, but his men should not have to suffer because of his wicked ways. I hope he shall find peace, but the lives of those he ruined by taking filthy coin will truly rest in peace now and the lives of the families who summoned the Highlander to do his work," Morgana said wistfully. "Do ye ken that yer Commander in Alexandria will want him followed? I can make a description of him for ye if it will be of help," Morgana offered.

"I ken ye would lass, but I would rather wait until the Commander orders it. I hope and pray that the debt of honor has been satisfied and that this Highlander can now return to his own life and perhaps to his own kin. There are many Scots in North Carolina they do say. Perhaps his family waits for him there," Jamie said wistfully.

*****

The next day Morgana and Jamie in the back of the wagon and Da driving, set off for their return home. The great beast Duncan was tied to the back of the wagon after Morgana had explained to him the reason his master could not ride. She would not have him think that the Macpherson had fallen out of favor with his prize steed. As they packed for the return trip, Morgana laid blankets and Jamie's saddle in the back of the wagon so that they could be as comfortable as she had been when she rode there with wee Jamie as they travelled to the Gathering. The outcome of this investigation was not what would have been expected when Jamie arrived to investigate the murder. Both murders had been ruled as unrelated to militia business and both cases were closed as far as both the Inspector and the militia Commander were concerned. The final verdict would rest with the coroner upon their return to Alexandria. The diary and the letter were both retained as evidence, as well as the service records of both men, copies of which would be sent to Jamie upon their receipt by the militia Commander.

The Commander assembled the men prior to their departure and publicly thanked Morgana for her gift of healing to the men of the company. Once again her gifts were shared openly and without reservation with those in need. The men shouted three hurrahs for the wee healer who had brought them more care in her three day visit than the surgeon had brought them throughout his tenure. She would be missed, but they were encouraged by the fact that a new doctor was on his way and it was promised that he was devoted to his profession and to the men that he would serve.

In two days time, they would be back with Mam and wee Jamie and they would begin plans yet again to welcome another Macpherson to the home of the laird and his lady.

Morgana settled close to Jamie as they set off for home. He smiled at her and brought her head down on his shoulder. "Ye charm the great beast Duncan with your loving ways and ye charm an entire company of men with your great gifts of healing, Morgana. Ye are the treasure of my life and if ever I forget to say those words to ye for one solid week, ye remind me at the end, mo gradh," Jamie said as he kissed her forehead.

"I am so thankful that ye are well and recovering from yer wound, Jamie. I am thankful for the men that I could help and most of all, that we are headed home. Wee Jamie will think us lost for sure; although I ken that Mam will have spoiled him rotten," she said giggling.

"Aye, he will be a holy terror and I shall have to beat him back to mind his Da," Jamie said laughing.

"As if ye would beat such a wee angel as Jamie," Morgana said smiling.

"And what of the great beast Duncan, eh? Have ye explained the mortal disgrace of watching his master ride in a wagon rather than on his back," Jamie said chuckling.

"Duncan and I have had our talk and he understands that his position has not been forfeit; but that ye are wounded and must have a care until yer leg heals. He will watch out for ye, as will we all," Morgana replied grinning.

"I will take ye up on that lass," Jamie replied. He closed his eyes and Morgana took his head down on her lap as he rested for a portion of the trip. Da turned to see his son wrapped around the wee Morgana and knew yet again that it was a fateful day when the tiny healer had been brought into the family. Lord, thank ye for the gift of Morgana and the joy that she has brought to Jamie, to her wee bairn and to her entire family. Watch over her as she carries the next wee one until he or she can be safely delivered into our hands. Amen.

*****

As Da brought up the brake of the wagon a day later, Morgana moved to the edge of the wagon so that she and Da could help Jamie leave the wagon on his crutches. He had become quite good with them and was moving faster with each passing day. Morgana took daily care of the wound and pronounced it healing very well. Soon Jamie would again be able to don his boots and walk and then ride without thought to the gunshot wound that had threatened his life at the hands of the very surgeon who had administered it.

They walked to the front door and Da opened it, calling for Mam and the wee Jamie. Mam came around the corner holding her grandson, a smile as wide as her face greeting them all home. Wee Jamie called for his Mother and she covered his cheeks and neck in kisses. He giggled and reached for her hair as he looked her full in the face. He glanced over at his father on the crutches and for the first time said the word "Da". Jamie was so taken with the fact that his son had finally recognized him that he nearly dropped his crutches. Morgana carried the baby to the settee where they both sat down so that Jamie could take up the baby in his arms.

"So ye are all back home safe; thank the Lord for it, I say," Mam said wiping her eyes with her apron. "Ye may spare me the terrible details of the case, just let me ken if the villain has been caught who did this to my son," Mam said frowning.

"The villain has been caught, Mam and has already paid for his crimes. We will tell ye as much or as little as ye wish to hear as the night carries on," Jamie said. He was kissing wee Jamie on his neck and the baby was crying out with glee. The smile that Mam saw on Jamie's face made the whole ordeal seem suddenly worthwhile. She sat down on the chair to watch her son and her grandson and the woman who had done so much for the family from the first day of her arrival.

"Yer Da has told me of yer wound in his letter, but not of who gave it to you, Jamie. Was it the man who was the murderer?" she asked warily.

"Aye, Mam, not only was the man the murderer, but the surgeon of the militia to boot. It is a long story and again, I can tell ye as little or as much as ye want to hear. He thought to wound me in the struggle with him and then to finish the job when he operated to remove the bullet. Our wee Morgana saved the day yet again, Mam. She and Da came marching in just as the man was preparing to take off my leg. She stopped that and then removed the bullet and nursed me back to health. I still canna put on my boot, but she tells me that soon enough, I will be walking without crutches and riding my fierce Duncan again. I believe her Mam, because ever since I walked into her wee cottage in Berkeley County, nothing but good has come of it. I hold the proof of that statement in my hands with our wee Jamie and soon, although she did not yet tell ye herself, we will welcome a second wee bairn into the family," he said as he placed his arm around Morgana.

"By all the saints, girl; ye are increasing and didna tell me?" Mam asked wide eyed.

"I dared not tell ye for fear that ye would not think it fitting for me to travel to the camp, Mam. I ken that Jamie was in trouble and I ken that I was the one who knew how to save him. There was nothing for it but to do what I must do," she said fiercely.

"Not only did she save my leg and my life, Mam; but she helped me to ferret out the root cause of the whole ordeal while she nursed the militia camp in the process. Our Morgana is a lion heart, Mam and I have kent it from the very first day that I met her," Jamie said smiling.

Once again, Jamie and Morgana had endured a trial that would keep Mam from sleep for the rest of the month and then returned to tell her that all was well. They both had guardian angels who watched over them, as far as she was concerned. She just hoped that they would always be so fortunate for the benefit of wee Jamie and the new baby not yet arrived.

Mam had dinner waiting for the threesome and they put wee Jamie in the highchair as they sat around the table. They all joined hands and Mam gave the blessing, thanking the Lord for the safe return of her family and to ask for blessings on Morgana as she carried their next child. Mam had heard quite enough about the case that they had just concluded. She talked through dinner of events that had taken place since they had left Alexandria. They could soon see that wee Jamie was not long for bed, so Da gathered them all back in the wagon and deposited them at their own home shortly after dinner.

211

"It feels good to be home, mo gradh. I feel as though I have been away for a lifetime and not yet two weeks," Jamie said as they carried a now sleeping Jamie to his room.

"Will ye go in to work tomorrow, Jamie?" Morgana said quietly.

"Aye, I asked Da to come get me in the wagon and he will take me down to headquarters where I will provide my report on the last unpleasantness. I do not ken whether the Commander will want to send a man on into North Carolina on the trail of the Highlander, but we will see what is what in the morning and go from there. I ken I canna make the ride in my current state, but he may wish the matter pursued further. There is a part of me that hopes the man is permitted to return to his wife and family. It was a debt of honor that he paid and ye ken as do I what that means to a Scot, even if others do not. It is over now, lass; and we must begin to prepare for the new bairn. Are ye well, Morgana after the trip and the ordeal of the past week?" Jamie asked worriedly.

"I am braw, Jamie; but just tired like ye and I think it will be good to be at home and to see my patients without fear of what one might tell me in confidence about murders and mayhem," she said smiling.

"Aye, it is good to be home, lass; that is for sure. Come and let us take our own bed now that the wee Jamie is settled in his," Jamie said. They both kissed the baby as he slept and Jamie made his way slowly back to their room. They undressed and Morgana heated water for them to bathe before bed. Soon they were in each other's arms and thanking the Lord yet again for his safe delivery of the case and of the parents back to the arms of their family.

*****

The next morning, Morgana woke to a thumping noise. She lay still for a moment and saw that the sun had already risen. It was past her waking time, but considering the trip yesterday and the stresses of the past week, she thought Jamie must have let her sleep. She put on her plaid about her shift and walked to wee Jamie's room to discover the source of the noise. When she opened the door, two sets of identical blue eyes looked up at her guiltily and with a start. Jamie had been given wee Jamie a horseback ride and the thumping noise that she had heard had been Jamie stomping on all fours to simulate wee Jamie on the mighty Duncan's back.

"The lad fancied a horsey ride, as he called it and well one thing led to another . . ." Jamie said with a guilty look. "I hope we did not wake ye, love. I thought to let ye sleep in this morning considering the week ye have had," Jamie said. The baby had slid down his back and was crawling around to sit in front of his Da.

"He, mama; he," wee Jamie continued grinning.

"He is trying to say horsey," Jamie said smiling down at his image. "We will try the horsey rides again after yer Mama has ye fed and dressed for the day," Jamie said with a smile. He gathered wee Jamie up into his arms again and kissed him on the neck which released a new set of giggles on the part of the baby. Jamie crawled over to the chair and gathered his crutches to raise himself to a standing position. "I hope that this will be my last week with the crutches, lass. I canna bear not being in the saddle, ye ken. It will be a sad day indeed when I must arrive at headquarters in the back of a wagon," he said wistfully.

"Ye are mending well, Jamie. Just remember what could have happened and ye will be happy for the recovery ahead of ye," Morgana said as she gathered up wee Jamie into her arms. "Will ye watch the lad while I finish dressing, Jamie?" Morgana asked.

"Oh aye, sit the wee lad down on the rug in the family room and I will watch him as ye get ready for the day. Have ye any patients to see this morning?" Jamie asked.

"Nay, they will not ken that I am back yet, but I expect Mam will get the word out this morning at the market," Morgana called out. They had much to do to get back to their regular routine.

Morgana was soon dressed and ready to face the day. She picked up wee Jamie and settled him in his chair as she brought his morning porridge to feed him. "Apples in the porridge, is it? Well, wee man, ye are to have a feast today," Jamie said as he sat down at the table.

"Our wee Jamie is not well pleased with the morning porridge, so I have added the apples to spark his appetite," Morgana replied. "Besides, his Da has apples with his porridge also," she replied grinning.

"Aye so I see. Yer Ma treats us like kings, wee Jamie. Best ye remember that and not give her trouble, ye wee rascal," Jamie said grinning at his image.

Wee Jamie returned the grin and endeavored to grab the spoon and feed himself, as he saw his Da do. Morgana had her hands full in getting the porridge into her son and not on his face, hands and head.

After breakfast Da arrived to take Jamie down to headquarters. Wee Jamie had managed to get his oatmeal on his head and face. She had waited to give him his morning bath and with good reason. She stood up straight for a moment and felt the first movement of the newest baby. He was making his presence known and she stopped her chores for a moment and placed her hand over the place of the movement. She marveled at the joy that had come her way ever since meeting Jamie. They may share adventures and they may come too close to danger during the course of their work, but she would not have traded one moment of her time with Jamie for all of the world. Now a second blessing was making himself known and her joy was only doubled.

AN EVIL MOON

*****

Da and Jamie arrived at headquarters before the usual work hour. Jamie climbed gingerly out of the wagon with Da's help and walked into the building on his crutches, Da following along with a case that contained all of Jamie's notes on the matter just concluded. Da sat down in the anteroom of the building and waited for Jamie's return.

Jamie walked to the office of the Commander and was shown in quickly. "Come in Jamie, come in; we are so glad to see you back and in one piece. I have had letters galore from the militia commander praising your work there and also if I might add; praising the activities of the fair Morgana. You two are quite the team and I have had nothing but praise for the manner in which you handled the investigation and the aftermath of your injury. How are you doing with that wound?" the Commander asked worriedly.

"I am doing well, sir; thank ye for asking. Morgana saved the day yet again when a far worse outcome could have occurred," Jamie said smiling.

"I will let you in on a bit of a secret. When the camp has concluded for the autumn, the Commander wishes to host a reception to honor both you and Mrs. Macpherson. He was most taken by her willingness to assist his men in the face of the woeful disregard of their former surgeon. It is unbelievable that the man would not only attempt to murder an investigator, but complete the job with his own malfeasance as a surgeon. Well, the two of you have done this unit proud yet again, Macpherson. I hope that Mrs. Macpherson will be pleased by the recognition," The Commander said smiling.

"Aye, Commander; she is a treasure for sure. She helped me when I was wounded and helped the men of the camp

215

when their own surgeon was too lost in his cups to see to his responsibilities," Jamie said heatedly. "I have my report here, sir if ye would wish to take a look at it. The man who reported on the surgeon's movements and crimes has moved on it seems to North Carolina. I do not ken if ye would wish me to follow him when my leg has mended," Jamie asked.

"The Commander has briefed me on that matter as well in his last letter. It is my feeling Macpherson that the debt of honor which you so properly explained has been settled. I can see no benefit in pursuing this man who could be in South Carolina by now for all we know. I believe the matter is closed by your excellent work yet again and by the confessions in the surgeon's own hand. I would like you to take several days off, Jamie and let that leg heal properly. I understand you are not able to wear a boot on that leg yet and you need to let it heal properly so that it does not become a perpetual wound. Take all of the time that you need and in the interval, I will give you a few files to review while you convalesce under the watchful eyes of your brilliant wife," the Commander said smiling.

"Thank ye, sir most kindly. We will have things sorted out with the leg at home and I will be ready to take on the next case when it presents itself," Jamie replied.

"Good to have you back again, Jamie. Please give my best to Mrs. Macpherson and the rest of the family. My adjutant will have the files that we spoke of for your review while you recover," the Commander said as he rose from his desk.

Jamie walked out to the assistant's office and took the files that had been presented for his review. He put them into his case and returned to the exit to find Da and to return home. He was glad that today was now over, at least at headquarters. He had not relished following the Highlander into North Carolina and as the Commander reasoned; he could have only told Morgana that North Carolina was his next destination. For all they knew, he could have been on a boat bound back for Scotland by now. The case was closed and two men who had betrayed Highlanders following the pivotal Battle of Culloden had themselves been dispatched to their maker to make amends for their crimes.

Jamie was relieved to return home as Da brought the wagon to a stop and helped his son again to his feet. Jamie felt like he could still sleep for a week. Apparently there was more to recovering from a wound than he remembered from his last such injury. That had been a saber wound to the neck that could have by rights killed him. He had not had Morgana by his side that time, but only the Lord who had saved him from death. To think that he might not have ever met Morgana and sired their wee man and the new baby was a thought that brought him no comfort. He knew now that Morgana had been waiting for him in far off Berkeley County and that the case that had taken him there had changed his life and the life of his family.

Da opened the door for him and Morgana came around the corner with wee Jamie. As soon as his son saw his Da again, he smiled a broad smile and motioned for his Da to take him. Morgana sat down on the settee again so that the baby could access both parents easily. "Was it a good meeting with the Commander, then?" Morgana asked worriedly.

"Aye, lass; it was a very good meeting indeed. He doesna wish me to follow the Highlander. We reason that he could have only said that he was going to North Carolina and could be anywhere by now. Besides, he wants me to let my leg heal properly and to take off some time to do so. So I am guessing that you and the wee man here will have to put up with me for a few days," he said grinning.

"The wee man and I will be that pleased to have ye home to spoil," Morgana replied. "We will see that leg right, mo gradh and see ye back on duty as soon as ye are able," Morgana replied.

"Ye are blessed to have a healer in yer own home, lad. Morgana will see ye right and back on duty soon. I must go home and report to Mam. We will come over this evening to visit with the wee lad, if it is agreeable. Mam misses the lad something fierce when he has been with her for a time," Da said taking wee Jamie into his arms. He kissed him on the cheek and promised that he and Mam would visit later on.

"I have cases to review while I recuperate, love. Would ye care to review them with me after ye put the wee man down for his nap?" Jamie said grinning.

"Could I, Jamie? Ye ken I like nothing so much as solving mysteries with ye," she said excitedly.

"Aye, I ken it well and it will give us both something to look forward to in the days ahead," he replied chuckling. It was like old times again, when he had visited her wee cottage to review the particulars of the case against the evil one who had terrified Berkeley County. Then his murderous spree had been brought to an end by the shared abilities of Inspector James Macpherson and the healer with the special gifts; Morgana Mackenzie Macpherson.

*****

Two weeks later, when Jamie's leg was well recovered and he could again wear a boot and pull into a saddle; a surprise celebration was held at the church honoring Morgana. The Commander of the Virginia militia had organized it to thank her for her kindness to his men. The men who lived nearby had been invited to attend and an event had been organized with the help of Mam and Pa using the church hall where Jamie and Morgana's wedding reception had been held. She thought only that she was going to a fundraiser for the church which would occur after the usual service.

When they all arrived with wee Jamie in tow, they moved to the church hall to find the Commander, Lt. Henderson and some of the local men who belonged to the militia. Men as far away as Richmond had also been invited and some had attended to thank the Macpherson family for the dual tasks of solving the murder case and providing healing to the men of the militia. Morgana was the most surprised of the group. The men applauded when she arrived and she was overwhelmed by their thanks. The Commander offered a few words before the guests sat for the dinner that had been prepared by the church women to honor Morgana.

"We had no idea when Inspector Macpherson's wife arrived that we were to receive two such talented people into our midst. The Inspector had come to solve a crime, as he has done in so many communities. When he himself became a victim of the murderer in our midst, Mrs. Macpherson arrived to nurse him and in turn to offer her healing skills to the men of our militia. I have here a resolution of thanks from the governor himself in appreciation of the efforts of this couple. If you would be so kind to step forward, I will present it to you both," the Commander said smiling.

Morgana and Jamie stepped forward, with Mam holding wee Jamie during the presentation. The Commander further asked if Mrs. Macpherson would be available to provide medical care next autumn during the same militia camp. "I have been given leave to request the services of both Inspector Macpherson and his talented wife, Morgana to the camp of the Virginia militia. The Governor believes and I agree wholeheartedly; that the presence of the Inspector will prevent any future unpleasantness while training proceeds and the presence of his beautiful and talented wife will keep the men healthy and hale to do their important work. I have looked no further to replace our prior surgeon and it would do me great honor if you both would accept our invitation," the Commander said smiling.

"I would be happy to do so, sir; provided I may also bring my wee lad and the other wee bairn who will be expected by that time," Morgana said smiling.

"We will make special arrangements to house you all should you but agree to join us, Mrs. Macpherson. My men have spoken of nothing else since you assisted us and I would welcome you and your wonderful healing skills during the next camp training," the Commander replied smiling.

That night, Jamie held his Morgana in his arms after baby Jamie had been put to bed. "Ye have made a life here, mo gradh, just as I ken ye would. Have ye been happy, Morgana even though it has all been new to ye?" Jamie asked worriedly.

"I have never been so happy as the time that I have spent here, Jamie. My business has been well received by the people of the church and all the people that Mam and Da ken. And now, to have the entire Virginia militia to treat; it is like something from a dream. My life was made for me the day that ye arrived at my wee cottage. I never ken how lonely my life was until that moment. I have never looked back, Jamie; but only forward to the future and to our happiness. By this time next year, wee Jamie will have a brother or sister, we will go to the Gathering again and ye will compete and make us all proud. From there we will head to the camp with the militia and we will have another memory to make. Thank ye, mo gradh for making all of my dreams come true," she said smiling.

*****

It may have not been one of Morgana's visions, but her prediction was an apt one. The next summer, Jamie again competed in the Gathering of the Virginia clans and again excelled in the heavy events. He had Morgana to thank yet again for saving his leg and for her healing talents that brought him safe and sound to the event the following year.

This year he had two wee lads who cheered him on beside Morgana, Mam and Da. Alexander Geordie Macpherson had been born during the year and was yet another replica of his father; auburn hair, blue eyes the color of Scotland lochs and a disposition which was as sunny as his brother's. Two future athletes were gifted to the laird of the Macpherson clan. They would grow up far from their father's homeland, but they would grow in freedom and in a land where their people's skills were lauded and history told for all future generations to learn and admire.

From the annual Gathering of the Virginia clans, Jamie and Morgana and the lads continued on to the annual camp of the Virginia militia. Jamie filled his days keeping abreast of the activities of the militia men and Morgana filled her days with the sick call of the men who met their annually to train and with the wee lads who had followed her to this place of training. The camp would become an annual event and all of the children of the Macpherson laird came to learn of both the ways of the Gathering and the way of the sword which their father had been instructed in since birth.

Morgana did not need to complete a reading to learn that she had found a forever home at Jamie's side. It was not Scotland, but it was a free land where their ways and the customs of their ancestors were practiced and accepted. It had all began in far away Berkeley County where the meeting of these two had been foretold. The reality was even better than the predictions had ever been. Two lonely souls had become one and a beautiful family had been the result.

THE END

NOTES AND AUTHOR'S COMMENTS

- **Scot's Gaelic – Dictionary of Terms**

I have seen alternate spelling of the terms noted, dependent upon their origin in the Scot's Gaelic or the Irish Gaelic. I have shown the popular spelling of these terms from the Google language dictionary in each case.

A leannan – Term of endearment for a baby
Bairn - Child
Braw – Grand, fine, super
Ceilidh – Informal social gathering where Scots folk music, singing, folk dancing and storytelling are held. Such events also accompany Highland Games where the test of physical strength and skills is held in competitive fashion. Competition of pipers is also a component of such events.
Dinna fash – Do not worry
Dirk – Knife instrument that is capable of ready use as a stabbing weapon that can inflict great bodily injury or death.
Ken – To know or understand
Mo Chroi – My heart or Love of my heart
Mo gradh – My love
Moran Taing – Thank You
Selkie – Mythical creature that is a seal in water, but assumes human form; found in Scot's lore.
Sgian dubh – Small, single edged knife worn as a part of traditional Scot's Highland dress; to be worn on the same side as the dominant hand, generally found in the tall sock worn with kilts and used historically for self protection.
Slainte mhath – To your very good health, toast over whiskey in the Gaelic.

- **Bella Vista** – The Bella Vista estate is an actual historic location in Berkeley County, WV. Referenced by the Society of Architectural Historians as the Frederick Seibert House and Distillery, it is dated to 1807 in their sources and 1805 in local history sources. I took some liberties with its construction date to place it within the time period of our story. I thought both its location near the base of North Mountain and its historical association with whiskey distilling would appeal to both James Macpherson and to Morgana Mackenzie as Scots from Highland heritage. According to local sources, a stone distillery and a tavern building were built on the site in 1800. One of the outbuildings served as the site of the fictional cottage of our heroine, Morgana Mackenzie.

- **Berkeley County, WV** – At the time of our story, Berkeley County was a part of Virginia, as indeed was the entire state now known as West Virginia. The division of the state occurred in 1863 during the height of the Civil War. The three eastern panhandle counties of Virginia, now part of West Virginia; were included as well as the western counties due to the presence of the B&O Railroad and the strategic importance of the railroad lines to the war effort. Berkeley County lies south of Washington County, Maryland and north of Frederick County, Virginia and is the gateway to the historic Shenandoah Valley. Berkeley County is the entryway to the Shenandoah Valley, which now covers two states, West Virginia and Virginia. Berkeley County because a county of Virginia in 1772, so was in existence before the advent of our story.

- **Highland Games** – The tradition of the games was brought from Scotland and includes the strength events, noted in the story; tug of war, shot put, caber toss, hammer throw. The ceilidhs are generally of the nature of music, dancing, storytelling and competition of the pipes, although such events can also be found at Highland Games where the traditions of Scotland were brought both to the United States and to Canada by Scots immigrants.

- The hero of our story, James Macpherson; is from Alexandria, Virginia. This city was chosen in particular as his home due to the long association of Scots connections to Alexandria. Alexandria was founded in 1749 by three Scots merchants from the original owner of the tract, himself a Scot; John Alexander.

- The original land grant was from Sir William Berkeley, Governor of Virginia, to Robert Howson, an English ship captain. In 1669, John Alexander purchased the land grant. In 1748, the three Scots; William Ramsey, John Carlyle and John Pagan petitioned the House of Burgess for a town located at the public tobacco warehouses. In 1749 the petition was approved and named Alexandria in honor of John Alexander.

- The Scots tradition continues today with the Scottish Christmas Walk in December and the Virginia Scottish Games in July, similar to the Highland Games referenced in the book. Sources – Alexandria, Virginia – Alexandria's Scottish Heritage by Jeremy J. Harvey and Brief History of Alexandria, Virginia.

- **The Saltire** – There are two flags in the nation of Scotland. The first is the saltire, referenced in the story. It is a blue field with a white saltire to represent the St. Andrew's cross. The second flag is the lion rampart, a yellow and red flag that is the royal flag of the Queen or King of Scots. The second flag is to be used only by royalty. The official saltire flag has its origins dating to 1385 and is considered the oldest known national flag in existence. Sources: Historic UK.com and Scottish History.com.

- **Macpherson Clan Motto and Tartan** – The motto of the clan is *Touch Not the Cat But a Glove* and was testament to the fierce nature of the clan. In the history of the Macpherson Clan, Ewan Macpherson of Cluny supported the Jacobite Cause, just as the Macpherson's of the story. After the Battle of Culloden in 1746, the lands of the clan were declared forfeit by the crown, as the laird had sided with the Jacobites who supported the cause of King James, the Catholic title holder to the crown versus King George II of England, the Protestant title holder. Ewan Macpherson was able to dodge the government troops who pursued him after the battle and its aftermath. His son Duncan fought for the government in the American Revolution and was able to restore the lands of the Macpherson clan back to him in 1784. The Macpherson tartan or plaid is red and green with the Macpherson Dress Tartan black, red and yellow. Jamie Macpherson would have worn the dress tartan on the day of his marriage to Morgana Mackenzie.

- **Thank you!** – As always, I wish to express my appreciation to my beta readers, Bill Hammond and Pam Swartwood for their always insightful questions and comments. I also love to hear from my readers with any questions or comments that you may have. My Twitter address is @DeborahHammon18 and I can be found on Facebook @dhammondbooks. The work of an author is a solitary one, but I love to interact with my readers and hear their thoughts on the characters that I love so dearly. In the words of our friends Jamie Macpherson and Morgana Mackenzie, moran taing; thank you! On the following page, please enjoy a teaser for the next novel *A Smuggled Heart*. Enjoy!

An excerpt of the next book by author Deborah E. Hammond, *The Smuggled Heart*

Edinburgh, Scotland – October, 1790

Alex McEwan walked into the cold darkness of the hidden warehouse; a tricorne hat fast to his head and a great coat about his shoulders. The hidden casks of brandy, wine and rum represented the autumn income for his operation. He was checking tonight as he would check on a nursery of wee bairns; putting it to bed for the night. The room was cold and damp; dampness in fact ran from the walls of the stone structure. It didn't affect him, however; this space was his pride and joy; something that belonged to him only and there were precious few things in his life that belonged to him alone.

He heard a rustle of feet which sounded vaguely like the scurrying of a rat; not uncommon in the cold darkness of the dank basement. That was not the sound that troubled him, however; it was the suppressed cry that followed that sound. "Who is there?" his booming voice called out. It reverberated off of the stone walls and even he could hear the anger in the tones. "Come out now and I will not call the Watch. Stay hidden and ye will soon see the inside of Tolbooth Prison," he added.

"I-I'm not hurting anything, sir. That t-thing scared me," the small voice answered.

"That thing was a rat. Have ye never seen a rat before?" he replied with a grin.

"N-no," the small voice replied worriedly.

"Well, then; I suggest ye come out and let me lead ye away from this place before he and his partner come back. They always travel in packs, ye ken," Alex said grinning.

The unseen visitor did not respond to that retort, but came around the corner of the far row of casks very slowly. The lad looked no older than twelve. The tricorne hat covered hair that was pulled back in a queue. The darkness prevented Alex from seeing the color of the eyes or of the hair, but by the size and sound of the voice, the lad was very young and very scared. "Where are ye from lad? I need to get ye back before ye are missed," Alex said patiently.

The chin of the young lad rose in defiance. "I'm not going back, sir; you can't make me," he replied belligerently.

"Hard master, eh? Well then, come with me, lad and we will get ye fed and puzzle it out," Alex said with a sigh.

The lad came from his hiding place and walked slowly towards Alex. When he reached his side, the torch carried by Alex reflected bright blue eyes and a height that did not reach his shoulder. The lad had on a shirt, vest, coat and breeches and wool socks. Clearly the clothing was not warm enough to prevent the shaking that was rattling the lad's small body.

"Come on, lad; ye are shaking so hard ye are making me cold," Alex said smiling.

Alex led the way out of the warehouse snug and climbed the steps to the tavern above. He heard a deep sigh from the lad who he led into the light and sound of the tavern above. Alex took a table in the back where his own back could face the cold gray stone walls and allow him to watch the inhabitants of the establishment. He quickly took in the tavern occupants with one glance. There was not a look in his direction; a positive thing as far as he was concerned. He liked to keep a low profile and was hoping this newest wrinkle would not create any attention in his direction.

"Two of yer specials, please," Alex said to the serving wench. She curtseyed and hurried to the kitchen with the order.

"Have ye eaten today, lad?" Alex asked frowning.

"N-no sir, I was waiting . . . for my friend to return. He was going to take me away . . . to my other family . . . but he never came back," the lad said worriedly.

"How did ye get into that room?" Alex asked patiently.

"M-my friend had a key. He said . . . I could stay there until he got back and if I stayed quiet, no one would know I was there and then I could get away, safe to my other family," the lad said.

"What's yer name then, lad?" Alex asked.

"A-Andrew, sir," he replied.

"Tell me then, Andrew; why do ye refer to yer other family in that way?" Alex asked frowning.

"Because, sir; that family doesn't care about titles and such," the lad said quietly.

"Titles, hmm; ye don't like titles?" Alex asked smiling.

"Well . . . some are alright I guess and then some . . . they just shouldn't ask for things that they shouldn't have . . . just because they have a title," the lad said frowning. The food arrived then and both were lost in silence at the power of the draw of the savory meat pies before them. The tavern might have some unsavory occupants, but the food was the best in this part of Edinburgh, in Alex' opinion.

Alex finished his plate; a thick piece of crusty bread remaining. The lad eyed it and looked at his own plate, then back again at the piece of bread. "Would ye like this crust of bread, lad?" Alex asked smiling, white teeth gleaming in his dark beard.

The lad swallowed and then grinned. "I-If you are not going to eat it, sir," he replied tentatively.

"Go ahead then, take it, lad," Alex said chuckling. "I hazard ye haven't eaten this live long day. Ye are fortunate I came along when I did," Alex said. He watched the lad take the crust of bread and wipe up the gravy from the meat pie. He closed his eyes in bliss and then opened them with a smile and a small burp.

"Excuse me, sir," the lad said smiling.

"Aye, wash it down with this ale, lad and then we'll get on," Alex said. He watched as the lad lifted the tankard, smelled it daintily and then sipped the ale. The lad made a face, coughed and then turned beet red in the face until the serving wench started beating him on the back.

"Ale gone down the wrong way, lad? Need some cider to wash it down, then?" she said with a laugh. She was a buxom lass who Alex had noticed as soon as they had taken the table. She was watching Alex with eyes that promised more than a quick resolution of the bill.

"Pay no attention, lad; ale is an acquired taste. Ye will need hair on yer chest and stubble on yer chin before ye can swill it proper," Alex said chuckling.

The lad frowned in response and sipped delicately at the ale pot again as though in defiance of both comments and both speakers.

"Alright then, lad; a cider to take with us. Tomorrow, I shall get ye back on the road to yer other family, as ye call them and I shall get back to what I was meant to be doing," Alex said.

"Where are we going now?" the lad asked wide eyed.

"To the rooms above, of course; ye canna set out in the dark of night for wherever ye are bound," Alex said jovially. As he moved towards the door, he did not see the panicked look or the bit lower lip of the lad who followed him to the tavern door and up the steps to the darkly lit halls above. Andrew had not counted on this bit of kindness or the new problem that it now represented.

Made in the USA
Middletown, DE
04 May 2022

64986230R00136